Not even the wildest Bayou Bachelor of all can resist the right woman.

Jeb DeVillier has a lot of explaining to do. True, he did steal millions from the sailboat business he ran with his partner, Brandon, and disappear to South America. But Jeb has a good reason—Brandon's sister, Jena Boudreaux. A decade ago, she broke his heart when she chose career over their relationship. Still, when he learns she's being held for ransom by drug dealers, he doesn't hesitate. He'll save her life, no matter what the danger.

When Jena called Jeb out of the blue, it was to ask him to give her last words to her family. She knew the risks when she took one final mission for the CIA. Suddenly, Jeb's riding to the rescue like her own personal Cajun knight. Yet now that they're both safe in New Orleans, he refuses to give her a second chance.

That's not good enough for Jena. Because when you find someone crazy enough to risk everything for you, the only sane thing to do is to hang on tight . . .

Visit us at www.kensingtonbooks.com

Also by Geri Krotow

Bayou Bachelors
Bare Devotion
Fully Dressed

BAYOU VOWS

A Bayou Bachelors Romance

By Geri Krotow

LYRICAL PRESS
Kensington Publishing Corp.
www.kensingtonbooks.com

LYRICAL PRESS BOOKS are published by
Kensington Publishing Corp.
119 West 40th Street
New York, NY 10018

All Kensington titles, imprints, and distributed lines are available at special quantity discounts for bulk purchases for sales promotion, premiums, fund-raising, educational, or institutional use.

Special book excerpts or customized printings can also be created to fit specific needs. For details, write or phone the office of the Kensington Sales Manager: Kensington Publishing Corp., 119 West 40th Street, New York, NY 10018. Attn. Sales Department. Phone: 1-800-221-2647.

Lyrical Press and Lyrical Press logo Reg. U.S. Pat. & TM Off.

First Electronic Edition: January 2019
eISBN-13: 978-1-5161-0604-2
eISBN-10: 1-5161-0604-0

First Print Edition: January 2019
ISBN-13: 978-1-5161-0605-9
ISBN-10: 1-5161-0605-9

Printed in the United States of America

To Mary Flynn Boener, LSCW, PhD, whose journey inspires mine.

Chapter 1

Rain battered the condo roof, and for the fifth time in as many minutes Jeb DeVillier reread the contracts from the many accounting firms eager for his CPA experience. He wondered which job he'd pick to start his life over. All four positions were out of state, far away from his native New Orleans, which had been his comfort zone for too long.

Away from Jena Boudreaux.

Usually the rain soothed him and gave him the peace he needed to think, but since he'd come back from Paraguay nothing had filled the crater in his soul.

Her face had been cut from lip to cheekbone.

No matter how many times he went over what happened last month—especially the part where he stole his best friend's money to save that same best friend's sister from certain death—he hadn't been able to justify his actions to himself. At the very least he should have told Brandon he was taking the company coffers to Asunción, Paraguay, to save Jena.

She could have died. Should have, statistically.

He'd saved Jena by getting the ransom to the Paraguayan drug cartel in time, gaining a lifetime's worth of stress in the process. His first trip to South America had been a matter of life or death. There'd been no time to think, no chance to second-guess. He'd received the alarming text from Jena and acted on instinct.

The image of her motionless figure, bloody and battered, flashed into his mind for the millionth time. Unlike any other memory in his life, this one didn't fade. It grew stronger, the utter despair it elicited strangling out any flicker of hope left in his battered heart.

And he'd realized that he could no longer see Jena as a fuck buddy, and in fact, that he had never seen her like that. It'd been sheer stupidity to agree to her proposal in the first place. They'd reconnected last year at Christmas, after barely having seen one another in seven years. Like a fool, he'd convinced himself that the years and space had allowed him to see their shattered adolescent and college relationship for what it was: growing pains with a childhood friend and first love, nothing more. But their red-hot chemistry was still there, and it'd been too tempting to turn down no-strings sex with Jena. He'd gone along with her offer, anything to be able to be with her. Even risking his relationship with her older brother, Brandon Boudreaux, his lifelong best friend. They'd kept their sex-only relationship secret, and it worked. Until it didn't.

After seeing Jena at her physical bottom at the hands of her kidnappers in Paraguay—a haunted ghost of herself—the bubble he'd been living in exploded. While he'd happily engaged in their very private, indeed clandestine, relationship, he'd also fallen for what she'd told her family: that she was in the Navy Reserves and got called to active duty as often as she did because she was doing refugee work in various spots around the globe.

And it made sense, on the surface. Jena had her degree in social work, and she'd said the Navy had assigned her as a general unrestricted line officer, which gave her the ability to serve wherever she was needed, whenever. Jena excelled at channeling her compassionate tendencies in the most beneficial way—he'd witnessed it firsthand when she'd helped the teen daughter of his work colleague early last year.

He grunted. That was when he'd had work colleagues. The destruction his split-second decision had wrought on the boating company he and Brandon had built from the ground up was immeasurable. The fifteen million dollars of absconded funds were easily counted, a solid figure to wrap his head around. And as rough as stealing the money was, it had bought Jena her life back. But the damage between him and Brandon— irreparable. Brandon had been his best friend, his chosen brother, much as the Boudreauxes had been his chosen family since the day Brandon brought him home after school to play Atari.

The only commonality he'd shared with the Boudreaux children was school. Jeb's family struggled economically. His father left when he was still in kindergarten, and his mother struggled with alcoholism until he was almost in middle school. Jeb had felt responsible for his siblings, but also craved the attention and security he thought the Boudreaux children had. He'd met Brandon Boudreaux in gym class at the local private Catholic school where Jeb was enrolled as a charity case. Their bond had been immediate, as had his friendship with Brandon's younger sister Jena. He couldn't remember his life without her.

How had the girl he'd known, the woman he'd thought he'd loved on and off over the last two decades, been an undercover CIA agent and he'd never had a fucking clue?

The not-knowing about her work wasn't what painfully stuck in his craw, though. He hated to admit the truth of it, even to himself in the small apartment he might very well lose in a matter of days. What crushed him was that Jena had never needed him, had only used him for booty calls. And he'd been too blinded by his attraction to see through it. To be fair, he'd used her for the same things, but deep down he believed that Jena needed *him*, what only *he* could offer her.

He'd been a fool.

Jena never stopped calling him her best friend. When they were kids, when they dated in high school, and then, later, college, she never stopped saying that he was the only one who really "got" her.

After seeing what kind of horrible human beings she'd fought and fortunately won against, he had to face facts. The young kids they'd been—and, yes, even the more recent fuck buddies—had been based on his assumption that Jena *needed* him. That he was a requisite part of her life. And he'd thought it would be that way forever. That Jena knew he was the one she'd always be able to turn to, no matter what. While that part was true, what wasn't was his fatal assumption: that Jena wanted to turn to him all the time.

Because Jena Boudreaux was a self-made woman who required help from no one, least of all her grade-school friend who happened to know her body better than anyone else.

He slammed his laptop shut, stood, and stretched. Hadn't he had enough counseling about his alcoholic mother to know that he was a classic caretaker, that his codependency had spilled over onto Jena for too long? Fuck, he'd destroyed his best friend's business, their relationship, and his own livelihood, all because of a single text from Jena.

Not the text asking him to tell her family she loved them, to let the FBI know what was going on. No, that hadn't been the biggest revelation. It was the short, three-word text that came two hours later, when he'd thought it was too late, that he'd never reach her in time.

I love you.

As it turned out, he'd arrived in Paraguay soon enough to get the liaison the ransom the cartel demanded.

But his ability to continue any kind of relationship with her was over. She wasn't the woman he'd thought, and he couldn't pretend he was still okay with playing the role of her sexual safety net. She'd never mentioned the text again, never repeated the words. She had, in fact, behaved as if she'd been delirious, out of her mind when she sent it.

As if the words meant nothing.

As he stayed by her side those awful hours until the medevac got her out of Paraguay, he'd realized that she'd only sent the text to make sure he acted on her SOS. Jena hadn't remained conscious for long, but when she was, she'd told him she was sorry for the text, asked him to forgive her for being so emotional. She'd needed him to save her life, had counted on him to do so. But nothing more. Who he'd been before that insight, the man willing to have a relationship with her no matter what the terms, died. They both deserved more, so much more, but they weren't going to find it with each other. It was time to make a life for himself that didn't revolve around Jena.

His cell phone rang and he reached for it, ready to ignore another call or text from Jena. He couldn't do it, couldn't pretend to be friends again, to be *anything* again. Not after his epiphany that he was wallpaper in her life, nothing more.

Brandon Boudreaux.

His former best friend.

"Hi, Brandon." His gut roiled. The guilt over what he'd done would never leave him.

"Jeb. Nice to hear your voice, man."

Silence stretched, mocked what used to be an unbreakable bond.

"Still there, bro?" Brandon's concern reflected in his somber tone. And damn it, it hurt that he still called him "bro." He didn't deserve the familial reference.

"I'm here. What's up?"

"I was hoping you'd be willing to come over for brunch tomorrow."

"At your place?"

"Yeah. I thought it'd be easier." Brandon sounded almost shy. They'd met at a favorite diner at least once a week when they'd had a solid relationship.

"I don't know.... I'm in the middle of a job search." Weak, but he had to come up with something.

"And no one's calling you on a Sunday, bro. Besides, I'm sure you've got a slew of offers by now. Am I right?"

Jeb waited a beat. *What the hell.* "Yeah, I lucked out."

"No luck involved. You're the tops at what you do."

"Brandon, I—"

"Nope. Save it. We can talk tomorrow. See you around eleven?"

Jeb wavered, on the brink of declining the offer. But leaving NOLA the right way meant tying up loose ends. A meal with Brandon could do that. "Sure, I'll be there." He hung up, headed for the shower. The fact that Brandon still read him so well, knowing that he needed to say again he was sorry, should bring him comfort. Instead, he felt the full force of his misery. But he couldn't fix what he'd done to their friendship.

Brandon didn't even know about his and Jena's relationship, or lack thereof. To Brandon, Jeb and Jena were childhood friends who'd dated on and off in high school and college.

He turned the water on full force and prayed the spray would knock some sense into him.

Jeb had built a life on taking care of others at his own expense.

No more. His tendency to overreach when it came to caring for others had led him to rock bottom. He might not have been attacked like Jena had, but her kidnapping was his crash point nonetheless. He was done with caretaking and enabling.

He was done with Jena.

* * * *

Upon touching down in her hometown of New Orleans after six months of life-threatening, career-ending adventure in South America, Jena Boudreaux wanted three things. She'd accomplished the first two: a long hot shower, followed by a grocery run that made Brandy, the ancient clerk at her local Piggly Wiggly, raise her brows, and it took a lot to rattle Brandy's cage.

"Haven't seen you in a while, Jena. Another Navy mission?" Brandy rang up Jena's eclectic order with her signature air of nosy detachment. Yogurt, chocolate, cheese, yogurt, eggs, more yogurt.

"Yeah. But it was my last. I'm getting out. My active duty time is up." True, except for the part about the Navy. It was the CIA she'd resigned from.

"Good for you. Staying here, then? For good?" The wizened woman's perfectly lined eyes regarded her with patience and a wisdom that comforted Jena. Brandy and Piggly Wiggly were as much a part of her as New Orleans and her family.

"Yes, that's the plan!" She paid for her order, throwing in a fresh bunch of flowers from the rack next to the checkout. Anything to remind her that she was more than the CIA operative she'd been for the better part of the last eight years. She had a life to live, things to do.

If only she could figure out what those things were. All she'd ever wanted was here, in New Orleans. Her social work degree, always her civilian cover, was what she planned to put to use now. But the thought of going back to work at the state government social services offices made her stomach sour. If she was going to settle, really settle down in her native city, it had to be to infuse energy and life into it. Her way. With the horror of her kidnapping growing smaller in her mental rearview mirror, it was time she found a job that utilized her degree. But what?

As much as her passion for social work and a full-time return to NOLA had been her carrot through the toughest missions she'd run with the CIA, they weren't everything. She'd figured out too late what everything really was to her. And in a terribly weak moment—okay, a life-or-death split second—she'd reached out to Jeb. And, worse, she'd texted him those three little words that she knew would be the end of their relationship. Jeb had never, ever indicated that he wanted anything more than their friends-with-benefits deal. But she'd needed him to know how bad it was for her in Asunción, that it wasn't some kind of bluff. So that he'd give her family her message. Her life was at stake, and even her CIA team couldn't reach her; the cartel had cut them all off from her.

She'd expected him to tell her family, and definitely alert the authorities, who'd in turn get the information to her team back at headquarters in Langley, Virginia. Instead, Jeb had blindsided her by draining her brother's company funds and paying the ransom to the sorry sack of shits that were the Jardin cartel. He'd flown to Paraguay to make sure the money was delivered via the State Department and refused to leave until he saw for himself that she was free.

Her weak moment had cost her brother his entire livelihood, along with Jeb's, since Jeb worked alongside Brandon as his CFO and effective partner. Boats by Gus—her brother's dream built from the bayou up—had closed, and Brandon had filed for bankruptcy.

It'd also cost her her relationship with Jeb. Their sexy-friends deal.

That part wasn't bothering her as much as knowing she'd hurt too many people by reaching out for help. She had no idea how she was going to make amends to Brandon or Jeb.

Jeb. He'd never acknowledged that last text, never reciprocated her sentiment. Had he thought she'd meant those three little words, that she'd really meant to put her heart on the line? Or did he think she'd used the words to manipulate him into coming to Paraguay? Either option appalled her.

The look of horror and shock on his face when he'd found her, right after the cartel's thugs let her go, told her all she needed to know. He was shut down, showed no signs of affection—only relief that she was alive and a determined set to his jaw that she'd seen when they were kids and he decided to climb the highest tree on her parents' property just to win a bet. It was Jeb's I'll-show-you expression.

She'd put too much faith into their lifelong friendship. He'd come to her rescue in Paraguay as only Jeb could, with nothing but total focus on saving her. But he hadn't talked to her since, and she knew she'd pushed him too far. He'd been good with their sexy friendship—they both had. Why couldn't she have accepted that and not sent that stupid text?

You'd hoped for more.

Yeah, she'd fantasized about them growing into more, why wouldn't she? She was gone so often on life-or-death missions, it was only natural she'd dream about her future. Jeb was the obvious object of her desires, as he'd always been. She did not need to feel guilty about the I love you text.

But she still did.

They were childhood friends, period. Sexy times aside, Jeb had never signed up for more than that with her. And she had to respect that, move on. No matter how much it hurt, no matter how much she knew there'd never be another man with such a shared history. Most people moved on from adolescent relationships—she'd just been slower to, that's all.

But she owed him a thank-you for saving her life, and an apology, a closure for both of them.

Back home from the Piggly Wiggly, she stared at her open refrigerator. Her favorite Greek yogurt was stacked in pretty rows, the banana flavor in front, with cherry vanilla in the back. She couldn't stop the smile. A full refrigerator said, "I'm home for good."

There hadn't been any yogurt while was a captive of the Jardin cartel. Her stomach twisted and her shame and humiliation rushed back, reminding her why she'd quit her eight-year-long career with the CIA. She sucked as an operative. Good undercover case officers did not get themselves kidnapped. Nor, once they were kidnapped and their life was in danger, did they text their childhood friend to tell him that they loved him.

A good agent didn't contact their childhood friend and ask him to bail her out, which she hadn't done directly, but, Jeb being Jeb, he'd taken matters into his own hands and had not only contacted the FBI and the State Department, but had also withdrawn a cool fifteen million of her brother's money to pay her ransom.

Jena winced at the memory of her CIA team leader finding out what she'd done. She'd seen her fate in her boss's eyes. That she'd already decided to leave the CIA didn't ease her hurt and humiliation; Paraguay was going to be her last mission without question now. Her opportunity to leave of her own volition had ended the second she hit send on the SOS text to Jeb.

That was over a month ago. She'd spent over a week in the Walter Reed National Military hospital in Washington, D.C., after the Jardin cartel released her; another two weeks of debriefing at CIA headquarters in Langley, Virginia; an additional week's worth of medical follow-up for the facial injury she'd sustained; and another three days to cut all ties with her tiny crash pad in Washington, D.C., where she'd stayed whenever a CIA op had come up. Her cover as a Navy Reserve Officer had worked perfectly, and her family and work colleagues in NOLA were none the wiser.

At least she had her dream job in her beloved New Orleans to come home to. She'd earned her degree in social work at LSU. If the CIA recruiter hadn't approached her on campus during her accelerated master's program, she'd never have sought out working for a government agency that wasn't local. She wanted to save the world, and for her, the world was NOLA. No matter how much of the globe she saw, New Orleans was her home. Jena lived and breathed Louisiana and her native city. It was what held her hopes high during the worst of missions, the darkest of nights, fighting for freedom in yet another godforsaken hellhole. Her hand drifted to her cheek, amazed that the stitches were gone, the cut's scar fading visibly by the day. The military doctors that treated her had used all kinds of magic medicinal and vitamin ointments, minimizing the reminder of her brush with death.

Jeb held your hand through the worst of it.

Yeah, Jeb. He'd been there for her, but he'd never said a word about what she thought was the last text of her life. I love you. What the hell had she been thinking?

That her time on the planet was up, that's what.

Her undercover work had opened her eyes and her worldview. In the end, it revealed to her that all she wanted from her life had always been here, ever since she was a kid.

Since Jeb had entered her life, when she was eight and he was ten.

Which brought her back to the third item on her want list.

Jeb. She had to find him, apologize. No matter how awkward or uncomfortable it would be for her, she owed him that much. He'd saved her life.

He'd basically ghosted her since she'd gotten back. Not that she blamed him; she'd made him a fugitive wanted by the FBI, if only for a brief time after Brandon had reported the missing funds. She'd used her contacts at the agency to help Jeb return and to ensure no charges were pressed against him. Brandon said he held no resentment over the whole deal. Sure, he said her life was all that mattered, that Jeb was still like a brother to him, that he understood the big picture of why Jeb took the money and ran to Paraguay after finding out she was being held for ransom. But his trust in Jeb had to have been shattered, and it was her fault.

Jeb. She sighed and tried to get her lady parts to chill out. She couldn't think this way, not if she was going to keep any semblance of pride and self-respect. All she had to do was get through the apology, then they'd never see one another again, save for infrequent family gatherings.

She locked the door of her small rental home behind her, appreciating that the former carriage house was still located in the middle of a very secluded garden. The late August morning sun cast a bright spotlight on the flowerpots, spilling with lantana and verbena, that lined the winding gravel walk. Her phone's ring broke the serenity and she grabbed it out of her bag, hoping against hope it was Jeb. That he'd finally come back around.

The initial disappointment that it was her brother turned to appreciation that at least he was still talking to her. "Hey, Brandon. What's going on?"

"Hi, sis. How are you?"

"I'm good." She still wasn't used to Brandon checking in on her as much as he had since she'd been back. So had her older brother Henry. They'd been shaken up, understandably, but there was nothing like a little kidnapping to make one's older brothers realize they still wanted you around. She giggled.

"What's so funny, sis?"

She didn't think Brandon would appreciate her dark humor. "Nothing. I'm walking to my car to run an errand."

"I called to see if you'd like to join Poppy and I for brunch tomorrow, at eleven. We're putting out a spread. Henry and Sonja are coming, too."

She wanted to ask if he'd invited Jeb, but it would be too obvious. Even with Jeb going to South America, no one in her family knew about the most recent incarnation of their relationship. And didn't need to, especially now that it was over.

"I'd love to. Did you invite Mom and Dad?"

"No, not this time. I thought it would be better to not do the Baton Rouge deal and make it just us for now. Things are still tense."

"I understand." It would take eons to ease the hurt their actions had caused over the years. "It'll be nice to spend time with you and Henry, and your women." She chuckled. "I'll see you then."

"Bye."

Her brothers didn't know the extent of her "issues" in Paraguay. They thought she'd been the victim of a random drug cartel crime. The front allowed her to keep her CIA work private for now, while explaining the fading but still visible scar on the right side of her face. Once her final resignation papers came through, she could tell them. They'd had enough to deal with on the family front while she'd been away this last time.

Since she'd returned she learned that Henry's wedding had been called off, which made her very, very sad. No one deserved a happy ending more than Henry and Sonja. They'd put up with so much abuse from Hudson and Gloria, whose racist ways had risen to the surface yet again.

Henry had always made it look like he was in sync with their father's business plan, taking over the New Orleans law office Hudson Boudreaux founded thirty years ago. Their parents had moved to Baton Rouge after Katrina, much against their children's wishes. Henry, Brandon, and Jena believed they should stay in their native city, that their father should devote his law practice to helping the disenfranchised victims of Katrina, the vast majority of whom were African-American. Unlike their children, however, all Hudson and Gloria thought about was themselves, and that meant getting out of the city, where another storm and flood were highly probable. Hudson started a new office in Baton Rouge, but agreed to keep the NOLA firm up and running, as long as Henry agreed to attend law school and work at the firm afterward, which Henry did, no questions asked. Henry had told Brandon and Jena he planned to take on more pro bono cases than their father ever had, and to do his part to make up for Hudson Boudreaux's cruel handling of post-Katrina life.

But then Henry fell in love with Sonja, a lawyer Dad had hired. Sonja was good enough to work at the NOLA firm, in Hudson's mind, but when the African-American beauty became his son's fiancée all hell broke loose. Jena's parents had acted like the asshole bigoted racists they were and proclaimed their dismay to Henry, who shut them down. Sonja was the woman for him, and he didn't give a river rat's ass what they thought.

Jena started her car and saw that her fuel tank was on empty. Impatience roared—she really needed to get this thank-you-apology to Jeb over with, like, yesterday. But then she reminded herself that gas only added another, what, three minutes to her journey? After what she'd faced in

Asunción, it was child's play. She let her mind drift again as she headed to the nearest gas station.

Brandon had never even pretended to want a law career, and in fact she'd wondered if he'd leave NOLA and completely sever ties with their parents. Instead, he'd found his niche in naval architecture and had managed to support himself and his employees while remaining estranged from their parents.

Jena had her own run-ins with her parents and their bigoted views. It was the impetus for her move on campus for college, and then her acceptance of the position with the CIA. She couldn't control her parents' twisted opinions, but she could get the hell away and contribute to national security—her way of setting her personal boundaries. Love for her parents was one thing, but she could never abide by any racist beliefs.

Jena was relieved when Brandon filled her in on the latest news. According to him, their parents had masterminded having one of Henry's exes show up at the wedding, which on the surface looked like the reason for Sonja jilting Henry. But it turned out that she'd left for reasons the couple wasn't sharing with the family. Thank God Sonja had more class and common sense in her pinkie than most folks had in a lifetime. Somehow, she and Henry had made up and were starting over. Sonja was pregnant and about to have the baby, and she and Henry were going back and forth about when to get married for real this time.

Brandon, the middle Boudreaux, had somehow reconciled with their parents during the course of the canceled wedding family implosion and had fallen for a famous former celebrity stylist from New York, Sonja's best friend, Poppy.

Both of Jena's siblings were finding a way to mend fences with her parents, on their own terms, from what she understood. If they could do it, so could she, but it'd be slow going. Hudson and Gloria were pieces of work.

Jena shoved down her self-pity over missing so much, not just this last six months, but every overseas mission that had cut her off from her NOLA life.

She was back now, for good. The niggling fear that she'd get a last-minute recall from CIA headquarters was down to a manageable hum. The odds of being asked to come back were slim, especially in light of her unprofessional behavior in Paraguay. Besides, no one wanted an agent who didn't want to be there. Of course she'd always answer the call to serve her country. But it was time for her to start serving her community full time, as a social worker. Social work was her first love, what she'd always looked forward to sustaining her life after the CIA.

That and Jeb. Their friendship was a nonstarter. She'd blown it and broken the code when she let her feelings come in during her ordeal in Asunción. His lack of acknowledgment of her admission hurt more than the slice to her cheek had. But as soon as she saw his ashen face and knew without a doubt he did not reciprocate, she'd shoved her disappointment down and convinced him it had been the result of being under duress, nothing more, and the way he'd readily accepted her explanation spoke volumes.

She stopped at a gas station, filled her tank. The mundane task soothed and grounded her—a reminder that she was truly home. The only big bad monsters to chase were of the social work kind—placing foster children, helping abused women, finding rehab placement for the fifth or sixth time for the addict who had finally hit their absolute bottom. She'd figure out the where and how after she finished her back-home list.

And apologized to Jeb.

* * * *

Jeb heard the familiar steps outside his apartment door a second before the doorbell rang. *Fuck.* He'd not counted on Jena showing up here, not when he'd made it so clear he was done with them, done with her. They didn't have anything to be done with, in fact, besides their no-strings sex agreement, goddamnit.

He wanted to blame Jena, blame her emotions for making this harder than it had to be.

Maybe it's you.

When he didn't respond to the bell, soft taps on his door sounded through the small apartment.

"Jeb, please open up. I promise I won't bite. I just want to talk to you." Her voice cut through him, and his dick didn't understand that they were through, that it was wasting its time getting hard.

He could stay quiet, pretend he wasn't here. How hard would it be? He'd ignored her texts, her calls, her pleading voicemails. Jeb needed space when he was troubled, always had. What he'd been through since Jena's text that her life was ending at the hands of a South American drug lord was the dark night of his soul. Hell on planet Earth.

Pounding, more solid this time, on the door. "Jeb."

Hell, she had that tone that meant she'd never leave. Would, in fact, camp out until he relented. And she'd no doubt seen his car in the street.

Damn it.

He pulled the door open and stared at her. Big mistake, as his cock still hadn't gotten the message that there'd be no more Jena and Jeb sexy times. And it wasn't only his erection that throbbed for her—his heart fucking ached. *Shit.*

She blinked her trademark Boudreaux blues at him, one side of her lush mouth lifted in a smile. The other remained flat, and he wondered if it was because of the cut. The scar wasn't as noticeable as he'd thought it'd be, but it was there, the pale pink reminder of the torture she'd endured. He'd never be able to look at her without remembering that night.

"Thank you for opening up. I know you don't want to see me, but I had to bring this by." She held her hands up and presented him with a freezer bag.

He stared at it, then looked back into her eyes. "I don't need any food."

Jena rolled her eyes and sighed. "Can I come in, Jeb? It'll only be for a minute, I promise."

He stood in place, unable to make his feet move. Seeing her was like it'd always been, but much, much worse. Lethal. Because as he looked at her he saw what he thought he had wanted a month ago: her total agreement that they were through, that they both needed to move on. Anger surged as he remembered the sleepless nights after Paraguay, sorting through his fucked up emotions.

Man up.

He cleared his throat, took a step back, and waved her inside. She stepped into the apartment and he smelled her shampoo, her flowery perfume, *her.*

"It's so freaking dark in here! Why don't you ever put lights on?" She moved to the switch and he found his voice.

"Wait." His plea scraped against his dry throat. It'd be easier if he couldn't see her eyes again. Or the pout of her lower lip. Or her Boudreaux nose—prominent on her older brothers but on her, decidedly feminine. Or the way her large breasts emphasized her small waist, how her hips flared under her dress. A perfect ruse to her sex, her sweet, wet hot pussy.

"Here." He moved to the window and flipped up the blinds.

Jena stood before him, all five-feet-seven inches of her. She was exactly seven inches shorter than him, and infinitely softer. Curvier. He looked pointedly outside at the green treetops, buying time. Because after one look at her it took all his resolve to keep his boundaries.

Only Jena had the ability to turn him on like an expert seductress—which, with him, she was—while also eliciting his most protective instincts. The woman was a fucking goddess.

And his best friend's younger sister, a sister who'd almost been murdered at the hands of evil men. Never had he felt more helpless than the three hours he'd waited in the US Embassy in Asunción to find out if they'd accepted the ransom and let Jena go.

Damn his erection, which wasn't going to make this easier. He wasn't about to explain to her that it was his first hard-on since he'd accepted they couldn't be together anymore. He'd googled it—he was in some kind of grieving process, according to his symptoms. Sex had been a regular part of his day, from his every thought to his being with Jena. But that was before Asunción, before he'd learned what a pathetic partner he made for her, even as a silent, secret fuck buddy.

Apparently he was moving on, moving out of his grief, judging from the hard-on that wouldn't quit. Relief would be impossible, with Jena right here in front of him. He had to get her out of here. Fast.

Rip the Band-Aid off, man.

"Jeb. You didn't even open your gift." Her tone belied the gravity of what they'd experienced together, what they'd both destroyed for different reasons.

He turned, walked to where she stood in front of the sofa, and faced her again.

"I promise you'll like it." She cocked her head in her unconscious come-hither expression, making a part of him wonder what harm there'd be in one little lick. A last kiss. He stood still as she moved, not resisting when she shoved the freezer bag against his chest. It was the closest they'd been since he'd held her, bleeding, in the hospital. Careful not to touch her hands, he took the bag.

And saw again the thin line from the corner of her mouth to her cheekbone. Where the thug had cut her with his knife, intending to permanently maim her. She'd been left for dead. The rawness of the wound had faded, but the memory of his terror at whether she'd live or die remained a permanent resident in his mind.

The plastic surgeon had done a good job, leaving her with the smallest mark possible considering the dozens of stitches the cut had required. He'd held her hand in the Paraguayan hospital while they stitched it, staring into her eyes, willing her to stay with him, stay alive.

He stepped back so abruptly the back of his legs hit the sofa and he landed on his ass. Jena stared down at him with her bright eyes.

The reminder of her tie to his best friend hit Jeb in the gut. Why had he ever thought it was okay to play with fire, to have anything but a platonic, brotherly relationship with Jena? Worse, why had it taken him seeing her near death to realize it?

"What's going on with you, Jeb?"

He swallowed. "Nothing." He made a show of unzipping the bag and pulled out the container of ice cream.

"It's your favorite. Butter pecan. I put some pralines in there, too, from downtown. Your favorites." If he didn't know better, he'd swear she was nervous. Jena never stated the obvious but just had, twice.

"Thank you." He remained on the sofa, grateful he'd showered and shoved into his jeans. She'd have to leave soon, wouldn't she? Jena wasn't one to miss subtlety, and he was being anything but. He wanted her gone.

"You're welcome. Here, give it to me—I'll put it in the freezer." He handed it to her, and watched her move to the efficiency kitchen, then open and close the freezer. He saw her cast her gaze about the counter, the small table. "You don't have a lot of food in here. Are you hurting for cash, Jeb? Until you get your next job?"

"I'm fine." He'd be damned if he admitted his financial situation to her. Besides, he'd be taking one of the half dozen or so positions he'd been offered, all out of state, within a week. He didn't need fresh groceries, not in NOLA.

"Thanks for stopping by, Jena."

"Oh, I'm not done yet, Jeb." She walked toward him and he remained pinned on the sofa, helpless to his body's reaction to her. Their relationship was over, but their primal connection? Never.

* * * *

Jena had expected to feel some sadness, even regret, as she thanked Jeb and gave them both permission to move on from the hell she'd put him through. She hadn't expected to feel like her insides were being ripped apart with a machete, though.

She sat on the opposite end of the sofa, facing Jeb but far enough away to assure him that she wasn't looking for anything more than conversation.

The fact that her body trembled with want for him was beside the point. Hadn't she just told herself she'd never control their sexual chemistry? Hormones didn't have a thought process, which was why she had to make this quick, before she screwed up her last talk with Jeb.

"I came here to say thank you. Really. You saved my life, Jeb. I wouldn't be here if you hadn't put your life on the line to come save me."

"No thanks needed. We've already been over this."

"Have we? All I remember is being in bad shape, with morphine messing up my thoughts and words. I owe you my gratitude. I can never repay you, except to wish you the best." She blinked, willing the tears not to fall, and grasped her hands together in her lap. In this moment, she knew what she'd pretended, what Jeb had already told her. They were over. For real.

He met her gaze and she saw the man he'd become. Unrelenting. Angry, but not willing to tell her why. Her own anger welled at how he'd cut her off so abruptly after Paraguay.

"I'm not ending our friendship, Jeb." That was sacrosanct. They'd gotten one another through everything for the past twenty years, since she was eight and he was ten.

"Jena, our friendship was over a long time ago. Way before Paraguay. Sex does not a relationship make." He sounded resolute, tired. "You don't want my friendship."

She swallowed. "That's not true."

"Stop. For both our sakes, all right? You got what you needed—your life. Thank you for the ice cream." He stood, and even dressed in a white T-shirt and jeans he looked as imperious as a general in full battle uniform. "I've got a lot to do. I'm leaving town next week."

Pain pierced through her frustration. What was her problem? Relief was the more appropriate response, wasn't it?

"Where—where are you going?"

"I'm not settled on a place yet. I have several job offers, and they start as soon as I decide."

She forced a smile. "I'm glad. Really. I'm happy for you." But she sounded deranged, even to herself. She *was* happy for him, wasn't she?

"Right. Well." He shoved his hands in his pockets and looked at the floor. She felt like a bug who'd lost her way home. Unwanted here, for certain.

She stood. This was different, the extreme awkwardness. As was the way he'd completely ignored that awful text she'd sent after her request for help. The I love you text.

"Jeb, one more thing I want to be clear on. That text, the one I sent after I first contacted you—"

"I get it, Jena. It was in the heat of the moment. You didn't mean it." He shrugged, and the weight of her sudden fury made her fight to remain standing, to not sag to her knees. He'd so carelessly tossed away what had been her truth in that moment.

"No. No, I didn't." Where was the relief she'd expected?

"We're adults, Jena. Let's leave it at friends, if you must." Had his face ever looked so grim, so done with her?

She didn't bother to filter her emotions, her thoughts. She couldn't. Her initial sadness morphed into unexpected anger.

"You're kidding, right?" She motioned her hand between them. "Your first instinct is correct. There isn't a friendship here, Jeb. We had an arrangement, and now we don't." She grabbed her bag and walked to the door, pausing only to throw him a last scathing glance before she slammed the door with all her might.

* * * *

Jena drove her coupe into Brandon's sleek driveway and let an audible groan escape her. As much as she wanted to blame her bad attitude on Paraguay, her angst wasn't from the mission gone bad, when she'd believed she'd never see the Spanish moss hanging on the Bayou trees again. Her discomfort wasn't from feeling as though she had to rip herself out of bed to get up and out early enough to make Brandon's brunch. And there was no question: she'd wanted to wallow in bed today after her last words with Jeb yesterday.

This pain ran deeper than any single event. It was the culmination of poor choices on her part. Decisions that had led to her life imploding last month.

Slamming the car door shut, she strode up the fancy half-circle drive, past her brothers' cars, and mounted the contemporary home's porch steps. Brandon hadn't lost his home—thank God—even with his coffers emptied. He'd paid cash to have the house built and had a new job that paid the taxes. She should feel some relief at this; she hadn't totally wrecked Brandon's life, just his boat business.

Guilt clung to her shoulders, weighed her every step. It was her constant companion since Jeb had risked life and limb to save her and gutted Brandon's business in the process, and it hadn't let up in the weeks since she'd returned.

The door flew open before she moved to open it. Brandon stood in front of her with a huge grin on his face. "Jena! Bring it in here, sis."

She was engulfed in a trademark Brandon "Gus" Boudreaux hug and, damn it, she needed the affection more than she wanted to admit. Tears pricked her eyes and she sniffed.

"What's this?" Brandon leaned back and looked at her. Before she answered, Henry, the eldest of them, walked up next to Brandon. They were all on the front porch, under a pergola draped with wisteria. She hugged her oldest brother, and noted that even the usually staid Henry seemed more demonstrative, his hug warmer.

"It's so good to have you back, Jena."

"Thanks." She backed up and eyed her brothers. "What's up with you two?" They looked at one another, but it wasn't with the usual "she wouldn't understand because she's a girl" glance she'd despised as a child.

"What's wrong? Is it Mom, or Dad?" She'd always assumed her mother would take ill first. Of course she would—she was a drama queen to the highest degree.

Both brothers shook their heads.

"Mom and Dad are fine. We need to know how you are, really. Not the 'I'm fine' crap you tell Mom and Dad. What can we do for you?" As Henry spoke, they both looked at her as if she were one of the frogs they'd catch as tweens and shove in front of her face, threatening to make her eat it raw.

"I'm good, really. I'm here, aren't I? What are you two getting at?"

Brandon cleared his throat. "It's just that you've been through so much, and it seems to us you've jumped right back into your job and life as if nothing happened."

She looked Brandon in the eye. He was the only one who came close to knowing what she'd gone through. Her work with the CIA was so classified that her entire family had believed she was in the Navy Reserves for the past five years. The only person in the world outside of the agency who had a clue about what she'd really done was Jeb.

"What did Jeb tell you?" He'd had no time to return her texts, but he'd managed to spill the beans to her brothers?

"I told them nothing." She jumped at the deep voice behind her and whirled to face the man who'd been her best friend since childhood, and who singularly had the ability to make her feel like a sexy seductress or a naive fool in the blink of one of his sapphire-blue eyes.

"Jeb! What a surprise." She swallowed and struggled to remain composed. To not reveal how badly yesterday had hurt. Even knowing they were over, she wanted to jump him and remind him of what they'd shared with ease for the last two years, before Paraguay.

But she had to shove it all down into the little place she always stuffed it into, because her brothers had no clue about them—no one knew. As far as her family was concerned, she and Jeb were old family friends. She was Jeb's best friend's kid sister. Period.

"Jena." He bent in and kissed her cheek, his scruff teasing her skin. Not turning her head to intercept his lips with hers was more difficult than surviving an extended round of waterboarding. Where had that impulse come from? Clearly her body still didn't understand what her head and heart knew.

A fucking chaste kiss on the cheek. All that had passed between them came down to that. She had no ground upon which to stand her anger. They'd never revealed to her family what existed between them before, so why would Jeb act any differently now? She'd barely escaped with her life thanks to his quick acting, and now Jeb acted as if nothing catastrophic had happened between them. Tears threatened again, for the second time since she'd stepped into her brother's home. She should run back out the door and drive until the hurt was behind her.

There wasn't enough highway.

Chapter 2

"What are *you* doing here?" She hadn't meant to sound so accusatory, but there it was.

"Brandon invited me." Jeb didn't meet her eyes, which stoked her anger. Since yesterday, the only feelings about him she'd allowed to surface were anger, anger, and anger.

"What did y'all want to tell me that was so important?" She pointedly addressed her brothers. Impatience tugged at her composure so near to Jeb. And why had Brandon invited him, anyway?

"We wanted to tell you a couple of things. First, as mentioned, there's been a big change in Mom and Dad since you left." Henry spoke up, taking charge.

"Yeah, my bet's on Dad having had a nervous breakdown, or Mom going through the change, but whatever. They've somehow seen the err of their bigoted ways." Brandon's wisecracking didn't hide his obvious bemusement at their parents' change.

"Wait—you're telling me Hudson and Gloria have admitted that they're racist asses? They told Sonja as much?" She looked at her oldest brother.

Henry nodded. "Yes and yes. It's true, Jena. They've come around."

"Whoa, don't go that far, bro. Dad's still wearing his IZOD polos from 1985." Brandon grinned.

"And Mom? How did she explain disowning you when you got engaged to Sonja?"

Henry's brows rose. "She apologized to Sonja. They say they're both determined to make it up to us. That's all I care about. Although I do think the fact that they're going to be grandparents made them figure things out sooner than later." Henry shrugged.

"It's still pretty damn late. And some things just aren't forgivable." She thought of the bitter arguments she'd had with her parents when they relocated to Baton Rouge after Katrina, abandoning their roots. And how as she'd grown up and realized they were racist she'd been so angry, so disappointed, so disgusted. "You're telling me that Hudson and Gloria are no longer bigots."

"Let's say they're working on it." Brandon's tone mirrored her skepticism. She angled herself to face all three of them. "Are you hiding Mom and Dad in the kitchen, too?"

"No. This is just us. Mom and Dad can pound sand in Baton Rouge for a while." Brandon spoke quietly and Henry gave a quick nod.

"Yeah, as much as they're trying to suck up to me, and especially Sonja, we all need a break."

Jena laughed and let the love her brothers always gave her buoy her heavy heart. "I agree. We need family time away from them right now."

Jeb remained silent, as he always did when it came to Boudreaux family matters, even though the three of them considered him family. Or at least, she had—until Paraguay, underscored by yesterday's discussion with him.

"The second thing we wanted you to know is that we're here for you, Jena. That's all." Henry played the oldest-brother role to perfection.

"What Henry said." Brandon hitched his thumb at Henry.

"Wait a minute." She looked at Jeb. "What did you tell them?"

He shook his head, but remained silent.

"Jeb's telling the truth, Jena. He didn't tell us anything, except that you were in a lot of trouble, getting kidnapped and all down in South America." Brandon spoke up.

Jeb shrugged. "I had to let them in on some of it, Jena. Your Navy mission got you in trouble with the drug cartel." Relief cut through her. He hadn't told them too much. Brandon knew more, of course—he'd had to be cut in, as he'd been briefed by the FBI on why Jeb had left the country. But Henry and her parents still believed she'd been a victim of circumstance, caught up in random drug cartel drama while she walked the streets of Asunción during her off-duty hours.

"I used Brandon's funds to get you back; that's not something you can expect to remain a secret, Jena." Jeb's calm demeanor stoked her resentment over being ghosted by him since she'd come back to the States, adding to his flat-out rejection of their friendship.

"No, but I'm having a hard time with how casual you're both being about it. My situation wiped out your business, and I'm sure you'll never trust Jeb again." The summer heat had only recently begun to let up, but it was hot enough to make sweat trickle between her shoulder blades. She pulled at her lightweight top, tried to will the stony fortitude she'd developed as a CIA agent to help her stay composed. Where was the thick skin that had been her trademark?

"That's not important right now." Brandon spoke as if they were still kids, figuring out whose turn it was to go first in a backyard game of kickball. Typical of Brandon to act so casual about something so huge. "I've got a new job, and I had some funds stashed away that Jeb couldn't touch. I'm good." Only Brandon smiled—Henry and Jeb looked as pained about it as Jena felt.

"Brandon, Jeb's right. Without Boats by Gus and your money, I wouldn't be here." She wasn't in the mood to deal with her brother acting all saintly. Especially when it was her mess that had caused him to lose his life's earnings. His entire business. His life, for fuck's sake.

"Hold on. No one told me to take the money. It was my decision to head out without telling Brandon what I was doing." Jeb spoke succinctly, putting any chance of Jena blaming herself for her brother's mess to rest.

"Jeb and I are cool, Jena. And frankly, it's none of your business." Brandon's lack of regret stymied her.

"You're good on fifteen million dollars being gone in a flash?"

"Of course I am. It saved your life—small price. And it led me to a new life, one I never envisioned for myself." Without hesitation, Brandon confirmed what Jena suspected the minute she'd met her brother's girlfriend Poppy two weeks ago. Her brother had met his match, and he had no regrets. But Jena did.

"I know, you met Poppy. And I'm happy for you. But you were going to meet her no matter what, Brandon." And he'd have had a helluva lot more to offer her had Jena not screwed up so royally and allowed the cartel to get the better of her. She'd only had to wait another seventy-two hours and her CIA colleagues would have rescued her. But she hadn't known it at the time, hadn't seen past what she'd believed were her last hours on the planet.

"There's some good news." Henry nodded at Jeb. "Tell them."

Jeb's stony expression revealed nothing. Where was the man she'd always been able to read? To count on as the one consistent source of understanding in her life?

It was as if that man had been lost in the Paraguayan third circle of hell—about where she'd left her CIA career and any sense of self-respect.

She'd messed up. Her only consolation was that she hadn't cost anyone their life. Except Brandon—she'd cost him his life's work. And Jeb—he was without work, too. Since finding out that Boats by Gus had closed up shop, she'd wondered about the relationship between her brother and his best friend. They'd been inseparable since the day Brandon brought Jeb home to play after school in their New Orleans backyard; Jena didn't believe Brandon would get over this that quickly. There was no way a best friend and confidante made off with your life's earnings without telling you and the bond survived intact.

And it was her fault.

"What is it, Jeb?" Her irritation made her voice sound harsher than she expected, harder than she ever intended. She was in no place to demand anything from anyone—but most especially Jeb.

"As you all know," he looked at her with intent again, letting her know he'd said nothing, "the FBI helped me get Jena out of Paraguay alive. They've also managed to get a portion of the ransom back, by intercepting the last bank exchange."

It was distributed in thirds. "So you have—"

"Five million. The FBI has retained five million dollars, and they'll transfer it to Brandon as soon as the red tape is cleared."

"A percentage of it is your money, too, Jeb." Brandon's quiet conviction angered Jena. How could he be so forgiving?

She had to take this reprieve, though, if it helped Jeb get his job back. "You wouldn't have taken the money without me reaching out to you, Jeb."

"We were partners." Brandon looked at Jeb. "We're not arguing about this. You earned that money, too."

"Bullshit." Jeb's harsh reply startled Jena. Jeb never swore, except when asking her to let him fuck her. *Stop.* She couldn't afford to revisit sexy memories.

She tried to shrug the errant thought away as if it were a horsefly. Problem was that sex with Jeb was anything but pesky. She bit her cheek hard, hoping that the pain would knock the tantalizing images out of her mind. How could she feel like this when Jeb was the last person she ever wanted to spend time with again? When she needed him to take his new job and get out town, out of her life?

"Hey, it's all good, folks." Henry attempted to smooth it over with his best lawyerly skills. "We've got to go inside, or Sonja and Poppy will wonder what happened to us. What Brandon and I wanted to say is that we're glad you're home safe, and if you need anything, we're here. I was worried you might have money concerns since leaving the Navy and not getting a paycheck recently. But from what Brandon just said about having money stashed away, he's your man for a loan." Henry and Brandon laughed, but she noted that Jeb stayed as silent as she, as if he, too, had more on his mind than money matters.

She risked a glance in Jeb's direction and immediately knew she'd made a mistake. White-hot heat smoldered in his brown eyes. For a split second, it was just she and Jeb, their attraction as sizzling as ever.

That was all it took—less than a second and she may as well have been pressed naked up against him, his cock pounding into her as she screamed out his name. Like they'd been in the shower last spring, before she'd had to leave on one of her assignments.

That was before she'd ruined everything with a single stupid text. Before she had a chance to shake herself out of it, Jeb broke eye contact and his stony, detached expression returned.

If she had any doubts about how rude they'd been to one another yesterday, they were burned away by the scorching disdain seeping from his pores as they stood too close on Brandon's porch.

She and Jeb were done.

After they entered the house, Jena wished she'd thought of something scathing to say to Jeb. To prove she didn't want to be near him any more than he wanted to be near her. Why had he come this morning, anyhow? He had to have known she'd be here.

It took some patience, but when she and Jeb passed one another in the small hallway between the kitchen and back porch, Jena saw her chance to speak to Jeb and went for it. She grabbed his arm and pulled him into the half bathroom off her brother's screened-in veranda. He looked at her and she leaned in, nose-to-nose.

"What the hell are you doing here?"

He reached over her and snapped the fancy blinds shut to prevent anyone outside from seeing them. His insouciance drove her mad, and she knew the tips of her ears had to be crimson.

"What's the matter, Jena? Isn't your return to your roots going exactly according to your super-secret plan?" His dark eyes glittered and his hair—thick and collar-length, contrary to the current shorter fashion—taunted her. Reminded her of how much they'd shared.

"My 'return'? You say it like I had any control over what happened...before."

"You had control over what you told those closest to you." She didn't think he meant just her family.

"You're still angry that I never told you I was CIA? I thought you'd understand by now that my job description was classified. I'll tell my family after my resignation is official."

"All I saw in South America was a woman who came as close to being killed as I ever want to see." His words rang true, but they weren't enough. He didn't mention that he'd cared for her, that her death would have affected him. She hated herself for wanting it.

She looked away from him, anywhere but into those eyes, and saw their reflection in the spotless mirror her brother paid a housekeeper to polish. At least, he had before he'd lost it all.

Jeb's back was to the mirror as he leaned against the sink, his arms crossed against his chest. Did he think she was going to harm him? She stood to his left, and when she saw herself in the mirror, her figure gave her pause. She was hunched over, the circles under her eyes pitiful.

Nothing had been easy since she'd returned home. Nothing.

"Jena." Quiet, commanding. The new side of Jeb she hadn't noticed before. The one he hadn't had to use, not before her frantic text when she'd been locked in that closet of a room, sure that her captors were returning to assassinate her.

She summoned her courage and looked at him. "What, Jeb? What now? Because if you're going to tell me again that we're through, save it. I get it, I get *you*. 'We' never 'were.'"

* * * *

Jena spit the words out, and Jeb took them as the sharply honed weapons they were. He deserved it. As mad as he'd been, mentally fuming at her for never revealing her line of work, or at least hinting at it, nothing topped the anger he had toward himself for not being more in tune with her.

Her hand moved to her face, and belatedly he noticed the tears. Goddamnit. "Jena, look."

"No, *you* look." She shook, her thinner-than-usual frame wracked with emotions. The attempt on her life was still taking a toll on her, no matter how tough she tried to act. "I trusted you. I shouldn't have texted you. It was a mistake. But for what it's worth, I really did think I had no choice—I wanted my family to know I loved them, and I knew you'd tell them."

He wasn't going to call bullshit, as much as he wanted to. She'd known exactly what would happen with her text. They'd always shared a close bond, and for the past couple of years they'd been exclusive sexual partners. Family friends with sexy benefits.

She absolutely had to know he'd find her.

"All's fair in war, right, Jena? I never had to tell anyone in your family bad news. You're alive, back home. Mission accomplished."

"And we don't ever have to deal with one another again." Her bottom lip trembled and, to her credit, she didn't draw attention to it by biting or licking it. Thank God. Was she emotional because she'd picked up on how he'd left out the other part of the quote? *All's fair in* love *and war.*

"Nope." God, was she playing him even now? Had that been what the past two years were about?

"Fine." She eyed him before she grabbed a tissue and blew her sniffles away. "You leave first. I'll follow in a minute or two."

He laughed then; he couldn't help it. "You mean like we did during the Christmas Eve party?"

She didn't laugh with him, though. Her stricken expression stomped the humor right out of his heart. Hell. His brain knew that Jena possessed supreme skills of manipulation and control—it was in her goddamn job description. Or had been, if what she said was true and she was no longer employed by the CIA.

Is this how she wanted him to feel? As if *he'd* hurt *her*, sliced open her heart and left it trampled on the dirt next to the big tree in her childhood backyard, where he'd carved a heart for her more than two decades ago?

Shit. The woman had been manipulating him since day one.

* * * *

Jena waited the prerequisite five minutes before she, too, left the bayou boat-themed bathroom and rejoined her brothers at the large island that dominated the immaculate contemporary kitchen. She noticed definite spots of bright color—potted flowers, fresh linens. Poppy's touch.

"Jena, help me make the corn casserole, will you?" Brandon grinned from the other side of the island, where Poppy stood next to him whisking eggs, her expression unruffled. Poppy struck Jena as a self-contained woman by the way she observed them all as if studying laboratory rats behind glass.

"Sure, bro." She took the cans of creamed corn he'd nodded at and picked up the can opener.

"There's a casserole dish in the cabinet next to the sink, Jena." Poppy smiled.

As she turned to find the ceramic dish, she bumped into Sonja, her brother's fiancée.

"Whoops, I'm sorry, Sonja!"

Sonja laughed. "No worries. It's hard to miss me right now." She rubbed her swollen belly. Sonja looked as cool as a cucumber, which was quite an accomplishment for a woman several months pregnant in the midst of the late summer heat. Not that Sonja hadn't had practice keeping her cool around their family—Hudson and Gloria had been complete jerks since the moment Henry announced his and Sonja's engagement. They'd been cool with the pair living together, but when Henry decided to marry Sonja, Hudson's dark beliefs surfaced.

Jena loved how Sonja and Henry were so open about how they'd fallen for one another immediately. They'd met at work, in the New Orleans law office owned by Hudson, and according to each of them, it had been love at first sight.

"How are you feeling, Sonja?" Jena wondered what it would feel like to be an aunt.

"I'm good. Tired, but nothing too unbearable."

"She's lying. That baby never stops kicking—he woke us both up last night." Henry's fatherly pride was sweet. Jena wouldn't have pegged her brother as touchy-feely, but obviously Sonja's pregnancy had changed him.

"So it's a boy?"

Henry looked caught in headlights, then his smooth attorney mask fell back in place. "No, we're waiting to find out." He kept chopping carrots for the crudités.

"How are you doing, Jena?" Sonja's soft voice cut across the chatter on either side of them.

"I'm okay. It's been an adjustment coming back this time."

Sonja's brow wrinkled. "Henry said you're done with your Navy stint, though, right? Will you keep working at the same place? For the state's social welfare offices?"

Jena sighed. "I don't know. I haven't been back to the office yet; I'm still on an unpaid sabbatical, basically. I've learned a lot more working for the state's child welfare system than I would have if I'd struck out on my own right away, but I'm tired of working for the government. I want something different. I may have to work there for a few more months, though, until I find another job." She didn't have any other options—she didn't have the funds to open her own nonprofit organization like she'd dreamed about each time she completed another undercover mission.

"You're a gifted social worker from all accounts. I know firsthand how thorough you are." Sonja's words were kind, especially since she'd helped Jena out with cases involving foster children and their biological parents' custody rights.

"Thank you. I'll never stop doing it; it's just a matter of which direction to take it in. Are you still interested in doing more pro bono work at the firm?"

"Definitely. The baby's starting to take priority, but after my maternity leave Henry and I are planning to address changing the firm's mission."

"That's fantastic! But what about my parents?"

Sonja smiled. "Henry has convinced your dad to sign the firm over to us. Your father only wants to be responsible for the Baton Rouge office."

"Yeah, Dad says he's going to spend more time doing charity work with Mom, give back where they should have in the first place," Brandon chimed in and Henry nodded.

"It's true."

Jena looked at Sonja. "I'm so sorry you've had to deal with their crap."

"It's not your fault, Jena." Sonja's grace was certainly something to emulate. Jena knew Sonja didn't blame her or Henry or Brandon for their parents, but Jena had never been able to shake the guilt-by-association.

"I do have to admit, it's a relief that they're finally figuring out what matters." It'd taken over a decade to get this far, and there was still a long way to go.

"You mean figuring out that they were complete asses?" Brandon handed Jena a large measuring cup with beaten eggs. "Here you go."

She poured the eggs into the cornbread mix, stirred in the creamed and regular corn, and then dumped it all into the baking dish. "I do love corn casserole. You're using Grandmom's recipe, I see."

"Not quite." Brandon reached over for the dish, and Jena slid it across the gray granite surface. Her brother doused the top of it with hot sauce.

"I hope we don't choke on it."

"Never. We're bayou born and bred."

"Have you thought of getting your doctorate, sis?" Henry spoke up.

"No way." Getting her master's in social work had been excruciating, balancing night school with her "Navy" schedule. She shuddered. "At least, not for now." She looked around the room, and no one reflected any type of disappointment. Quite the opposite. Her brothers and their partners all looked like she'd given them the answer they wanted. But why?

She sought out Jeb's gaze before she remembered that it wasn't her place to do so any longer. Apparently he'd forgotten, too, as his eyes were on her, and she watched his cool assessment melt into something hotter. Primal.

This had to stop, but how? She offered him a small smile, a way of saying sorry. As if they stood a chance of moving into a casual friendship again.

Jeb looked away, and the loss of warmth made her shiver. No matter what he did or said, they'd always have this connection—which made it smart to break it all off completely now, while they were both young enough to move on. Except she felt like she was eighty, and in truth they didn't have a hell of a lot to move on from. Their relationship had been shallower than she'd thought.

Brandon coughed. "Um, that's what I'm trying to tell you, Jena. You've mentioned in the past that your dream is to run your own social work business, maybe an NPO, I don't know—you'll figure that part out."

A tiny glimmer of hopeful comprehension dawned. What was her brother saying?

Brandon cleared his throat. "Dad's signed over the NOLA law practice to Henry. He and Sonja are opting to eventually turn it fully nonprofit, or at least take on a heftier amount of pro bono work. Did I say that correctly, you two?" He addressed Henry and Sonja, who smiled as if they'd won the lottery. Sonja's relaxed posture, with her arm resting on her baby bump, underscored her belief in the work she and Henry were going to do.

"We definitely need more time to transition fully to nonprofit, but we've already been able to take on cases that need our help." Henry placed his arm across Sonja's shoulders and she reached up and grasped his hand. A stab of envy hit Jena's solar plexus and she closed her eyes and sucked in a deep breath as her training had taught her to do when faced with something unpleasant. But no amount of training eased the constant heartache that had plagued her since Jeb found her in Asunción.

"Dad offered to help Brandon get back on his feet," Henry began.

"Which I turned down, even before we knew that Jeb hadn't blown through all of the money. Taking financial—or any other kind of support from Mom and Dad isn't in the cards for me. No matter how much they're changing."

"Now that you have some resources again, will you quit your new job?" She couldn't imagine Brandon working for someone else. He'd been his own boss since they were kids, really.

"I'm not certain. I was hoping Jeb and I could explore some new opportunities, or even start over with Boats by Gus. But it doesn't look like that'll happen." Jena noticed that Jeb didn't voice support for Brandon's words. The weight of how her failure in South America had affected her family blanketed her with exhaustion. As Jeb remained silent, Brandon turned his attention back to her.

"I may have a business opportunity for you, Jena."

"I'm not a boat builder!"

"This would be a social worker job."

"I'm fine with my job for now." It was futile. She knew both Brandon and Henry had heard the lie, and Jeb, though silent, always saw through her bullshit.

"Having my life blown apart, then put back together in such a wonderful way, gave me time to think." Brandon stared at Poppy, wrapped his arm around her small waist, and pulled her up against his side. He kissed her on the mouth before he turned back to Jena, who fought against squeezing her eyes tight and covering her ears. It wasn't younger sister icks from seeing her brother and his girlfriend's open affection, either—more like the pangs of regret she got when she watched Henry dote on Sonja and her burgeoning baby belly. She was alone in the world.

Brandon didn't seem to notice her private pity party, though.

"Hear me out, Jena. I want to open a facility in NOLA that offers help to those who need it most. Sure, I could sign a check over to any one of a dozen charities, but there are so many cracks in the system that need filling. How many times have you told us that? I'd love to see you go after your dream. Let me help you get there, at least to start. I'd be a ghost contributor in the long run."

Jena blinked, shook her head. "I think it's great that you want to make a difference, Brandon, but I don't want your money. I totally support whatever it is you want to do, of course. But I have my own career." Hadn't she always found her way? Until last month, but she wasn't counting that. Couldn't.

"But you've said yourself you're ready to move on from working for the state." Brandon dug in his heels.

"For God's sake, Jena, have some common sense about it all." Henry grabbed a celery stick from a large stainless steel platter and dunked it in bleu cheese dip. "If you don't want to take the money outright, then look at it as a loan. You're not getting any younger, and you'll want to get this idea of yours off the ground as soon as you can. That way you'll be set for the rest of your working life. Aren't you the one who always emphasizes the timeliness of social work? There are children and their families to save right now, today. Time's a-wasting."

"Henry's right. Let me help you go for your dream, Jena. You've done your time in public service with the State of Louisiana and the US Navy. It's your turn," Brandon chimed in.

"It's still public service, the social work center you've talked about starting over the years." Jeb's voice wrapped around her like it always did. His observation revealed he hadn't missed one iota of the conversation—or of her desires when she'd confided in him about her career dreams. They'd had the best conversations, right after the hot sex.

Would memories of their sexy times ever die?

Brandon named a figure he was willing to donate.

Jena gasped. "You don't have that kind of money to throw around right now, Brandon. And I don't want to talk about this in front of everyone."

He held up his hand. "I know it sounds like an exorbitant amount, and you may not use all of it. But I'm going to need the tax break if I'm going to get Boats by Gus going again. And take it from someone who's run his own business for over a decade: It takes a huge amount of personal investment, and time, before you'll see a turnaround. I'll provide annual private donations as well, but it won't be enough to keep it all going. That'll be your job."

"I haven't agreed to anything here." She'd fought enemies of freedom and found placement for the least desirable foster children abandoned by their parents and the state, but at the Boudreaux table, she'd always be the little sister. The girl who needed a little extra boost.

"The reason I'm bringing it all up here is because Henry and Sonja have already agreed to help with the legal side of it all."

"Whatever you decide, Jena, we're going to support it. It's a way to evolve your family legacy in New Orleans, too." Sonja's reasonable voice shook Jena more than her brother's forthright offer. If she refused, she was sinking an entire family vision. Crap.

But if she agreed, she'd be able to start her new life now—no waiting, no searching for an in-between job to shore her regular household bills. A surge of hope mixed with anticipation swirled around her insides. It was the most promising thing to happen to her since she'd come back to NOLA.

"Let me get this straight. You're going to donate funds for me to find a place to build and run a community social service nonprofit. No questions asked, no telling me how to do it?"

Brandon nodded. "Exactly."

"When can you have the funds ready?"

He grinned and looked at Jeb briefly. "Already have them. From the funds that you didn't need for the ransom."

"Okay. I'll need to find a building first."

"That won't take long. The real estate market is flooded with old office buildings." Henry began to carry the food out to Brandon's veranda.

Jena waited until everyone else was outside, then spoke to Brandon alone. "You're not doing this because you feel sorry for me, are you?"

He barked a laugh across the granite island. "Sister, pity's the last thing that I'd ever feel for you."

She let a slow grin form before she held out her hand. "Okay then. I'm in. Deal."

Brandon clasped her hand and they shook.

* * * *

Jeb watched the Boudreaux siblings parry back and forth over the delicious brunch. Brandon's veranda looked like a hotel restaurant, complete with floor-to-ceiling windows that converted to screens to accommodate the Louisiana humidity and temperatures.

He was careful, so very careful, to keep his observation of Jena to a minimum. He had no doubt that each glance he gave her was filled with his self-disgust at going along with her ruse that she'd "needed" him. But keeping his eyes off her was next to impossible. Their attraction continually hummed, invisible yet palpable.

"Did you hear that, Jeb?" Brandon's voice roused him.

"Sorry." He shoved a huge scoop of omelet into his mouth. "Too busy enjoying the fixings." Although the food tasted like balance sheets—nothing could break through his rumination.

"Brandon asked if you know anyone who'd be willing to work the financials for Jena, for a lower salary at first, but then more as the project gets off the ground." Poppy's head tilted at an angle that reminded him of a cat waiting for a mouse to emerge from a gutter spout. His stomach tightened.

"Since I've been working the books for Boats by Gus for most of my career, I don't have a lot of CPA contacts in town. But I'm happy to search the professional database I have access to."

"You're getting ready to leave soon, aren't you?" Henry's question was fair, but discomfort tugged at his gut.

What was his hang up? He'd already told her he was leaving. He wiped his face with the bright linen napkin—definitely a Poppy touch in Brandon's previously minimalistic décor.

"Yes. I'll be flying to Atlanta on Tuesday."

"Atlanta?" Jena's face looked...frozen. Did she think for one minute he'd stay any closer than two days' drive or a plane flight away? He mentally shook himself. Jena didn't care where he went.

"Yes." He named a national accounting firm. "They've given me an offer I can't refuse."

"Congratulations!" Brandon's cheer was sincere, and soon the others chimed in. But Jena remained quiet, withdrawn.

"Thank you."

"Well, damn, there goes my proposal." Brandon casually reached for his drink. Jeb recognized it from when they'd worked together, taken out a client they were courting. Brandon was slick and polished in the art of a business deal.

Jeb decided to beat him to the punch.

"I've never worked with a nonprofit before, so I'd be a terrible choice." Henry's brow rose, and Brandon nailed Jeb with a glance. "I'd never think of allowing you to forgo such a lucrative opportunity, bro. You've earned every cent you're going to earn in Atlanta. At some desk, with no view of the bayou." Brandon softened his jab with a smile, but Jeb's insides began to itch. He had no reason to stay here. He had every reason, in fact, to leave, to get out while his heart and pride were still somewhat functioning.

Poppy began a conversation with Sonja and Jena, clearly moving the group to safer territory. He took advantage and spoke solely to Brandon.

"I'm sorry, but I'm not the man for the job."

"I never said you were. Let it go, it's okay. You've done enough for our family."

Jeb knew Brandon wasn't lying, that he was indeed grateful that Jeb had acted quickly enough to save Jena's life. But it still gnawed at Jeb that he'd broken the friendship code with Brandon. He'd had no reason, other than his own sheer panic over Jena's situation, to not tell Brandon why he was taking the money.

If he helped out Brandon this one time—in fact, helped the entire family as they launched their do-gooder project, would he assuage the guilt that still plagued him?

His stomach flipped. It was the only sign that this was what he was supposed to do, because every fiber of his being—besides his gut—was telling him to get the hell out of Dodge and run. Drive. Fly. To anywhere but New Orleans. Anywhere there wasn't even a slim chance of ever running into Jena again.

Brandon clapped him on the shoulder. "I mean it, Jeb. Let it go. It was a stupid idea on my part—I still hope you'll think about working with me again someday. I get it; you need to strike out on your own. That's fair."

"I'll do it." The words escaped his dry mouth, and he immediately felt a rush of relief. Yes, this would be his payback to Brandon. "But only for a month. I have a thirty-day wait option in my contract with the Atlanta firm."

"Are you sure?" Brandon's excitement was evident in his sparkling eyes, but he stayed stock still, as if afraid the smallest movement would make Jeb change his mind. Brandon's belief in him was humbling, and it shored up his resolve to do the right thing.

"I'm positive. You have me for thirty days."

"Jena's project has you for thirty days." Brandon let out a sigh of relief as he corrected Jeb. "Thank you, bro. It means the world to me."

"My privilege." It was going to be his private hell to have to see Jena for another month. At least it'd be in the light of day, with other people around. No place for temptation.

Because no matter how sure he was that they were through, Jena's presence remained a siren song to his dick.

Are you sure it's just your lust?

He ignored his conscience, like he suspected he'd have to do every day of the next month.

Chapter 3

"Jeb's agreed to be your numbers man, Jena!" Brandon beamed as he loudly announced Jeb's commitment to the group. Sonja and Poppy cheered, Henry nodded with approval, and Jena's mouth gaped open.

"What? No, you can't do this, Jeb. You've got to take the job in Atlanta. I'll find someone. There are always college grads looking for placement." She'd covered her surprise with refusal in the blink of an eye.

"But they don't have the experience I have." Jeb wasn't going to back down now. "And I can help with more than the numbers. When Brandon and I got Boats by Gus off the ground, we each did everything, from mopping floors to hanging roof shingle."

"That's not necessary." Jena's chin jutted out and angry sparks danced in her eyes. "Brandon's providing a generous amount to start with. I'll be fine."

"It's for the entire community, Jena." Jeb stayed calm, met her fiery gaze, ignored the way his body wanted to soothe her. "And don't fret; I'll be gone in a month, if not sooner."

Mollified, she reached for her iced tea and said no more. Jeb stood up. "I'm going to hit the desserts. Can I bring anybody anything?"

No one answered, so he walked into the dining room, where Poppy had arrayed a mind-boggling dessert buffet.

Jeb helped himself to a second slice of Poppy's peach pie, wishing he'd never agreed to come today, yet at the same time knowing he'd done the right thing by offering to help. He'd thought of the Boudreauxes as his own family ever since he'd become fast friends with Brandon in elementary school. After college, it seemed natural for he and Brandon to work together, as they both brought different skill sets to the table. Brandon had the vision to build boats, and Jeb loved numbers and sales.

"Here you go." He startled as Jena spoke next to him, then spooned a dollop of whipped cream onto his pie—but her demeanor had nothing to do with sweet.

"Thanks." He moved to go back to the veranda, anywhere but next to her, where her scent drove him crazy. And he could feel her body heat along his side. *Too close.*

"Not so fast." They were alone. Chatter from the veranda trickled in, but no one would hear their conversation.

"We've said all there is to say, Jena." He didn't want a repeat of their earlier bathroom rendezvous. Hell, he'd been nanoseconds from saying to hell with his resolve to not touch her. And if he touched her...

"You're kidding, right?" She stared at him, using her infinite well of patience. Except Jeb had a new perspective. Even though Jena had always made him feel like he was the only man in the room—in her life, in the world—he knew it was a lie. All of it. She'd hidden a secret life from him for years. It was one thing when she'd broken up with him toward the end of college, told him they both needed to move on.

He'd tried to. And for a while, he'd convinced himself that he had.

"We are nowhere near done talking, Jeb. But enough about that—what made you say "yes" to Brandon?"

"I've already explained my answer, and my terms. I can help for a month. That's it."

If not for the Boudreauxes, he wouldn't have had a safe place to hang out as a kid. He wouldn't have become best friends with Brandon, and he wouldn't have the career experience he did, no matter how disastrously Boats by Gus had ended.

"Why are you agreeing to this? To putting us through this?" The tortured gleam in her eyes made him want to kiss her, hard, then take the whipped cream and...

"Hey, you two, save some pie for the rest of us." Henry stepped up to the banquet and helped himself to more dessert. "God, I love peach pie. Poppy used Mom's recipe, according to Brandon."

"Thanks for leaving me to sink out there, bro." Jena poured herself iced tea, adding three slices of lemon. It was always three slices. She liked tart, and her favorite dessert was key lime pie, but she'd take lemon meringue in a pinch.

"You okay?" Henry's concern made Jeb want to sink through the floor. Had he groaned aloud?

"I'm good." Jena squared her shoulders.

Henry's blue eyes were back on Jeb. "You're not going to change your mind about this, are you?" Henry was slick—like Hudson, a gifted attorney. Jeb knew when he was in over his head.

"I'm not going to tiptoe around it, Henry. I owe your family. You've always been here for me. And I'd like to do my part." It wouldn't kill him to help Jena out, see the NPO get going. Thirty days. Then he'd leave. Because having to work with Jena every day and maintain the distance he required for his sanity? It'd be his undoing.

"You can't do it because you feel you owe anyone, Jeb. It has to be something you're passionate about, or you'll be miserable. Trust me, I've been there."

And Henry *had* been there, working in his father's firm on cases he didn't care about. Since Sonja had come into his life he'd made changes.

"Thanks, man. I'm not a social worker, but giving folks a hand has always appealed to me." Jeb didn't want to talk about it anymore, because the smooth-talking Boudreauxes were not good at taking no for an answer. Especially Jena, who sipped her tea as if she had all the time in the world. As if she hadn't spent the years since college risking her life for her country.

What had Jeb ever done, besides survive?

Henry cut an extra slice of pie for Sonja and walked away with two heaping plates. Resigned to Jena's interrogation, Jeb leaned against the furniture and took a bite of the pie. Jena loved the chase, so he'd end it before it started.

"Go ahead, Jena. Shoot."

Her thumb pinged against her sweating glass, and she shifted on her feet. "I won't take advantage of it. If you decide to work with me, I mean."

"I know. But I won't be working for *you*, per se. I'm doing this for Brandon." Jeb still smarted at how she'd brushed off her I love you text too easily for it to have meant anything but what she'd said it was—a frantic cry for help during a desperate time.

"You know? How do you know? To be fair, you haven't ever seen me in a professional capacity. I'm very businesslike. Nothing like how, how..." Her cheeks looked like the skin of an overripe peach. But he had no desire to ease her discomfort.

"I've seen you in a professional capacity my worst nightmares couldn't have produced. Is that what you meant to say, Jena?"

She blanched. "I can't apologize enough for the hell I put you through, Jeb."

"Forget about it." God knew he'd never forget seeing her so beaten and broken, not knowing if she'd survive the ghastly cut on her face. Knowing he'd have no reason to go on if she didn't make it. The irony hit him square in the gut—she'd survived, and he had all the more reason to leave.

"I'm only helping out as a kick-start deal. Temporarily."

She nodded, her mouth in a grim line. He resented that their ease, the complete unself-consciousness between them, was gone.

"I know you want to help my brother out, but forget it. This will be my project, and I don't need you. You're right, we need to move on with our lives." Her blue eyes regarded him with a coolness he'd never experienced from her, not in the two years they'd agreed to their sexy friendship. This was the detached woman who'd dropped him like a hot potato senior year of college. He realized now that by then she'd been recruited by the CIA. She'd picked her career over him, a youthful choice he didn't fault. He'd wanted space between them then, too. For different reasons. He hadn't been ready to face the very adult emotions Jena stirred in him.

It didn't matter now.

"I've already agreed to do the numbers for you, Jena."

He walked into the kitchen and put his half-eaten pie in the sink. Jena didn't follow him. It was what he wanted—for her to forget about him, because it helped him forget that he'd been such a freaking fool.

* * * *

Jena sat in the cushioned stainless steel chair closest to the veranda's door, allowing her a full view of the Boudreaux brunch while providing a close escape hatch. She'd survived her share of dangerous assignments, and she knew that her need for control over her circumstances was heightened because of Paraguay. It wouldn't last forever, but until it was gone she found comfort in being close to the door. And farther from Jeb.

He was sitting next to Brandon, and she could overhear snippets of their conversation. Enough to know that Brandon wanted Jeb to think about working with him again, even if he wasn't coming out and saying so. Jeb's expression hadn't changed from the careful neutral mask he'd worn since Paraguay. He'd only lifted it for a few brief seconds in his apartment, when she knew he was warring with his lust for her. She'd fought her desire that day, too. And even today, thinking it was the last time she'd ever see him, her body wanted him.

How was she going to accept working with him for a month?

She bit her lower lip, the pain grounding her, keeping her from going down the rabbit hole. She had a life aside from Jeb, and it was damned time to start living it. Brandon's offer had come at the perfect time. If things were a little tense between her and Jeb, so what? It was only temporary. Jeb wouldn't break his one-month promise, she was certain. He wanted out and away from her, too.

"Do you want the whole family there when the baby comes, or the next day?" Poppy's question rose above the many conversations.

Sonja looked at Henry with a slight widening of her eyes. Jena smothered a laugh with her hand. Her brother was so private, she was sure the thought of anyone else in the birthing room made him apoplectic.

"We're going to keep it just us in the delivery room, but we'd love to have everyone meet the baby right after." Henry used his best attorney voice, and Jena gave him silent props. It hadn't been an easy road for him and Sonja, with their parents being such racist fucks for too long. As she watched the un-drama unfold, a tremor of realization snaked through her: If the decades-deep sin of her parents, which had blown their family to smithereens, was able to be addressed, and her siblings were willing to work together to begin a new family legacy, what was her problem?

Why hadn't she been able to keep Jeb as more than a fuck friend? More painful to ask herself: Why had she ever settled for only that?

Chapter 4

Jena thought she'd need weeks to find the right place to launch what she'd begun to think of as The Refuge House, but Brandon had a definite location in mind: an old home that she happened to agree was the perfect spot. Brandon had given her an address to check out in the Garden District. She'd assumed it was a real estate agent's, but she'd been pleasantly surprised to discover the house that her brother had miraculously found—with a little help from Poppy, she later learned.

The renovation began within a week of their brunch at Brandon's.

"Why did you pick this place again?" Jena shouted over the cacophony of drills, hammers, and shouts as the construction crew worked inside the old Victorian.

Brandon's eyes lit up, and it was like looking into a mirror when she was revved up about a mission, or a new client she could find the right aid for.

"This is the center of some of the neediest folks in New Orleans, Jena. But it's far enough away to be safe for them. If we're in too rough of a spot, it might be harder to get the volunteers we're going to need. And I wanted a place that was near all the other, bigger services, like the Salvation Army and Goodwill. It has to be a place where the after-church crowd won't mind stopping, too."

Her brother got distracted by a loud bang and went to investigate. A worker had dropped a can of paint.

She'd been impressed by the house's fresh coat of paint, the gingerbread trim, the colorful detail work, all of which had clearly been accomplished to lure the buyer—her, with Brandon's funding—inside. While the bare bones of the structure appeared solid, she counted one, maybe two, walls left. Whether it was Katrina or age or both, the house had practically been destroyed. She eyed the wooden stairs, which had what she'd bet was the original railing.

"Is the upstairs as bad as this?" A too-familiar voice, too close. She took a step away before she turned and faced Jeb. At her silence, he nodded at the steps and repeated his query.

"No idea." Just like she had no idea what the hell he was doing here. She'd made it clear she didn't need him on site for at least two weeks, bringing the total of their time together to two weeks. Her palms grew sweaty and her heart vied for position with her tonsils. She refused to look at his eyes any longer than she had to, and instead checked out his clothing.

She'd seen Jeb in a suit, in boat clothes, in business casual—he looked especially hot in khakis and a button-down, sleeves rolled to mid-forearm, revealing his dark hair. His naked body was no stranger, either, as familiar as her own—until he'd put the kibosh on their arrangement, which her sexual frustration damned him for.

As well as she thought she knew him, she'd never seen him in construction gear. The waistband of his worn jeans slung low from the weight of his tool belt—so low that his white T-shirt struggled to stay tucked in. He wore a short-sleeve plaid cotton shirt over it, and his deep chestnut locks were covered by a hard hat.

"Tell me you're working for the contractors."

"Ah, no can do. I'm here to help you get your dream started."

"Jeb, we had a deal." Unspoken, maybe, but nonetheless. She hadn't expected him to show up so quickly, to jump in.

"I struck no agreement with you, Jena. I shook Brandon's hand. We all do what we have to do."

"Hey, Jeb!" Brandon waved at him from across the room.

"Gotta go. I believe you're my boss, as of today. And I'm holding you to your promise."

"Promise?"

"You said you wouldn't ever be anything but professional at work." He turned and walked across the house to a cluster of contractors. Jena felt out of place in her work clothes—dress slacks, presentable blouse, basic jewelry. This was her business, her dream come to life. But it felt as though she were the quiet one, the person who had no idea what she was doing.

* * * *

"We're going to need five separate rooms downstairs, and upstairs can be whatever we want. Were you thinking of making this a halfway house?" Robyn Jones, a noted local architect, directed her question to Jena. Brandon had pulled all his networking strings to get the top talent in NOLA to pitch in for The Refuge. Jena was eternally grateful. Her CIA work had kept her too far from NOLA, too out of the local business loop. Brandon's help was immeasurable.

As had been Jeb's. So far, he'd accomplished the work of a paid contractor.

Jeb, Jena, Brandon, and Robyn stood around the makeshift meeting table—plywood atop four sawhorses—in the far corner of the downstairs, where the drywall had been replaced and fresh coats of cream paint dried. The architect projected her images onto the wall.

"Yes, that's the direction this will go. I've spoken to several local charities, and the heroin epidemic is making empty beds a top priority." Jena chewed on her bottom lip. "Tell me, Robyn, how many beds do you think we can fit upstairs?"

"With the required bathrooms, eight, maybe ten, tops. The city code might allow for bunks, but I'm not sure that's what you're going for."

"But this won't be a rehab center, will it?" Jeb studied Robyn's blueprints.

"Not at all," Jena said. "I thought about it, because there's certainly a need for it. But that's not the business I'm interested in. We'll take in folks who need a place before a rehab bed opens up, or right after they get out of treatment, when they're waiting for a halfway house."

"If you take in addicts, you're going to need medical staff. Security, too." Jeb's observation, while completely fair, pissed her off. If anyone knew about security and how to provide it, she did.

Or had. This was where she wanted to be; social work was her calling. But it didn't stop the former CIA operative in her from speaking up from time to time.

"Jeb's right." Brandon had uttered those two words exactly five million times since they'd come together and started work on The Refuge. She hadn't told anyone her idea for a name, not yet.

"Isn't he always?" Jena muttered under her breath, wishing the construction workers were still there, but they'd knocked off an hour early so that the architect could come in. She took a swig of her bottled water. "We need to make several decisions today, like where the walls are going up down here, and if we want to proceed with the living quarters upstairs. I know where I'd like my office to be, and the other three executive suites. They'll be simple, nothing over-the-top. I want maximum space for the waiting lounge and the kitchen."

Jeb's brow rose. "The kitchen?"

She nodded. "People need to eat, and I see us providing meals in rotation with other shelters during holidays and heavy need times, like winter and when the next hurricane hits. It's easier if we set up a commercial facility now, rather than later. Am I right?"

The architect nodded, her smile highlighted by ruby lipstick. "It might require going back into what used to be a butler's pantry and using that space—are you okay with that?"

"Why wouldn't I be?"

"If you want to retain any historical status to this property, some of your proposed changes might not fly with the city board."

"I think the time for historical classification was before the inside was gutted." Her brother's vocation shone at times like these, and she appreciated the clarity.

She sighed. "Brandon's right. We'll keep the outside as close to the original as possible, but we're going forward with this work. This is about the future of New Orleans, and for that we're going to need a fully modernized office space and shelter facilities."

"Jeb, do you have anything?" Jena didn't want him to think she'd leave him out because of her personal feelings.

He scratched his head, his hands speckled with dried paint. Thinking of all the physical work he'd done over the past several days made it difficult to keep her from fantasizing about everything she knew his hands were capable of.

"Honestly? No. Other than getting this place put together, I'm not going to have much to do numbers-wise until your first client walks in the door." He leaned down and pulled several thick files from his briefcase, contradicting what he'd just claimed. He slid the files across the plywood, one to each team member. "I worked up the costs for every category of client, from homeless to addict to domestic abuse victim. You'll see the charts with the associated charges. I don't know a heck of a lot about health insurance, but I made some calls, did a little research. The basic copays for counseling, intake, and referral services are listed."

"When did you find time to do this?" He'd been at the house as much as she had over the past two weeks, often ten, twelve hours a day. And they were very physical days. Most evenings, she collapsed after her shower.

"We're all putting in extra time about now, aren't we?" He didn't meet her eyes as he looked at his laptop. "If you all turn to page thirteen, you'll see what it takes to feed anyone we shelter. I think the commercial kitchen is a requirement."

Jena heard Brandon and the architect chime in on Jeb's observation, saw Jeb's smile at a quick comment the builder threw in. Thank God they couldn't see inside her mind—or worse, her heart, where she still ached for what might have been with Jeb.

* * * *

Jeb knew he was being an asshole, but this was pure survival. It was bad enough that he and Jena worked in the same building each day. At least he'd been able to get wrapped up in the physical construction part and not have to deal with her one-on-one. This business meeting was the most intimate environment he'd faced her in since that day at her brother's, and he planned to keep it that way.

"You've got a talent for numbers." Robyn the architect leaned over his head, looking at the spreadsheet on his laptop.

"As you do for city zoning laws and building code." He was fairly certain that she didn't need to know every accounting detail to build the best facility for the center—and that she didn't mean for her breasts to be right next to his right cheek. And yet, they were. His nape tingled, and— damn it—he didn't stop himself from pinpointing the cause.

Jena stared at him and Robyn, her displeasure marked by the curl of her sweet lips. No, just lips. No more sexy adjectives where Jena was concerned. *Jena lied to you, never fully trusted you.* If he repeated the saying like a mantra, he'd reprogram his attraction to her. He'd read about it on a post-apocalyptic relationship site.

When he didn't take the architect's feminine bait, she straightened and walked back to her computer. "I'm done with my presentation." She looked at Jena, whose detached expression was back in place.

"Thank you, Robyn. You've gone above and beyond your job description."

Was it just Jeb, or had Jena just verbally speared Robyn the architect? More likely, she'd aimed the jab at him. That explained the tight ball of nerves in his gut. He and Jena had been linked by some invisible cord since they were little kids. To expect that to dissipate because they'd called off the last variation of their relationship was insanity.

"We're making good progress this week. I'm hoping we'll each have our own offices by next week, so we can install the furniture." Jena stood, and he told himself he wasn't fazed by how loosely her business casual clothing hung on her frame. It wasn't his problem if Jena hadn't gained back the weight that the stress of her ordeal in South America had caused her to lose so precipitously. He watched her as she shifted her attention to Brandon, who came by when his regular job permitted it.

"So, what do you think?" Jena asked him.

"I think you're doing a fantastic job. You really don't need me around anymore. Have you come up with a name yet?"

Jena nodded. "The Refuge House."

"Nice and to the point."

"Thanks."

"Are you still set to have the first client in two more weeks?" Brandon looked up from the one of the folders Jeb had handed out.

"I'm hoping it will be a lot sooner than that." She looked at the architect. "When is the earliest we can have the front reception area and extra waiting room done?"

Robyn clicked through the slides she'd already presented. "If we go with this more basic design, we'll be ready by the end of next week, or early the following."

Jeb eyed the space around them. They had made a lot of progress, but he knew the rest of it wasn't going to be any easier. Of course, he wanted the space to remain unfinished until after he'd moved on. It'd be easier to leave before he became too invested.

Before he spent too much time around Jena.

Frustration made his fingers drum on the plywood surface. He couldn't leave for Atlanta until he finished this project. From the figures he'd run, it'd be months before that happened. He wouldn't be around to see it come to full fruition. He'd agreed to thirty days, period.

He dreaded the remaining weeks in an office space with Jena. It was one thing to hold up his personal vow when they barely spoke to one another, but once the clients came in, Jena would need resources. And she'd come to him, expect him to pull the money out of thin air. He'd have to see her, deal with his emotions every goddamn day.

"Where are we on the funds so far?" Brandon got to the jugular of the shelter.

"We're good." Jena tapped her pencil on her notebook. Her cleavage taunted him, reminded him of all they'd lost—all he'd lost. The scent of her skin, the warmth of her mouth on his cock… "Right, Jeb?"

Shit. She'd caught him red-handed, and by the glimmer of amusement in her eyes, she knew it.

"Since the Boudreaux Foundation is covering all initial start-up costs, yes, we're good. But we need to start bringing in money as soon as we can. We're supposed to be fully solvent, with your funding only as a backup, right?" He tossed his query to Brandon, who looked a little stymied. Had he caught the waves of sexual tension between his sister and Jeb?

"Good to know." Brandon stood. "Thanks for keeping me in the loop. But I have to say, this is your baby now, Jena." He left the room. The rest of the group began to stand and pick up their supplies.

Jena's face was flushed, and she refused to look at him. Instinct told him that he'd upset her—or, worse, she was still feeling the attraction between them. Jeb's about-face on their friends-with-benefits deal was pure instinct, nothing but animal survival.

The same animal reaction tugged at him, nudged him to go talk to her as the meeting broke up, make small talk, anything to mend the chasm between them.

A split he'd willingly made. Jena was his lethal addiction, and what did his friends in recovery say? One day at a time. Yeah, one day at a time he'd stayed away from her, and he needed to do it again now. Get up and walk through the door and go back to his apartment.

"Jena." He spoke quietly, unable to resist.

She jumped and whirled around, the rickety table shaking from her sudden movements.

"Jeb. Geez, you're like a cat." She smoothed her hair, her attempt at composure. He knew. Whenever Jena was nervous, she had to keep her fingers occupied. Fiddling with her hair, a beverage glass, or silverware were her prime choices.

"Sorry—didn't mean to startle you." Yet he had meant to give her zero warning that he was close. As if he stalked her.

"I thought everyone had left." She looked around the room, anywhere but at him. It should relieve him to not have to look into those eyes, but, like any craving, it wasn't an easy urge to break.

"They have. I took out a bunch of the trash." He'd loaded the bins in the back and still needed to pull them out to the curb for the pre-dawn pickup. "You shouldn't hang around here so late."

She smirked. "What do you think I'll do when we open the doors for good?"

"Delegate." He didn't like how she always took on full responsibility for everything—but he adored her for it, too. Had adored her. Christ, he had to get a grip on his own demands. They were done, and she was his past.

She shrugged before gathering up her papers and heading toward the big room behind the stairs, the planned kitchen. Jena stopped at the railing and looked at him. Her eyes caught the soft glow of the sunset, visible through one of only a few original windows. Standing a foot from him in the historical space, it was easy to trick himself and think that they still could be friends. That he'd learn to trust her again, forget how foolish he'd felt when he fully realized the extent of her undercover work. The risks.

"Eventually, we'll have to hire more social workers. Until then, it's my job to close up shop each day...and night. Besides, we're not in a rough part of town. I've never felt threatened after dark."

"Once word gets around about how spiffy this place is, you can't be certain a thug wouldn't cause trouble." His gut tightened at the thought of any harm coming to her. "Of course, you're trained to take down threats."

He saw her wince, and a part of him—the old part that died in Paraguay—would have believed she regretted not telling him what she really did for a living.

"I've got to work late tonight, because work on the kitchen starts tomorrow."

He nodded. "The experts are descending."

She flashed him a quick grin. "You're great at what you've helped with, like painting. But it's the law—we have to employ certified utilities contractors."

"Why do *you* have to work late, though?"

She sighed. "I haven't picked out the colors for the flooring or walls yet. And I have to figure out what's worth spending the big bucks on—a commercial stovetop, sure. But do we need a single or double refrigerator? Will it fit? Things like that."

"Let me help." His offer hung between them. He shifted, leaned his hip against the stair railing.

"Jeb—"

"No strings attached. We know how to do that part."

Her pupils dilated, and he couldn't help remembering other times he'd watch her body react to his touch.

She shook her head. "You and me working on anything more than what you agreed to...it's too hard."

"I'm not asking you to go to bed with me, Jena. There isn't even a bed in this place yet." He didn't mention the times they'd had sex in places without a bed, like her kitchen counter or his shower, but from the flush on her face, he didn't need to.

"Fine." She turned and walked out of sight. It was fire play, for sure. He should turn, pick up his briefcase and tool belt, and go home. But the thought of his empty apartment and a night of crunching numbers or streaming his favorite show until his mind went numb didn't appeal to

him as much as the prospect of working with Jena on something other
than keeping their sex life secret.

And planning a kitchen was way better than chasing her to Asunción.

* * * *

"It's big enough for a commercial fridge, width-wise. But I don't know
about the depth." Jena stood in the small space meant for the refrigerator.
She'd more than half expected Jeb to have headed home by now, but
he'd patiently taken measurements of every inch of the kitchen, offering
his ideas freely.

And he hadn't made a pass at her. Not even a flick of his eyes roaming over
her figure like he usually did. Or had done, before finding her in Paraguay.

"Here, let's re-measure." Jeb used a carpenter's tape measure like another
man might play a guitar. His long fingers had calluses she didn't remember,
no doubt from the hours of construction work and painting. The shackles
of paint on his clothes weren't anything she'd consider sexy, but on Jeb...

"It's going to be a super tight fit, but I think it might work. If you
consider the number of beds you'll have, and the extra room for temporary
cots during weather events, you won't regret going as big as possible with
the appliances."

"True."

"And you have the funding. That's a given."

His words rankled her. "That's the point, though. Like you said earlier,
The Refuge needs to be completely self-supporting. Brandon's generosity
is great, and I admire what he's wanting to do. But any good NPO or
charity operation works from sound financial principals, which means
we don't touch the original endowment, ever. We get an expert to help us
with investments and we get busy with grants."

"You're a grant writer, aren't you?"

She was touched he'd remembered. "Yes."

"Why the sidelong look, Jena?"

"I didn't think you knew a whole lot about what I do." Too late, she
wished she would have used her filter. Damn it. They'd been getting along
well, too—no tongues or longing body parts involved. A first.

"We never talked a whole lot, did we? After college, I mean." He didn't
pick up on her comment, and relief and gratitude relaxed her shoulders.

"It's never going to be easy between us, with our history, is it? But we
had a childhood friendship."

"We did. And it seems to me we messed up when we allowed it into other areas."

"Other areas?" She tried to tease him and immediately regretted it.

"Sorry. I hear you." Loud and clear. He was done with their physical relationship, which meant she was, too.

His eyes were bright in the kitchen's bare bulb lighting. His dark hair and olive skin took on a golden hue. "We do better as friends, Jena."

She swallowed and damned the stinging in her eyes. "And now, we're business partners."

"Correction—colleagues. You're my boss."

"Teammate. The Refuge is a team operation."

"Whatever you say, Captain." He smiled, and she found the sense of togetherness in the yet-to-be-built kitchen, both of them fully clothed, to be more intimate than any sex they'd shared over the past two years.

Jeb held her glance for a split second longer than expected, then looked at his watch. "It's late. I'll walk you to your car."

"Sure thing."

As she drove back to her apartment, she let the tears fall. One more time, she'd grieve the what-could-have-beens, because all she'd ever get from Jeb was what they had returned to tonight: their lifelong friendship.

It might not have been her first choice, but she'd take it.

Chapter 5

The next morning Jena decided the work crew needed beignets to soothe the constant hammering and pounding of construction. Jena picked up the delicious fried dough from Café du Monde. Her apartment wasn't far from The Refuge House's location in the Garden District, but morning traffic downtown gave her time to think—and promise herself she'd be grateful for the new friendship forming between her and Jeb. He'd made it clear from day one of the project that his time on their team was temporary. It was time for her to grow up and take things at face value, no matter what her body wanted.

Okay, maybe there was another part of her that wanted Jeb still, too— for far more than sexy times—but where would it lead? To more disappointment and regret?

"Hey, thanks for the treats this morning!" Robyn slid into the seat next to Jena at the plywood table. "We really need to get your furniture in here, at least for your office."

"As soon as you put up the walls, I will."

"I'm working on it. Hey, do you want to get lunch?" Robyn regarded her with piercing green eyes offset by dark tortoiseshell glasses. "I imagine it gets old, being around so many guys all day."

Jena laughed. "Sounds good. We can walk over toward Magazine Street and have our choice."

Twenty minutes and a hot, muggy walk later, they were in the air-conditioned comfort of a local home-cooking restaurant. Jena had never taken the time to develop close friends, because she couldn't share her life with them. But ending her undercover work meant it was time to begin a new life, and girlfriends were part of it, she hoped.

Robyn sipped her iced tea. "Have you lived in NOLA your whole life?"

"My whole life. My parents moved to Baton Rouge after Katrina, but I was in college by then and stayed here. How about you?"

"I'm originally from Biloxi, but my dad's job—he's an oil engineer—brought us here."

"Do you have a big family?"

"No, it's just my dad and I. My mother died back in Mississippi, before we moved. Breast cancer."

"Oh, I'm so sorry. That's awful."

Robyn's glance moved around the eclectic décor before she settled back into the conversation. "It was. I was only twelve, and it was the worst time in my life. Ever. But my dad's been great, and I still have both of my grandmothers. I go back to see them in Biloxi when I can."

"What made you want to be an architect?"

"Ever since I played with my first set of Legos, I was hooked. It's kind of in my blood, with my dad being an engineer on the rigs."

"Is he gone a lot?"

"Not as much as he used to be. He's mostly on the land side of things now."

"Do you live with him?"

Robyn giggled. "Oh, no way, girl. I'd drive him nuts. And he'd put a serious crimp in my dating life!"

Jena smiled as the waitress delivered their food. "It's good to have your own place."

"Yes."

They ate in companionable quiet. The hush puppies were the best Jena had tasted in forever, and she realized her appetite hadn't been the greatest since she'd returned. It was wonderful to enjoy her meals again.

"So Jena, what's between you and Jeb?"

"What?" Jena answered with a mouthful of hush puppy, hoping she'd heard Robyn wrong.

"You two have an obvious connection."

"We do?" She wiped her mouth, stalling.

"I'm not blind. You have a silent communication going on."

"You didn't let it stop you from flirting with him."

Robyn laughed. "No, I didn't. And, as I'm sure you noticed, he wasn't interested. At. All. Which made me think that maybe you're more than work or family friends."

"We are all of the above. Jeb has been a part of my family since we were in elementary school. But he and I are friends, period."

"Uh-huh." Robyn took her explanation at face value, and Jena immediately knew she'd found the first friend of her new life. If she and Robyn became close, she could always confide in her later. But for now, it was hard enough reminding herself that she and Jeb were friends. Period.

* * * *

Jena and the architect came back into the office laughing like high schoolers, and Jeb felt a distinct flip of unease in his chest.

He was the one Jena usually laughed with. She'd had friends in school and college, but since they'd reconnected two years ago at her parents' annual Christmas bash, she'd been more of a loner—which, after learning that she was basically a female James Bond, made sense.

And it made him more than a little bit sad for her. He cherished his bond with Brandon, and he had several other friends he hung out with on the weekends. It hadn't occurred to him to push his and Jena's time together into something more than sex.

And now he'd ended that possibility for both of them.

He waited until she put her bag down before he approached.

"What can I do for you, Jeb?" There was a quiet joy emanating from her that he hadn't seen in…years. All because of lunch with a colleague?

"It doesn't have to be now, but I'd like to go over some figures with you. I did a prospectus for the first twelve months, with client goal breakdowns."

"Client goals?" She paused, then sat in the cheap folding chair. Were her bruises gone? It'd been over a month since Asunción, but her skin had been so battered.

"Yes. I thought it'd be helpful for you to have an idea of the volume we need in order to keep afloat the first year."

She let out a short laugh. "We're not selling widgets, Jeb. I can't place numbers on client load. There's no telling who we'll have, and it's going to vary greatly depending upon season, weather, economic realities."

"It's a business, Jena." The worst thing to say to a social worker. Before she protested, he held up a hand. "Hear me out. This is why you need a full team. You're the expert care and client need manager. I'm your temporary numbers guy. You take care of people, I take care of the resource management."

"You're not hearing me, Jeb. This isn't a boat factory." Her voice remained calm, low, but it was like a verbal Molotov cocktail—and it ignited frustration he didn't know he harbored.

"I know that." He unclenched his jaw. "More than you realize, I know that. You're the one who said The Refuge needs to be self-supporting. I'm telling you how to get there."

"Fine. Figure out another way. I'm not running a social welfare operation around quotas."

Anger sparked, but it wasn't a quick reaction to not being heard, or having his words twisted out of context. The embers of his resentment over what she'd kept from him had never gone out.

"We can go over this later. Maybe we're not hearing each other." She saw it, too, saw the depth of his fury.

He turned and walked out the door.

* * * *

"While I appreciate the work you're doing to help Jena out with The Refuge House, we need to make this right between us, Jeb." Brandon eyed him over a plate of pulled pork and beef brisket. The noisy smokehouse had seemed like the perfect meeting place, since it was in between the docks where Brandon worked and The Refuge House.

Jeb took a swig of his lemonade before he answered. "You'll never trust me again, Gus." He slipped into the nickname Brandon used on his business, Boats by Gus. Thank God at least five million had escaped the cartel's bloodstained hands.

"If you'd stolen the money for any other reason, you'd be right. I'd never trust you again." Brandon was as bullheaded as Jena. He saw what he wanted, ignored the rest.

"I could have mentioned it to you, before I left." Even as he slow-pitched Brandon the opportunity to hit it out of the park, Jeb knew he'd had no time to do anything but get on the next flight out of NOLA. He'd barely made the transfer in Miami, and once on the ground in Asunción, his entire focus had been to save Jena.

"Stop fighting me on this, Jeb. We've been friends since…"

"Since forever."

"You've never told me how it was, when you got there. Or how it was to find Jena in that hellhole basement."

No, he hadn't. The visits with the State Department at the US Embassy, meetings with both US and Paraguayan law enforcement agencies, were all a blur. And Jena's condition when they'd let her go—he forced his brain to stop. He couldn't go down that mental alleyway, or he might never come out of the despair he'd fought through the last month and a half.

"You were there when I got back, with the FBI." Jeb didn't like remembering the first week back. He'd been arrested at the NOLA airport and taken to the county jail. Turned out communications between federal and local law enforcement weren't as immediate as he'd assumed.

"I'm sorry you got locked up, man. If I'd known you'd saved Jena..." Brandon shook his head. "It's like the whole family was affected by Jena's work, even if we didn't know about it."

"It was. The fact remains that you and I are the only ones who know mostly everything."

"You think she was working for the CIA?"

Jeb thought before he spoke. Of course he knew she'd been employed by the agency, but she hadn't told Brandon yet—couldn't, until her resignation was official, so neither could he. "No idea. All I know is that she was working for the government, on something classified."

"I have to wonder if she was ever even in the Navy. We never saw her in uniform. She made it seem like she did short-notice missions as needed, for the Reserves."

That's what Jeb had believed, too. One day she'd tell Brandon and Henry what her real job had been. Until then, he had no reply.

"As for me being arrested, it wasn't a picnic, but I survived." He'd been in the county jail for less than twelve hours. "It's not your fault the different factions weren't talking to one another."

"But it's on me that you were arrested in the first place. If I'd waited a week longer to file the charges, you'd never have gone to jail."

Jail was nothing compared to what Jena had been through. "To be honest, I was already so exhausted and jet lagged, it didn't matter." A lie. The county jail had only served to remind him of Jena's ordeal, how close they'd all come to losing her.

"Tell me, Jeb. What happened when you found her?"

"I had to speak to all the embassy folks, like I told you." He pushed his plate away, unable to look at food as his stomach sank. It never failed—any thoughts of Paraguay made him want to hurl. He had nothing against the nation, which had looked pretty enough. It was the hell seared into his memory that soured his perspective.

"You said it took two days of wrangling."

"A day and a half, yeah. Then the local police had to agree to stay out of it. There are so many layers to an international kidnapping, I had no clue."

"But you got through them, bro." Brandon's use of the childhood nickname made Jeb feel like an imposter. A true brother wouldn't have made a move without telling the other, especially when it involved an entire business.

"Somehow, yeah, we got through the red tape. The transfer took all of thirty seconds to go through, but then it took the cartel another hour to release her. They didn't get the call that the money was in their account on time, so they started to…"

"Hurt her." Brandon's face was white. "The FBI agent told me, after you'd given your statement."

"They tortured her. When I saw her, I thought she was dead." Her face was bloodied and her body limp. "But head and mouth injuries bleed the most."

"She's okay, bro. She made it. You got her out of there." Brandon's words, meant to comfort, only underscored the depth of all their fears. They'd come too close to never seeing her again.

Jeb blew out a long breath. "We got out of there after she was seen by the embassy doc at the local hospital. I couldn't go with her—she was taken out on a life flight, a service the embassy had access to. Then a Foreign Service Officer drove me to the airport to catch my flight out."

"You had no idea you'd be arrested here?"

Jeb laughed. "None. In fact, all I was concerned about was when and where Jena was going to get her medical care." She'd been flown straight to Washington, D.C., and transferred to Walter Reed. The medical staff on the life flight had stopped her bleeding and stabilized her until a plastic surgeon tended to her. He only knew that because the embassy employee had kept him up to speed until he boarded his flight.

"There's hardly a mark on her face. And she seems to cover it with makeup okay."

"She has a scar, but you're right, it's faded so much already, and there won't be much left of it before long." Except he'd always know what had happened, how she'd suffered. Rage blinded him and he forced himself to breathe through the emotions that crested over him, threatening to turn him upside down again. *She's safe. Jena's okay.*

"Jeb, it's okay. Jena's out of there. You saved her." Brandon's voice grounded him, and he looked at his lifelong friend.

"How did you know I was—?" He didn't have to say what or why; he and Brandon had a connection that was almost scary at times.

"You're about to crush that glass in your hand." Brandon nodded at Jeb's lemonade, and he relaxed his fingers and took his hand off the vessel.

"It catches up with me sometimes. How close we came." Cool relief washed over him. He'd shared his fear with no one.

"To losing her." Brandon nodded. "I know. If my parents ever knew, it'd kill them. For the record, my folks would have raised the money from their friends, you know. They've been racist asses for most of their lives, but they do love their children, as best they can."

"I do know. I also know that would have taken too much time. You know what they did to her when the money was five minutes past their demands. If I'd waited—"

"My sister would be dead."

Jeb nodded. "Yes."

"Do you know for sure that she's done doing this kind of, uh, work?"

Jeb nodded. "She says she's done with the Navy, and it appears to me she's thrown herself into The Refuge House."

"How's that going, you two working together? Besides what I've seen." Jeb tensed. Did Brandon suspect anything between him and Jena?

"Fine. Good, actually. Jena's a stellar professional."

"She is, and she's found her calling with social work. But it wasn't enough to keep her from getting into dangerous work with the Navy, or whomever she worked for."

"You know as much as I do—she said she's done with that part of her life." And he had to believe her—anyone who'd seen her as battered as she'd been would. The thought of her ever doing that kind of work again was worse than the anxiety the memories of Paraguay triggered.

"How long do you plan to work there?" Ah, here it was. Jeb knew Brandon as well as he knew himself. Like him, Brandon was a fixer. From the way he was staring at him, he saw Jeb as his current project, he'd bet.

"Another couple of weeks. My Atlanta life beckons." He paused, then forged ahead. "I can't thank you enough for not affecting my career over what happened."

"No thanks needed. You were working under extenuating circumstances. Speaking of which, would you let me know before you drive out of town?"

"Why do I get the feeling this isn't about a farewell party?"

Brandon shook his head. "You're a gifted accountant and executive. I want to know when you're leaving because I want to counteroffer your new job. I'm hoping you haven't already signed on the dotted line."

"I haven't, but I did verbally accept. I've got thirty days to back out, which I see no reason to. Why are you so determined to get Boats by Gus going again? I thought you were set with your new job." Jeb knew Brandon had taken a high-level position with an international ship building company in NOLA. As a naval architect, his skills were highly desirable.

"'Set' is a matter of perspective. I enjoy it enough, and it's challenging, but it's nothing like what we did with Boats by Gus. We were a good team, Jeb."

"We were." Until he'd changed everything.

"You say I'd never trust you again, and while I'm sure I might be jumpy about funds and accounts for a while, there are ways to have a third party oversee that for us. I don't want to lose the working relationship we had, Jeb. I designed my best sailboats knowing you were at the helm of the business side. And our flat-bottom boats were the best. The factory's waiting for us to start again."

"How are you going to do that while working at the shipbuilder's?"

"I'll quit. But not until you're ready to partner up again."

Jeb stared at his last remaining best friend in the world. It'd be incredible to be back with Brandon, working his dream job. It'd also be a fucking nightmare, a constant reminder of how quickly he'd dropped it all to go after Jena.

The woman he'd never be able to have.

Brandon saw the reluctance and leaned back, both hands on the table. "Don't answer me yet. Hell, don't give me an answer for a year. I'll wait longer if I have to. Do what you need to do with Jena at her center first. Go to Atlanta, try the new job. But promise me you'll take another look at coming back to Boats by Gus."

"Whoa—I'm working at The Refuge House for *you*. You're the one that put me over a barrel about it." They both laughed. "I have to leave, Brandon. It's the right time for me to start over, like you have."

Brandon didn't reply right away, just let Jeb's words settle.

"Remember when my father caught us smoking out back, behind the shed?"

"Oh, my God, how old were we? Twelve? I thought we were both going to get the belt, for sure." The belt and other forms of abuse were part of Jeb's home life until he'd found escape and salvation with the Boudreaux family.

"Naw, Dad wasn't that kind of disciplinarian. He was more into making sure we understood consequences." Brandon referred to the community service Hudson signed them up for after the cigarette incident. They'd spent the next four Saturdays helping the neighborhood hermit, Mr. La Croix, clean out his house, a hoarder's haven and their torment. The worst part wasn't the piles of decades-old newspapers, or the six feral cats that roamed the stinking place. Mr. La Croix had suffered early lung and tracheal cancer. His tracheostomy tube had horrified them, as had how he'd smoked through the man-made opening at the base of his throat.

Jeb laughed. "Poor Mr. La Croix."

"Are you kidding? Poor fucking us." Brandon grimaced.

"I never picked up a cigarette again. And I can't stomach cigar smoke."

"Same." Brandon's eyes crinkled, revealing the depth of his sincerity. Regret yanked on Jeb's awareness. He knew Brandon like he knew himself. Leaving NOLA wasn't just about leaving Jena. He'd be letting go of life as he'd known it. He wanted to make sure he left nothing unspoken with Brandon. Maybe he'd been too harsh on himself about taking the money. Like Brandon said, he'd saved Jena's life.

But if he healed his friendship with Brandon and agreed to work with him again, he'd forever be tied to the Boudreauxes.

"You've gotten serious again." Brandon playfully punched him on the upper arm. "That bad in South America, huh?"

"You've no idea." He slid his empty glass away.

"Sorry, man." Brandon looked around for the waitress and waved her over for the check. "Take your time. When you're ready to move on from The Refuge, or Atlanta, all I ask is for first dibs."

Jeb didn't say anything, but he didn't want his silence to imply consent.

"I can't promise anything right now, Brandon."

"Fair enough. Let's meet up again soon."

"See you." They clasped hands, gave one another a brotherly hug.

Damn it if a huge lump didn't clog his throat.

Chapter 6

Jena looked up from her desk—her real, solid desk that had been delivered earlier in the day—as Robyn walked through the opening that would become her office doorway. Jena's immense gratitude that Robyn had remained involved, even after they'd signed off on her plans, made her smile.

"Hey, Robyn. What's up?"

Robyn placed two pieces of card stock in front of her.

"Good morning. These are the chips for the wall paint. The first set is a typical health services office palette, and the second is more along the lines of the historical vibe of this house."

"There's no question I'd rather go with the Victorian colors." Their clients deserved to feel like they were coming home. This wasn't a medical facility, and she didn't want the upstairs to resemble a hospital ward. She fingered the eggplant and mustard chips. "Do you have any idea what color the original rooms were?"

Robyn shook her head. "I don't, but I'll bet we could get information from the historical society, or at least the library."

"Those photos will all be black and white."

"We can actually guess on some of the colors using a program my firm has. I'll see what I can find out." Robyn crossed her hands over her chest. "What do you think about your space?"

"I love it!" And she did. Her office was down a corridor from reception, the last and largest one in the facility. "I can't believe they've gotten the walls up so quickly. Thank you so much for staying on, Robyn. It means a lot to me, and the community. Your work is going to make a difference for so many people."

Robyn sank into the easy chair across from Jena's desk. "I'm glad to hear it. But after the kitchen extension is complete, I'm afraid I have to move on. My firm gave me an extra two weeks here, tops."

"You must have a long line of clients eager for your talents."

"You seem quiet lately, Jena. Is everything okay on the personal front?" Robyn's expressive eyes touched a place in Jena's heart that she'd forgotten existed: the girlfriend chamber, where men couldn't reach no matter how great they were as a partner, or brother, or friend. Or more.

Nope, not going there.

"It's good." She still wasn't ready to spill it all, but as Robyn sat patiently, clearly open and nonjudgmental, an emotional dam broke. "I've been better, actually. Without going into it, I had a pretty complicated job with the Navy Reserves. I was out of the country for several months, on my last deployment, and it got riskier than I'd expected. I'm finding the transition back to regular life a little difficult." It was scary how easy the lies still came—necessary lies, but she'd never been more aware of how much of her life since college had been a total sham. At least, the parts she presented to her family. And Jeb.

Robyn nodded. "I totally get it. My cousin was in the Marines for five years and she's still not the same. I have no clue what she did, other than go to the Middle East, Iraq or Afghanistan, for a year at a time, twice. My auntie and uncle were so worried. So were my Dad and I. Have you thought about getting some counseling?"

Jena bit back a grin. She'd had to undergo extensive debriefing at CIA headquarters, and at Walter Reed, before returning to New Orleans. They'd also sent her to see a psychiatrist who specialized in special ops trauma, at the National Military Hospital's Bethesda, Maryland, location. It was counseling on speed. Not that she was able to share that, though.

"I did see someone for a bit. Like I said, it's not anything super heavy right now, just an awareness that I'm in the middle of a career and life change. Moving on from my past."

"I'm here for you." Robyn looked at her watch and stood up. "I have a meeting with the contractors on the extension in five minutes. The roof's not measuring to spec."

"You'll work it out." Jena knew there were no mistakes in Robyn's plans—they'd been checked and checked again by her firm. "And Robyn, thanks for listening."

"Anytime. We need to get a cocktail night on the calendar. Part of your stress is probably from the long hours. Take it from me: work can be a salvation, but it can also be the death of you."

Jena laughed. "Don't I know it."

* * * *

Jeb stood just outside Jena's office, plywood in hand, ready to frame the doorway so the door could be hung later today. He'd stopped to look at a text from Brandon and unwittingly overheard the tail end of her conversation with Robyn.

"Hey, Jeb." Robyn smiled as she left the office and walked past him.

"Robyn." *Fuck.* All he'd had to do was put the damn beams on the floor outside Jena's office and walk away unseen. Now he had to say good morning to Jena—he was certain she'd heard him reply to Robyn.

"Jeb. What do you have here?" Jena stood in the doorway, her eyes missing nothing, from the two-by-fours to the caught look he knew was on his face.

"We're hanging your door today."

"Doors are important, aren't they?" The sparkle in her eyes told him all he needed to know.

"I wasn't eavesdropping."

She shrugged, her go-to defensive gesture. "Wasn't anything to hear."

"Other than you're leaving your past behind you." Goddamnit, he needed to work on his filter.

Her chin raised and he fought to remain in place. He wanted to take one, two steps back. Hell, he'd turn tail and run to escape—

Escape what? His heart pounded and his palms suddenly dripped sweat, making his phone slip from his hand to the floor. It wasn't unlike the panic attacks he'd experienced after he'd returned from South America, gotten out of the county jail, and sought refuge in his apartment. The after effects of seeing someone you cared about as still as death, short on blood.

He bent to pick up his phone and found he'd been beat, again. Jena's hand grasped the cell and his hand covered hers. As if his brain was a step behind, his rapid pulse blocking his ability to function. As if he'd downed a tranquilizer. Then his serenity snapped back into place. Jena's touch, like magic, cured him even when she didn't intend to.

The instant spark of attraction that ignited from their physical connection didn't escape his comprehension.

Or Jena's, her eyes wide and her mouth parted in surprise.

"Oh." A soft sound, let out on a breath scented with toothpaste and pastry. Jena's sweet tooth knew no bounds, and sugar was her go-to when stressed. She crouched in front of him, giving a beautiful view of her slim knees, her frothy lemon skirt hiked up and exposing a solid length of thigh.

"Jeb. Stop." The barest whisper, but she wasn't moving away, didn't let go of his phone. He kept ahold of her hand, wondering if he'd forgotten how soft her skin was or had never fully appreciated it before.

"Hey, kids!" Hudson Boudreaux's low voice barked down the corridor, the unfinished walls echoing the sound like a clap of thunder.

Jena dropped his phone as she jumped up and back. Jeb let go of the wood beams as he heard the unmistakable crunch of his phone's screen.

"What are you doing here, Daddy?" Shit, she never called Hudson "Daddy." Usually it was "Dad," or, more often, nothing. He might as well have held a big sign saying, "sexual tension zone here," with an arrow aimed at his dick, which was harder than the two-by-fours he'd dropped. He avoided looking at the elder Boudreaux for a few breaths. Jesus, he was glad to be in his loose, worn cargos. If he'd worn jeans, the entire staff would have seen his erection.

"Now, that's a fine good morning." The bold words didn't match Hudson's hesitancy. "I didn't mean to bust in, but I've been curious about your project. You didn't tell me much about it on the phone the other day."

"That's because it's my project." Jena wasn't cutting Hudson any slack, and Jeb didn't blame her. But he did recognize a man trying to do the right thing, no matter how late.

"Hey, Mr. Boudreaux. Welcome to The Refuge." He felt Jena's gaze and chose to believe she was happy he'd stepped in.

"Nice to see you, Jeb. Putting in doors today? I thought your talents were more with the books." Hudson sized up the beams, the door space, and looked at Jeb, who fought against the wood in his pants.

"Yes, sir. I'm doing the books for the initial start-up, and lending a helping hand where I can."

Hudson nodded. "Good man. You always were, Jeb. If only I'd had half of your wisdom at your age." Melancholy edged his voice.

"Robyn, our architect, dropped off paint chips. Why don't you come look at them?" Jena was way too flustered to not be as moved as he'd been by their close call. A zap of satisfaction that had nothing to do with his cock warmed his gut.

A reminder of why he needed to keep his time at The Refuge as short as possible. He'd never be able to be around Jena and look at her as just a colleague. Even "close family friend" was too close, yet so far from how he reacted to her.

He had to keep his focus on the Atlanta job, only two more weeks away.

* * * *

Jena hid in her office for the remainder of the day, taking breaks only for lunch and to see the progress in the kitchen. When she had to walk past Jeb, she took extra care to leave plenty of room, not wanting a repeat of their morning mishap.

She clicked through yet another grant application, proofing her grammar before hitting "submit." It'd be great to have a fully dedicated grant writer on staff sooner rather than later. She wanted to devote her time to the client base, at least for the first couple of years, until The Refuge was on its feet.

Her encounter with Jeb had stung. First, she wondered how much of her conversation with Robyn he'd overhead. Shame flooded her cheeks with warmth as she painstakingly went over what she'd shared with her new friend. "Moving on with my past" wasn't something to feel badly about saying, was it? Or believing?

Hell, Jeb was the one who'd cut their relationship off, told her they were through with their previous arrangement. Guilt gnawed at her and she reflexively touched the scar on her cheek. Barely discernible with her fingertips, its quick healing still surprised her. But before her face had been expertly put back together, the slice from her mouth to just below her eye stitched with precision, Jeb had been there to get her through the worst.

He'd come with a team of rescuers. She knew this from the after-action reports and what she'd been told during her debrief in D.C. But she didn't remember any of it. She only remembered lying on the dirt floor of an abandoned house in a forgotten part of Asunción, thinking her life was over, being grateful she'd texted Jeb. She'd asked him to tell her family what had happened, that she was sorry and would always love them.

And she'd told Jeb she loved him, too.

Then he burst through the basement, letting in the daylight along with the hope she might live after all. He'd been all she'd dreamed about, back when she thought she loved him. In high school and part of college, before she made her commitment to her country and decided to cut him out of it. The sex-only relationship they'd shared the past two years wasn't what she'd clung to in the dark basement that was her prison for two weeks. It was the bond they'd had from day one, running across her family property in the middle of the hot, muggy summer. Canoeing through the bayou, shrieking at the alligators and snakes, delighting in the hushed silence that was NOLA in autumn.

Her little girl heart had loved Jeb with no reservation, adored him as her older brother's best friend. When childhood evolved into adolescence, she'd fought the confusion over her feelings toward Jeb. No longer just friends, she realized that no other boy measured up to him. Once they figured out they were a couple, they'd kept it secret, as much as two teens could.

The office grew quiet, the contractors gone until morning. Hudson had left early, told her he'd return next week. It was hard to blame him, as the drive to Baton Rouge was over an hour each way. She closed her laptop and promised herself she'd get in extra early tomorrow to get the grants finished. Robyn was right—she needed to expand her horizons beyond work.

One last pass through the house, flicking off lights as she went. Humming from the kitchen stilled her steps, made her think twice.

Jeb.

She pushed herself to walk into the kitchen, and at first she didn't see him. The original kitchen walls had been stripped, and fresh drywall was up, ready for paint. The spaces for the commercial appliances were taped off, only days from delivery. The most noticeable improvement was the lighting—completely modern and fully functional, not one inch of the kitchen center, where a large, stainless-steel-topped island was planned, was in shadow.

The humming continued, and she knew Jeb was in the room past the kitchen, the extension that would serve as a pantry and office supply area.

"Hey." She raised her voice, not trusting herself to walk into the enclosed area. Not after how her heartbeat and desire had spiked from his simple touch this morning. Jeb didn't have to tell her twice—she got the message loud and clear when she'd shown up at his place hoping to apologize. Still, it was going to take more time to teach her desire that things had changed.

How can you do that when you haven't let go yet?

Stillness, then quiet steps. Jeb walked into the main kitchen and stopped several feet from her. His eyes revealed nothing, and she noticed they didn't sweep over her like they used to.

"I'm heading out and wanted to lock the place up. If you think you'll be much later, I can leave you the key."

"Yeah, I'm going to need another hour or so. I want to paint the first wall in the storage room before I call it quits."

"Okay. Well, here you go." She took the front door key off her ring. "It'll be easier when the electronic system's in place." They'd each have their own fob to scan and unlock the front entrance, or the back door off the kitchen.

"It will." Nothing else. Had she made that much of a fool of herself? Did Jeb think she was going to jump him?

Because damn it, she wanted to. She wanted this man, from the long brown locks of his hair to the tips of his toes inside his construction boots. This was why she should have listened to her instinct and just gone home. Left the key on the plywood conference table with a note.

"Here." She held the key out, unwilling to walk toward him, lest the shaking sense in her center show in her legs. Her hand was *trembling*, for fuck's sake. "Never mind—I'll leave the key on the meeting table. See you in the morning."

She turned to walk out of the room, and she really, really meant to do it.

"Jena, wait." His hand touched her shoulder, and she didn't know if that's what spun her back around, or her need, or both. What mattered was that she couldn't—wouldn't—look up into his eyes. So she stared at his chest, three inches in front of her.

"Take it." She shoved the key between them, willing him to take it. Willing herself to stop thinking with her vagina and ignore the pounding between her legs—the need that only Jeb filled completely.

His hand reached to take the key but instead closed around hers, and it was this morning all over again. The shock of the sensation of his skin on hers. The warmth from his body, as if it reached out to her whether he wanted it to or not. Her body was straining to push up against him. Her mind found her baser instincts, clawed for a quick reason to get away before she blew the professional demeanor she'd used as her shield.

Jeb took the key, but instead of releasing her hand he drew it up to his mouth. Her gaze followed, and when he pressed her palm to his lips, white-hot heat shot straight to her pussy, weakening her knees. She looked into his eyes, and any attempts to stop the inevitable went up in a flash of the sexual connection they shared. His eyes were half-lidded, his pupils dilated despite the overhead lights. Jeb was a man on fire.

Her body fell against his as his arms wrapped around her, pulling her to him in perfect timing for his lips to take hers fully. Jena let go of all the reasons she had to not do this, to remind herself that she and Jeb were over. His tongue was too persuasive, his hands too gentle as he stroked her back the way he knew she loved.

The kiss grew more heated, and she pressed her hips into his, groaning in frustration when she felt his erection but wasn't tall enough to grind her heat against it. Jeb spun her around in one quick move, and her back connected with the kitchen wall. He grasped her thigh but didn't have to lift her leg as she wrapped it around his waist. His erection pressed into her, and she thought she'd come while dressed, right there in the unfinished kitchen.

"Jeb!" He took advantage of her cry to move his attention to her throat, trailing his tongue down, down into her cleavage. When his free hand pulled her dress off her shoulder and reached in to grasp her breast, she gasped. The sensation of his fingers flicking her nipple while he ground his pelvis against hers was more than she could bear. Her breast was out of her bra, fully exposed to his ardent gaze and luscious attention as he twirled his tongue around her nipple, turning the rosy areola into a tight raspberry. The heat between her legs grew, and her pussy pulsed for him.

"Do you like that, Jena?" Before she could form a coherent answer, his hand was under her skirt, between her legs, his fingers pushing past her panties. When he touched her wetness, his groan vibrated through her chest.

"Oh, my God, Jeb, please, please—"

"Please what?" He didn't make her tell him, didn't wait. He knew what she wanted, what she needed, as he plunged two fingers into her slickness and played in her heat, stroking and rubbing her swollen sex as only he ever knew how to do.

"That. This. Oh, Jeb." She leaned her head against the wall, pushing her shoulders into it so that she could bring her pussy closer to the pleasure his fingers promised. His mouth found the spot where her throat met her shoulder and he lightly dragged his teeth across her skin, his tongue swirling in time with his fingers. His thumb pressed on her clit, and the pressure hit her without warning and she screamed, the waves of her climax making her buck against his hand. Jeb covered her mouth with his, absorbing her cries.

He pulled back when her vocalization turned into raspy breathing, his face shocking her into stillness. She'd seen him turned on, his expression filled with want. She'd seen the shock and horror on his face when he'd found her, near death. But she'd never seen Jeb express such a primal need for her. His eyes blazed like a man with a fever, and he had a singular purpose stamped on his perfect features.

"Jena, I need this. Now." He waited for her, waited for her decision.

"Whatever you want, babe." Her voice wobbled with her need. She knew why he'd asked—because as much as Jeb was totally unself-conscious in bed, he was always a gentleman. She turned in his arms and lifted her skirt, pulled her panties off and kicked them aside. Placing her hands on the wall, she looked over her shoulder at him, her bare ass exposed for his view alone. "Is this what you want?"

His groan was more like a growl, and without hesitation he unbuckled his pants. She heard his zipper next, then the crinkle of a foil packet. *He'd brought a condom to work.* Her pussy clenched in anticipation, and she fought against the urge to turn and take his hard cock in her mouth. There'd be time for that later—right now, they were both so turned on and tuned into one another that there was no other way through their need than this.

"Hurry, Jeb."

"Babe." His hands were on her hips, drawing her up and against his hard length. His fingers moved over and inside her, spreading her slick heat in preparation for his next move.

"Jeb, please." She barely got the words out, the tight curl of tension so taut, so focused on his touch.

"What, babe?" The tip of his cock was touching her pussy. She groaned, long and hard, her walls clenching and unclenching as if he were already inside—

He shoved into her in one single thrust, his hugeness and steel heat plunging into her very essence. She came before his pelvis touched her bare ass, before he'd retreated to plunge into her again and again, making her orgasm pummel through her only to start again, sending her into the place where all she felt—all she knew—was Jeb.

The third wave of pressure started to press deep inside her, where Jeb's cock filled her again and again, his hands clutching her hips. Her fingers pressed against the wall, and she pressed back against him, countering his thrusts. She never wanted it to end.

Chapter 7

Jeb held on as long as he could, praying he'd last through at least one more of Jena's cries. But he was only human, and her pussy was supernatural in its heat and slickness as it clamped around him, giving him sensations that were the definition of ecstasy.

"Come again for me, babe. Don't hold back."

"Jeb." She turned his name into two sobbing syllables, her head twisting as her fingers splayed on the drywall, grasping for purchase. He lifted her hips higher and plundered her pussy with his cock, his need to be one with her far beyond sex or connection. His destiny and his fate were wrapped up into this moment, this time that was fleeting and infinite all at once.

Sweat dripped into his eye and he welcomed the sting, the slight distraction. It allowed him to hold off for one, two thrusts more. Until her pussy convulsed around him and her breathless cries ripped out of her, echoing off the bare wall. Jeb let loose his release then, an outwardly generous gesture but in reality purely selfish. Because he had his most intense, most satisfying sex only when Jena was fully sated.

He groaned, long and low, then laid his head on the curve of her back, just above her full ass. As his breath came back he kissed her back, moving up her spine with his mouth.

Jena sighed and straightened, and he took advantage of her position to fully cup both of her breasts. One was still in her bra, under the dress, and the other completely naked and so, so soft in his hand. He eased the break in their most intimate connection as he slid out of her, pressed his chest against her back.

Her hands covered his and she laid her forehead against the wall, still breathing heavily. He inhaled her scent, rubbed his cheek against her hair.

When she turned in his arms, he waited, needing to see her face, her eyes. Jena's eyes never let him down—they told him exactly how she felt.

"Hi." She grinned shyly, and he saw something in her eyes he didn't recognize. "That was...unexpected."

"Jena." He wasn't a sentimental man, didn't think he'd ever be moved to desperate behavior for a woman—like Brandon seemed to have done to win Poppy over, and how Henry not only took Sonja back after she'd jilted him and put his heart through the wringer, but now acted as if it was the best thing that had ever happened to him.

But the lump in his throat wouldn't allow more words. He soaked in her beauty, the wide blue eyes full of something he was unable to name, the glow of her skin that he knew he'd caused, the swollen red lips that he'd only begun to taste. It'd take a lifetime to explore the depths of Jena Boudreaux.

"What are you thinking?" She spoke in a whisper, and he cupped her jaw with one hand and stroked her heated skin with his thumb. His gaze caught on the scar, silver in the shadow his body cast between her and the bright lights, and he kissed it. Thanked his Maker that the cut hadn't killed her, didn't hurt her any longer. He refused to allow his mind to see her when she'd gotten the cut, before it'd been repaired. When he hadn't known if she'd make it. He couldn't speak, not yet, so he let his body do the talking.

He kissed her. And she opened her mouth to him, fully and without hesitation. With total trust. He told her everything he couldn't find the words for, willed his emotions into each tongue stroke, each touch of his lips to hers. It wasn't the frantic kiss of need from earlier, or the purely sexual kisses they'd mastered over the past two years. This kiss was purely theirs. Jeb could stay here, in this moment, forever.

Her giggle stopped him. He pulled back and waited for her to open her eyes.

"What?"

"We're standing in the unfinished kitchen of The Refuge, half-dressed, and you still haven't, um, taken care of business." She looked pointedly between his legs and he took a step back.

"Right. Be right back." He went into the restroom just off the kitchen and cleaned himself up, and when he returned to the kitchen, he brought her a damp paper towel.

She was already put back together, and she gave him a rueful smile. "Thanks." She took the paper towel and disappeared into the restroom. He let out a sigh—of what, he wasn't sure. Relief, probably. They were back on familiar territory with the after-sex clean up, a return to things they'd always shared.

Unlike the emotions that had passed between them as they'd come together in the kitchen.

* * * *

Jena rinsed her face several times in cold water, not ready to listen to her heart about what had just happened between her and Jeb. She couldn't. Of course they had amazing chemistry—that hadn't changed. But what had passed between them just now wasn't physiological. Their bodies had done their part, sure, but the heavy lifting was more emotional. Something deeper than a childhood bond. Something she didn't ever want to name. Because if she did, her plans to move on, to accept Jeb's previous line in the sand, would be impossible.

And he'd been very clear that their sexy friendship was over. No more friends with benefits. What had just happened was a statistical anomaly. It had to be.

She didn't even bother to smooth her hair—she looked like a woman who'd been made passionate love to, and she had. So what?

Bracing herself to let Jeb know that she wouldn't make more of the kitchen sex than need be, she walked out of the bathroom.

The kitchen was empty; Jeb nowhere in sight. She walked into the conference room and immediately saw what he'd left on the plywood table.

The key.

* * * *

Jeb couldn't let the rest of the night pass without talking to Jena. He'd completely fucked up. He'd had to get out of the kitchen, away from The Refuge, after they'd made love. It was too intense to face her before he processed whatever the fuck was going on in his head.

But fucking Jena…he'd never regret that. Especially because what had passed between them in the kitchen was new, something beyond what they'd normally shared before Paraguay.

A text or phone call seemed callous after the intense intimacy they'd shared, so he steeled himself to show up at her place. He'd visited the upgraded carriage house several times when they'd enjoyed their friends-with-bennies agreement. His car didn't fit in the tiny space between hers and the red-brick house, so he left it on the tree-lined street. The original main house had been divided into several condos over the last decade, and the carriage house in the back of the property was its own condo. He knew Jena rented, and he also knew that she hoped to someday have a place like the one in which she'd grown up: in the city proper, with a huge backyard and property to spare for kids and dogs. He walked through the property to her place, and the myriad trees snapped his mind back to one particular tree on the Boudreauxes' New Orleans property. Would that tree even still be there, after Katrina and the storms they'd suffered through since?

Funny that he hadn't thought of the oak—the tree that he and Jena had deemed *their* oak—in years. Not when they'd dated in college, nor during their no-strings tumbles, nor in Paraguay. It was as if that part of his life and their relationship had been forgotten, or left dormant for a long, long while.

He reached her front porch, a tiny square of paved rocks, and knocked on the painted white wooden door. The house was so solidly built that he didn't hear steps before she opened the door.

"What are you doing here?" Her face had that hopeful look on it again, goddamnit. Regret twisted his insides. She was in a set of pjs he'd never seen—or, if he had, it hadn't mattered to him because all he'd thought about before was sex. And more sex. The top was a plain pink T-shirt, but on Jena it looked like spun silk. Her nipples poked through, and he forced his glance south, anywhere but on her breasts. The pj bottoms were shorts that revealed her long legs—the same legs that he'd lifted and wrapped around his waist while he'd plunged into her.

Jesus.

"Sorry to bother you after hours. We need to talk." Her brows drew together, and he shook his head. "Sorry. Let me start over. I need to talk. I'm here because I can't leave things where they're at."

She didn't step aside to let him in, didn't budge, in fact. Her arms came up to cross over her chest, taking away his view of her breasts. Fuck. She'd seen him look at her, and he knew she'd thought he'd stopped by for one of their usual get-togethers: the sexy kind.

"You made your thoughts pretty clear, I'd say. I found the key." Her lower lip jutted out just slightly. No one else would have noticed, but he did.

"Yeah, about that—I had to get out of there, Jena. I totally blew it, and I'm sorry."

"Sorry you had sex with me?"

"I've never been sorry for being with you, Jena. But things are different now. I told you that I didn't want to continue our relationship, and then I went back on my promise."

"Your promise?" She laughed, but it wasn't her naturally deep belly laugh at all. It was more like a sharp crack of lightning, a wake-up call. She was pissed.

"It wasn't a promise, just the reality of where we're at." God, could he sound any fucking weaker? He squared his shoulders. "We had our fun. It was only a matter of time before we moved on. Your adventure in Asunción brought things to a head sooner."

"Nice choice of words, Jeb." Her lip curled. "You insist on always making it about sex between us. That's fair—we never signed up for more than that. Paraguay, and my old job, complicated things for a bit. But that's the point, Jeb. My reaching out to you when I thought I was about to be sliced and diced by a vicious drug cartel was a blip. If you look at the big-picture view of our relationship, we've never shared a whole lot more than good sex."

He stared at her and forced his mouth closed. When had she turned into such a pragmatic person? *Probably the minute she signed on with the CIA, jackass.*

He opened his mouth again to speak, but a huge bug assaulted him, hitting his cheek with a loud buzz. He swatted it away and it hit the ground near his feet, its shiny brown shell intact as it scuttled off.

"Ugh! Motherfucker." He detested palmetto bugs. They were ubiquitous in Louisiana, and natives took the giant cockroaches with wings in stride. But he'd never been able to. Since living with his mother in that rundown apartment, where the cockroaches coexisted with them, his stomach had always turned at the sight of them.

Pure humor echoed around him in the form of Jena's laugh. Since they were kids she'd tormented him with bugs whenever the mood hit her, and especially if he'd done something to annoy her. After he recovered the composure his disgust had stolen, he couldn't help it: he laughed with her. Like sex, laughing had always been a natural no-brainer for them. Their senses of humor were similar, on the same wavelength.

Relief eased the tension that he'd arrived with. Jena got it, got him. They might even be able to salvage their friendship this one last time after what had happened in The Refuge House's kitchen. He'd move on, as he'd planned, and it wouldn't be difficult.

Jena's laughter faded and her eyes flashed with something completely foreign to the warmth they'd just shared. Anger, yes, but more. Disdain?

It was his only warning before she slammed her door in his face.

* * * *

"Wow." Robyn eyed Jena as if she were about to explode. "Are you okay?"

"I'm good." She sank down next to Robyn on the sofa and grabbed her glass of pinot grigio. It'd gotten warm, so she poured more from the bottle they'd put on ice. "I wasn't expecting that, though."

Robyn, also in pjs for their first girls-night-in together, popped a chip into her mouth and thoughtfully chewed before she replied. "When you two are at work, there's no sign of this, this depth of emotion. I mean, it's obvious to me that you have sparks, and booty calls wouldn't surprise me, but what just happened, Jena?" She gulped her wine.

Jena considered how much to tell Robyn. Their friendship was new, and she didn't want to burden it with the heavier stuff she'd been through with Jeb. Of course, she couldn't tell her about the ransom, about what had really happened in Paraguay. But she didn't have to flat-out lie, either.

"We grew up together. Since my older brother Brandon brought him home, I thought he was also mine."

"You have two older brothers, right?"

She nodded.

"Yeah. Henry is the oldest, the one who took over my dad's law firm here in the city. He's with Sonja, and they're about to have their first baby."

"You're going to be an auntie!"

"Yes. I can't wait." And she couldn't. But she didn't have to like being around Henry and Sonja and seeing how good it could be between two people who were meant for one another. "And Brandon's with Poppy, who you might have heard of as Amber—the stylist from New York."

"OMG, you are totally killing me here! Amber Kaminsky is your sister-in-law?"

"Not yet, but yes, close to it. They haven't said their vows yet. She's left that life and says she's found her place here with Brandon."

"Tell me something, Jena." Robyn pulled a slim leg up under her, settled back into the sofa. "Are your brothers super protective of you? Because you're a girl and you're the youngest?"

"Yes and no. They think they know what's best for me at all times. They thought I was stupid to join the Navy Reserves, for example." And they would have had a shit fit if they'd known she'd really been with the CIA. "But they've always minded their own business when it comes to my personal life, if that's what you're asking."

"My point is that if Jeb thinks he's crossed a family line by being with you, he's going to fight whatever he really feels, deep down. He won't want to betray the male bonds."

"You may be right. But it's not that creepy, icky feeling about him being part of our family. I never looked at him as a brother. Ever."

"What did you look at him as?"

"At first? My buddy, my friend. In high school I had a huge crush on him. We went to prom together, but it wasn't over-the-top romantic or anything." That had been in college, and was short lived because of her focus on her future as an undercover agent. A future that didn't have room for a partner, and definitely not Jeb. He'd have fought her tooth and nail if he'd known then. "If anything, Jeb's more protective of me than my brothers are."

Robyn tilted her head. "It'd be totally natural for you two to be together. Have you ever thought of that? Instead of the friends-with-benefits deal you had?"

"Naw. We're lifelong family friends. We just got off-kilter when we tried to make it more than that. I shouldn't have agreed to our sexy-friends pact for as long as I did."

"We haven't known each other long, and while I have a good feeling that we'll be good friends, I don't want to overstep." Robyn's clear, straightforward manner was as refreshing in a social setting as it was when she presented a blueprint at work.

"But?" Jena grinned.

"What I'd want you to tell me, if I were you, is to think about why I stayed in the relationship for so long as it was. A friends-with-extras deal is okay for the short term, or once in a blue moon. But from what you've described, you saw one another regularly. Like, two, three times a week?" She waited for Jena to nod.

Jena groaned. "More like four or five."

"Holy fuck, girlfriend. You had more of a sex-with-a-little-friendship-on-the-side agreement."

Jena looked at Robyn, revelation dawning. "You're absolutely right."

"But again, the real question is why, Jena? Why did you allow yourself to be with only one man for that long, a man who made it clear he wasn't interested in anything but sex? What's keeping you from going out there and finding someone who wants everything you have to offer?"

Jena sipped her drink. "Let me ask a question."

"Answer mine first."

"Ouch. Okay. I suppose I'm a bit commitment-phobic. I don't want what my parents have, or had. They've kind of gone through their own identity crisis, and now they're the happy couple I thought a real relationship would be. But for most of my life they've been hot and cold, lots of bickering, too much work. Life is enough work, you know? I don't want to come home after beating my butt only to have to struggle to find a comfortable zone with my partner."

"Preach it. I totally get what you're saying. But there's usually another reason we don't go looking for something new."

"Yeah?"

Robyn nodded. "We're either too afraid to break from our comfort zone, or…" She exaggerated her leading comment, waving her hand in a circular motion for Jena to jump in and finish the sentence.

"Or…hell, I don't know, Robyn. Or what?"

Robyn grinned. "Or we're happy where we are. You didn't bother looking for anyone else because for you, there wasn't anyone else. Jeb is it."

Jena quickly picked up a decorative pillow emblazoned with a French bulldog and tossed it at Robyn. "You're right, we're still in the beginning stages of our bonding process." And she refused to consider Robyn's theory. She couldn't. It was too hard to look at anything about her and Jeb without immediately feeling the unique mixture of befuddlement and hurt that only happened when she thought of him.

But her heart heard, and it whispered its own reply.

Maybe.

* * * *

Jeb hadn't seen red like he did when Jena's door shut with a bang in a very long time. With the exception of the Paraguay deal, where all bets were off, Jeb considered himself level-headed, a calming factor in most situations. Cool and calculated were in his job description as a CPA and CFO.

He ran along the paved river embankment, relishing the early morning quiet. New Orleans was a 24-7 city, but sunrise was sacred to him. As a boy, sunup had meant he'd survived another night of his parents' drinking and fighting. They'd be passed out and he was free to move about the house, get something to eat if there was cereal in the cupboard, and play outside on the stoop.

In college he'd earned the nickname "Sunny" because he was up before the sun, studying while his roommates slept in. The full ride scholarship—thanks to the track and field program—had demanded his devotion to daily practice, which often meant two training sessions a day, one at dawn.

His body stretched, reached, and pounded the pavement. Sweat dripped into his eyes and he swiped it away. He was near the end of his run, and the finish usually left him in a better spot mentally than when he'd started.

But ever since he'd been back in the country, nothing cleared his mind.

He slowed to a walk a half a mile before his favorite smoothie shop, needing the cool down—and more thinking time. He'd agreed to meet Brandon, and he had another five minutes.

"Hey, sunshine, get in!" Brandon's car pulled up alongside him, and his cheerful smile as he leaned toward the open passenger window mocked Jeb's inner turmoil.

"I'm all sweaty."

"Do I look like I care?" Brandon held up an old beach towel. "That's what this is for."

Jeb opened the passenger door, shook the towel out over the seat, and got in. Brandon had the air cranked up, so he shut the vents.

"Sorry about that. We can go with the outside temps." Brandon clicked off the air conditioning and opened the windows and sunroof. Brackish air filled the front seat and Jeb let his legs savor the break from the concrete. "How far did you go today?"

"Eight."

"Eight *miles*. Man, you're a stud!" Brandon made a left onto the street where the café sat amongst several other restaurants. "Would you rather we blow off the healthy stuff and go get beignets? You've certainly burned the calories for them."

"No way. I've been craving a strawberry banana smoothie the entire run."

"Okay, just asking."

"You still have your sweet tooth."

"I do. So does Poppy—you should see the ice cream and chocolate she brings into the house."

"She doesn't look like she eats a lot of junk."

"She doesn't, not all the time. She's helped me get better about my eating habits, and she's very disciplined about working out. But if she's feeling blue she tends to crank up the chocolate consumption. It lets me know that I either need to try to get her to talk it out, or stay the hell out of her way!"

Jeb wondered if that's where he'd gone wrong last night. Maybe he should have stayed out of Jena's way.

Brandon pulled into a spot in front of the smoothie shop and they got out. "Thanks for the lift. I was going to go home and change before we met, but then I decided I needed the extra few miles instead."

"I don't care how you're dressed." Brandon wore similar gear, but instead of Jeb's cargo-type running shorts, he had on basketball shorts. "I'm headed to the gym after this."

They ordered their drinks and took them outside where, while hot, it wasn't as oppressive as the heat the day was bound to bring. August in New Orleans was both Jeb's favorite and most hated time. He much preferred the cooler months of winter and early spring, but he also liked that the tourists stayed away during the dog days of summer. Except lately, he'd noticed there didn't seem to be a lighter season.

"It gets busier down here each year, doesn't it?"

"Yeah. Used to be August was low season, but with COOLinary going on, forget it. Food's half the reason most people visit here." People came for the restaurant festival, but they also came for the party atmosphere of the French Quarter: a combination of continual live music and free-flowing booze.

"How's work at The Refuge going?"

"Fine. We've got the rooms walled in, and we're looking to be done with the kitchen next week."

"That's quick, just like you thought it would be."

"Stop trying to play it cool. It's not your strong suit."

Brandon laughed. "You can't blame me for trying."

Jeb looked at his friend, and regret swamped him. "It'd never be the same, Gus."

"I'm not looking for the same. We already did that. We've both gone through a lot, both changed since you took the ransom money for Jena."

"What you've been through is on me."

"Not really. What we've all been through—you, me, and mostly Jena—is because of a horrible event halfway around the world. Drug cartels aren't known for logic or compassion. You were the freaking bomb in how you acted. I have to be honest: I would have fucked it up."

"No, you wouldn't have. You'd have gotten the text like I did, and you would have headed out of town on the next plane."

Brandon slurped the rest of his smoothie through his straw. "Nope. I would have called the police, or the FBI. Probably both. And I'd have been too late."

Jeb had no reply. They'd already talked about it, and they both got it—Jena would have been killed.

He rubbed the back of his neck. "She's safe. I keep reminding myself of that whenever I feel the panic of those days, that long week, creep in."

"That's why you're running the longer distances again, isn't it?"

"Yeah. I don't know. Probably. Hell, my head's been screwed up since I took the money and ran with it." Since he'd gotten Jena's text, but he wasn't going to verbalize that. His decision to steal and run, then to help get Jena out of that place, had been all his own.

Brandon looked at his watch. "I've got to go. Poppy's meeting me at the boatyard. I'm still doing the custom yachts, but at a much slower production rate. She's doing their interiors."

"I'm glad you can still do that, Brandon." He knew that Brandon's full-time job was at a large shipbuilding company in NOLA. Brandon said he'd learned a lot there and that it wasn't so bad—he had a decent salary. But Jeb had seen his friend at the top of his game, running a multimillion-dollar production facility. It had to be tough to take the pay cut and lose his creative license.

"Me, too, bro. And it'll be a lot better when you agree to come back." He winked at Jeb before he stood up and threw his cup into the recycle bin. "You want a lift back to your place?"

Jeb shook his head. "No, thanks. I need the walk."

Chapter 8

Jena drove up to Baton Rouge the next Sunday for family dinner. A laugh escaped her as the breeze whipped her hair around the car. Having the sunroof open on a warm summer day, with the air conditioning blasting at her face, was an indulgence. A fun one.

She hadn't asked if Jeb would be there or not; it wasn't something she'd ever asked before, and she didn't want to raise any curiosity. Not after her father had witnessed their combustible chemistry firsthand.

"Gah!" She pounded the steering wheel. If her father had been holding a lit match, it would have blown up The Refuge when he found them reaching for Jeb's phone. Hudson hadn't said a word, but she'd seen the bemusement in his expression. As if it wasn't much of a surprise at all, seeing her and Jeb hot for one another. It made her wonder how many other times her parents or brothers noticed there was more in the air between her and Jeb than a childhood friendship.

There was nothing to make a go of, anyhow. Never had been. Okay, maybe back in college, before she'd been recruited into undercover work. But they'd been so young, what were the odds anything they'd started back then would go the distance?

They'd never know.

She prepared herself to face her parents anyway—just in case Hudson had said something to Gloria. Her mother had begun to worry about her never "settling down," and despite Jena's protests that times were different, that she was different than her mother in so many ways, Gloria wouldn't hear any of it.

The house looked as beautiful as it always had—Gloria didn't do anything only halfway. But Jena had noticed a more welcoming vibe, as if the house had settled into becoming a home now that Hudson and Gloria had opened their minds and hearts.

Jena wasn't a fool—she knew her parents weren't going to instantly turn into diversity poster children, but they'd made a big step by apologizing to Henry and Sonja and the entire family.

The front door was locked and she didn't get any response when she rang the doorbell. Puzzled, she walked around to the back via the long, winding gravel path her mother had laid around several flowerbeds and groves of trees.

But there wasn't anyone by the pool, either, or on the veranda. She shot off a text to Brandon, since she was certain he and Poppy were coming. His reply was swift.

Sonja's having the baby. We're all in NOLA. Sorry, sis.

Brandon gave her the hospital address and told her to take her time driving back—the baby apparently was taking its time, too. Whatever that meant. She sighed. Getting back into the groove of being a permanent Louisianan was going to take a while. She'd been going on missions for the better part of a decade. No one was going to realize she wanted to be a part of their lives instantly.

They'd forgotten her. Of course they had. No one was used to her being around, and it wasn't personal. But it felt like it.

She turned to leave, but the day was so hot, the heat oppressive as all hell. Her sundress was easy enough to slip out of, and she could swim in her underwear. Or... She looked around the property. No one could see into the very private backyard pool area.

But Sonja might give birth to her niece or nephew at any moment—although Brandon had said it was going slow.

She promised herself a fifteen-minute dip, no longer. Without further delay, she grabbed a beach towel from the veranda, still unlocked, and stripped off her clothes. She dove into the twelve-foot-deep end and let a grin split her face under the water. It was about damned time she acted more like a fun-loving woman than the deadly serious agent she'd been for too long.

* * * *

Jeb pulled up to the Boudreauxes' and his stomach sank when he saw Jena's car in the circular drive with no sign of either brother. It wasn't that he was afraid of seeing her again, exactly. It was more of a self-preservation tactic. Work tomorrow morning would be safe, as there would be an entire staff of contractors and the employees she'd begun to hire. And he'd never let himself be alone with her again, so that ruled out another kitchen disaster.

He pocketed his car keys and hit the doorbell, hoping against hope that Hudson would be the one to open the door. He'd converse with him until the other Boudreaux men showed up.

No answer. They had to be around back. He walked around the side of the house and the first thing he noticed in the backyard was that no one was there—the veranda looked empty, and the laughter that was a part of the usual Sunday dinners was absent.

The water's splash drew his gaze to the pool. More like a resort, the Boudreauxes' pool looked as if it'd been prepped for a fancy magazine shoot. Lush plants and flowers surrounded the river-rock edge, and the small waterfall at the far end came from a hot tub he'd only been in once, when there'd been a family get-together.

What he'd never seen in the luxurious pool was Jena, swimming laps as if she were still on the school swim team. Unlike when she was in high school and college, however, she wasn't wearing a swimsuit.

Go. Now. Get. Out.

His mind screamed while his feet turned to lead weights. He tried to summon the soundtrack from every slasher movie he'd seen, but instead all he heard was the water lapping over Jena's skin as she stroked across the length of the pool, oblivious to him.

Maybe he was wishing her naked, and in reality she had on a skin-colored swimsuit. He ripped his gaze from her and immediately saw the chair with what looked like a dress and underwear.

Jena was naked. In the pool. Alone.

He didn't know how he summoned the strength, but, as if through his own pool of pepper jelly, he turned and began the walk back to his car.

Keep going. One step, two... The legs that had moved him across eight miles of NOLA yesterday morning struggled to make it the few hundred yards to the side of the house, where he'd be out of her range of sight and—better—he wouldn't be able to see her, either.

"Hey!" For the second time in three minutes, he froze. Maybe she was yelling at a snake. He took another step away, doing the right thing. Leaving Jena alone.

"Jeb!" Closer, the pat of wet feet on the rocks, the squeak of the gate. "Come back here."

He braced himself. *Look at her face. Do not look down.*

But when he turned around, Jena was wrapped in a big pink towel. Not that he looked anywhere but at her face—where her eyes flashed.

"What the hell were you doing? How long were you watching me?"

"Hey, wait a minute. I wasn't here to watch you. No one answered the door so I came around back. There's no crime in that."

She clutched the towel high against her chest, leaving him no chance of seeing her cleavage. He kept his gaze on her face anyway. "Why did you leave without saying anything? You saw me, right?"

Lying had its virtues. But she'd known him for most of his life. And she could read him like a neon sign at midnight in the French Quarter.

"I did."

She looked at him, and he saw the lines around her eyes. Not the smiling ones he loved to cause when they were together. Jena was tired.

"No one's here. Wait, give me a minute." She whirled around and stretched the towel out like bat wings, then rewrapped it. When she faced him again she'd somehow tucked it under her left arm, in the secret way only women seemed to know. It was the same with bath towels and her long, long hair. He'd seen her wrap it up like a frothy dollop of whipped cream, never failing to make his fingers itch to undo it. Now her wet hair hung in thick lengths around her shoulders.

"You look a little out of it, Jeb. Did you go for a long run today?"

"Yeah."

"And you haven't hydrated enough, have you?"

"I did." No, he hadn't. He drank plenty of water, but sometimes his long runs made him a little more susceptible to the heat and humidity.

"You look like you did that time in college, after the 10K."

"I didn't think you'd remember that."

"I'd never forget seeing you dry heave like that. Come on." She jerked her head at the pool.

"What? No. I've got water in my car. I'm leaving."

"You need to cool off, Jeb." She put her hands on her hips, and miraculously the towel didn't move. Not that he was looking. "Look, I promise I won't come in the water with you. You've got it all to yourself. Let me get you a sweet tea out of the veranda fridge."

He was too mentally exhausted to care, so while she sauntered off to get his cold drink, he went ahead and got into the pool. Almost as soon as the cool water hit his skin he began to feel more like himself. The confusion about whether to stay or go vanished, and his leg muscles loosened up.

"Here you go." Jena handed him a plastic cup and straw before she sat on the pool's edge, her calves in the water. Jeb sucked down the drink in two gulps.

"I don't think your mother's iced tea has ever tasted this good."

"So you're feeling better, I take it?" She motioned for him to give her the cup and she refilled it from the pitcher she'd also brought out. When she gave it back to him she surreptitiously glanced at his waist below the water.

"Don't worry. Not everyone is as comfortable in the buff as you are." He'd left his boxers on. The tea was cold and smooth against his parched throat. "I feel stupid. I hadn't realized that I'd let the heat get to me."

"Maybe you were distracted?" Her grin threw him back to college. It was her saucy, devil-may-care smile that he credited as the reason he'd originally fallen for her, as a kid, when he'd carved that heart in her parents' huge oak tree.

"No offense, but I ran long yesterday and this morning. I haven't been able to get out after work, so I pushed it too much, I guess. How did you know?"

Her eyes narrowed and her lips pursed. He didn't think he'd asked a tough question.

"It was my job to know." Her quiet answer carried over the water. He sank onto the ledge that rimmed the pool, providing seating. His back was to her, her legs next to him.

"You mean with the CIA?"

"Yes." She scooped some water, let it fall from her hand. "It's not classified that I was employed by the agency. At least, it won't be in due time. When I can tell my family, I will. But until then…"

"You don't want me mentioning it. I haven't, and I won't."

"I know." She looked at the waterfall across the pool and he sipped his tea. He didn't know the last time he'd felt so relaxed. The constant hum of the sexual chemistry was there, of course—it always was. But he wasn't going to act on it. The price was too high; each time he was with her, the fall afterward was too hard. It sliced too deep, reminded him that he'd never have her.

"By the way? I knew you were getting dehydrated because you were pale and clammy."

"I should know better by now. Thanks for getting me in the pool. I needed it." He took another swig of tea. "Where is everyone, by the way?"

She kicked her feet out, splashing. He wasn't going to linger on her pink toenails. Or wonder when she'd found time to pamper herself, which no one deserved more than her. "Sonja is having the baby. I would have turned right around to go back, but Brandon says it's taking a while. I was hot, saw the pool, and jumped in."

"It is a perfect day for a swim. So you're heading back to NOLA now?"

"Mmmm." She pulled her knees up, sat cross-legged with the towel between her legs. His fingers trembled with the need to shove it back and explore Jena's most intimate parts.

Instead, he moved his hands through the water, sank deeper so that his shoulders were beneath the surface.

"I wanted to tell you about my real work for a long time."

"Yet you didn't. And that's okay, Jena. I get that you were working on national security. I didn't need to know." But he'd sure have liked to. To understand that she wasn't on some Navy supply ship, taking aid to a natural disaster or manmade catastrophe site. As if knowing would have made a difference. He grunted in frustration.

"You never wondered, when we were...seeing one another the last two years?"

"No. I trusted you."

He looked out of the corner of his eye and saw the crisscrossed scars on her shin. Without touching her—that would be disastrous—he nodded at her leg. "Those scars, what are they from?"

"Running through brambles with you when we were eleven, after we'd rung the Devereauxes' doorbell and hid behind their wall."

He burst out laughing. "I forgot all about that. That's right, you fell and ripped up your pants."

"Not all my scars are from my work." She half frowned, and he saw the skin of her scar stretch.

"Your cheek has healed incredibly well."

"I had the best plastic surgeon in the world."

"Does it still hurt, though?" He knew his knee surgery site still bugged him, years out. His torn ACL in college cross country had needed surgery, and it effectively ended his competitive running career. He was grateful he was still able to run recreationally.

"Sometimes. I'm fortunate it's summer. Maybe in the winter it'll bother me, when it's chilly and damp."

"What about the scars on your back?"

"You noticed those?" Genuine surprise spiked her voice.

"They're hard to miss." Especially the one that looked like someone took a scoop and left an indent just above her right shoulder.

"You never asked before." She hugged her knees, keeping her bottom flat so that her towel did its job and kept her privates covered. "The one that looks like a bullet wound? It's not. It's from getting thrown into a rusty piece of rebar. Yes, by a bad guy, and don't worry, my partner at the time took him out."

Jeb didn't ask what "took him out" meant. He didn't want to risk interrupting her words. She'd never shared this part of her life with him before, and he couldn't expect there'd ever be a time she would again.

Her sigh echoed around the pool's high brick landscaping. "The three lines near the base of my spine? That was a gunshot. I'm lucky to be alive and walking, let me tell you. That happened early on, within my first year with the agency."

"Yet you went back for more."

"It's seductive. The training was like nothing else I'd ever experienced. And believe it or not, most of the work was boring. Stakeouts, so to speak. Waiting. A lot of waiting. And a lot of analysis, working with analysts who are highly skilled at ferreting out a life story from the tiniest crumb of intel. It was easy at times to think that the lulls would last forever, that my first few missions were anomalies. That's when I got most of my scars, when I was a rookie."

"How long do they consider you a rookie?"

"Not long enough. The last couple of years have been more intense. The missions came one after another, and it was getting harder and harder to come back to the social work position I had with the State of Louisiana and pretend I'd been on yet another Navy deployment. It's one thing in the middle of a war that's on television and all over the Internet every day. But we're not at that pace anymore, at least not as far as the public sees it."

"What made you want to quit?"

"I never intended to make it a career. It's hard to not be in the thick of it, to just let it all go, but that last mission sealed the deal for me. My operator days are over, and I have no regrets."

He looked at her then. "None?"

Her eyes shone, reflecting the light off the pool surface. She met his gaze with steady calm, and something else he'd never felt from her before.

"I can't regret reaching out to you, Jeb, no matter what it cost you and my brother. It saved my life. Do I regret that you risked your life to come get me, saw me at my weakest, my most broken?" She glanced away, her face shrouded in doubt. He waited.

"No. Someone had to see me like that, to get me out of there, and there's no one else I'd have chosen."

He swallowed. "I didn't risk my life, Jena."

"You spent a day in the county jail!"

"An administrative glitch. Sure, it wasn't the best day of my life, but it wasn't the worst, either." The worst had been the thirty-six hours of not knowing exactly where she was, and if she was still alive. That had defined hell for Jeb.

"The end result, regardless, is that we're both here now, going after new dreams." He set down his cup and swam out to the middle of the pool before he turned and faced her again. "You can come back in, you know. I'm not going to touch you." Unless she wanted him to.

The sun reflected in diamond-shaped undulations on the water's surface. Silence stretched between them. She was thinking about it. Weighing the pros and cons. He forced himself to concentrate on the water, the iced tea, anything to keep his erection from becoming a distraction. He'd always want her, but it wasn't fair to say she'd be safe in the water and then sport a raging hard-on through his wet briefs.

Jena stood, and he caught a glimpse of her inside upper thigh, the creamy flash against her pink towel the definition of temptation. Anticipation swirled in his gut, and his cock abandoned his silent do-not-get-hard order. The sun blazed, but the water gave respite from the heat.

Jena picked up her dress and turned to face him. "I don't think that's such a good idea, do you? I mean, you're this close to going to Atlanta, starting your new life. Why complicate it? We've said what we needed to say."

He watched her, unable to speak.

"I'm going to head back. Enjoy yourself as long as you'd like, of course. I'll be at the hospital until the baby comes if you need me. Otherwise, I'll see you at work tomorrow morning." She padded out of the pool area and disappeared into the veranda, where he assumed she'd get dressed.

She'd left him with sexual frustration to add to his dehydration woes. He swam into the deep end, stopping under the mini waterfall. He'd hoped that the pounding water would massage his shoulder and neck muscles—but getting rid of his desire for Jena was too tall an order for hydrotherapy.

She didn't come back, not that he'd expected her to. As he lay on the warm chaise to air dry his briefs, he went over their poolside conversation. They'd been facing front, not looking at one another. Not touching. Yet this afternoon had been one of their most intimate times ever.

Chapter 9

Jena tried not to go over the pool conversation with Jeb as she drove back to New Orleans, but, like a favorite song she couldn't get out of her mind, all she heard was his voice.

The bridge across Lake Pontchartrain seemed endless; the blue water that normally soothed her only made her check the clock again and again. She'd be at the hospital within the next twenty minutes, where, according to Gloria, Sonja still hadn't had the baby.

A brown pelican skimmed over the bridge, appeared to hang motionless for split second, then dove into the lake, reappearing seconds later with a huge fish flopping in its pouched beak.

Like the bird, she didn't have a problem committing to the necessities of life. She knew that undercover work wasn't her lifelong ambition and had jumped into The Refuge project with enthusiasm. Her personal life was another matter. She and Jeb had moved on, had to. And she'd find someone else, according to statistics.

But she'd never fallen into a clear demographic, never been average. Neither had her relationship with Jeb.

* * * *

Jeb took his time drying off in the shade of the veranda, still half hoping that Jena would walk around the corner of the house and tell him that she hadn't been able to stay away.

The Boudreauxes' new house in Baton Rouge was incredibly nice, but it was nothing like the rambling old place they'd grown up in. He was prejudiced, since he had so many great memories there. Running around the property with Brandon and Henry, until Henry started to notice girls and GI Joe didn't hold his interest. Jena, a quintessential tomboy, never left Brandon's side—that evolved into Jeb's side as the years went by.

He shoved on his cargo shorts, free-birding it, as his underwear could only get so dry in the humid air. As much as he was a part of the Boudreaux family, there were times—like now—when he knew he wasn't blood. If it were Brandon and Poppy's baby on the way, he'd be there, because Brandon was like a brother, even after all they'd been through over the ransom money. As long as Brandon wanted him there.

He wasn't going to the hospital, and didn't want to—except he wanted to be there with Jena. To see her face light up when the little tyke showed up. And her smile when her family was together and things were going well—that was priceless. Especially after the years of strain and acrimony over the way Hudson and Gloria behaved. First leaving NOLA right after Katrina, cutting their losses and turning their backs on the screaming need of the devastated city. Then being complete assholes to Sonja once she and Henry became an item. As far as Hudson was concerned, it was fine for Sonja to work at the Boudreaux law firm, but marrying into the family as an African-American was another thing altogether.

Had been. Hudson and Gloria had to come up against losing all three of their children because of their racism before they finally cracked and saw the light. Now they were cleaning up their mess, and it was a big, hot one. Jeb stayed out of it all, grateful that the Boudreauxes had taken him in, fed him, invited him on so many family trips. It had truly changed his life as a kid; without them, he wouldn't have known what summer vacation could be. His mother hadn't sobered up until he went to college, so he owed the Boudreauxes a huge debt of gratitude. But not for their bigotry—he had no doubt that if he'd been a kid of color, his presence would have been tolerated, not welcome.

Out of respect, he made sure the veranda was neat, with no evidence of he or Jena having been there. Once in his car, he didn't let his mind wander to the what-ifs or his time spent with Jena. Instead, he focused on the way she'd opened up to him today, no sex involved.

One thing with Jena: It was never predictable.

* * * *

Jena walked in to the maternity ward and immediately sensed the tingle of excited anticipation. Several groups of families were gathered in various spots. In the lounge area, in front of labor and delivery rooms, at the nurses' station. She knew which room to find her family in thanks to a text from Brandon. Spying Poppy as she leaned against a wall, she walked up to her.

"Hey!" Poppy's eyes widened at Jena's greeting and they embraced, two women with no idea of what Sonja was going through since they didn't have children. "How is she doing?"

Poppy sniffled, and Jena noticed the tears in her eyes. "It's been a long day. It looked like the baby might come quickly, because of the intensity of her contractions. But her uterus wasn't talking to her cervix, apparently, because she's not dilating at a good enough rate. They've induced her with a drug, and she's in so much pain!"

Jena knew Poppy and Sonja were BFFs from college, and she placed her hand on Poppy's shoulder. "It has to be hell to see your friend going through that."

Poppy nodded. "It is. I came out here to give her some space, to be with Henry. Brandon's off getting coffee for everyone, and your parents are in the cafeteria."

Jena looked at her watch. Dinnertime. Between her swim, her talk with Jeb, and her drive back, she'd lost the afternoon. "Why don't you go get a bite to eat? I can wait here, and I'll text you as soon as you need to be here again."

Poppy nodded. "That'd be great. Thanks, Jena."

"No problem."

Jena hadn't thought about what she might encounter, showing up for the delivery, until this very moment. She'd seen her colleagues through life and death situations, performed trauma first aid on agents shot with lethal weapons. Those agents were still alive—a major feat for the ones shot with automatic assault rifles, the weapon of choice for many illegal organizations and nations. How hard could helping Sonja have a baby be? Besides, Jena was only the auntie. She didn't have to see anything that would embarrass Sonja—she was here to offer her support.

The butterflies in her stomach were left over from her talk with Jeb, for sure.

She walked into the hospital room to see Henry, her usually calm and in-charge elder brother, bent over at Sonja's side, holding her hand and looking into her eyes like an Olympic coach giving last instructions to his favored athlete.

"You've got this, babe. I'm right here. You're not alone."

"Get the hell out of my face!" Sonja's beautiful features contorted in a mix of rage and pain as she panted through a contraction. If they were two strangers, Jena could stay detached and even see the humor in it. But this was her brother and the woman he loved. And she loved her soon-to-be sister-in-law, too. Henry and Sonja weren't legally married yet, but they were closer than any couple she'd ever seen, except maybe Brandon and Poppy.

A painful twist in her gut threatened to draw her deep into her pile of regrets that led to her being single with no prospect of a life partner. If she'd never taken the job with the CIA...

No. This wasn't about her, or Jeb. It was about the new baby coming into the Boudreaux family.

She had a split second to back out of the room unseen, but running had never been her style. Henry must have felt her sisterly stare, because he looked up and gave her a huge smile.

"Hey, sis. We're getting ready to have a baby!" She thought her brother was on thin ice but went along with his forced positivity. Except it wasn't forced—Henry was tired, sure, but also very excited.

"Come join the party, Jena." Now that the contraction had passed, Sonja looked like the cool, self-possessed attorney that she was. With a huge bump on her belly, covered by a sheet. The room echoed with the sound of a heartbeat, and Jena assumed it was the baby's, as it was too high to be an adult's.

"Look at you two!" She walked over and kissed Sonja's forehead, careful to not bump the bed. She knew from firsthand experience that when you were in pain, any slight jostling could be excruciating.

"You're as beautiful as ever, Sonja."

"Stop. I feel like a stuck pig. I need this child out of me, yesterday. Oh, boy." She grimaced, and Jena looked at her hand as it clenched Henry's.

"Come on, babe. Relax your face, breathe like we've practiced. You've got it. I'll count."

"Don't fucking count!" Sonja's voice was amazingly strong and deep for a woman in so much discomfort. Jena thought about making a joke about Sonja's ability to spin her head in a full circle, but squashed it.

As Sonja's contraction eased and she once again became her serene self, Jena looked at Henry. "What can I do?"

"Make sure Mom and Dad are kept busy."

Sonja turned to her, eyes beseeching. "Yes, please, Jena. I want your folks to feel as much a part of this as possible, but I do not want them walking in on the delivery and seeing my whole self displayed."

Jena laughed. "I hear you. Okay, well, I'll go find them, and we'll wait to hear when the baby arrives." She walked around the bed and gave Henry a quick hug, but he was less than his usual warm self, his attention totally on Sonja.

As she left the room, a nurse entered, and she heard her ask Sonja how she was doing.

Her intensive first aid training with the CIA had prepped her for more than saving agents injured in the line of duty. She'd been able to read the room, figure out that while she wasn't needed right at the delivery, she was needed to help keep the family together while they waited for the first Boudreaux grandchild to appear. A sense of belonging enveloped her. This was why she'd come back, why she'd had the pull in her gut that had told her to let go of the CIA work and return full time to NOLA.

"Mom, Dad." She slid into the seat across from them in the cafeteria. "Anything good here?"

Gloria clenched her coffee cup. "I had the broiled catfish. It was good."

Jena groaned, as did her father. "Mom, that's awful! If you're going to have catfish, have it the right way."

Hudson grinned. "They have it fried, along with some damn good hush puppies, over there." He pointed to the quick-order counter. "I'm buying, honey. Help yourself to whatever you want."

"I'm good, Dad, thanks."

"We're sorry we didn't text you. We were so excited to get the text this morning, and then we were in a hurry to get out of our house." Gloria always did the explaining for both of them.

"It's fine. You had a long drive here." She had no doubt they'd driven the seventy miles in record time, as her father had a lead foot.

Gloria tilted her head. "Your hair's a mess. Did you go swimming?"

"You know me well, Mother. Yes, I took a quick dip. Your flowers look stunning this year, by the way."

"Was Jeb there, too? We forgot to tell him we left early as well." Hudson spoke without the usual tone of self-righteousness he'd taken on after they left NOLA, after Katrina.

"He did show up, yes. But he's not coming here, I'm sure."

Gloria sipped her drink. "It feels like he should be here. He's been part of the family since forever. Remember how darling he looked when Brandon brought him over for dinner that first time?" She smiled at her husband.

"I do." He turned to Jena. "Honey, I want to clear the air between us. About Jeb."

Oh, fuck. He was going to bring up the hallway incident. Judging from the concerned look on Gloria's face, he'd already told her. Double fuck.

"Dad, stop. It's not what you think."

"I'm not thinking anything, sugar plum." Sugar plum? He really had made a complete life turnaround. Not only had Hudson dumped his bigoted, racist ways, he'd resorted to calling her by her childhood endearment. She'd hold out on giving either of her parents a pass, though. It took a long time to turn a huge ship around, no matter the captain's intention.

"Dad. Mom. Today's about Henry and Sonja, and your very first grandchild."

Hudson nodded once. "Yes, it is, Jena. It's about family."

"Spit it out, Hudson." Gloria's exasperation appeared fueled by her impatience for said grandchild to make his or her appearance. Henry and Sonja had kept them all in the dark about the sex of the baby, said they wanted everyone to have a surprise to look forward to.

"I'm getting there, Gloria." Hudson patted his wife's hand before he turned his focus back on Jena. "We want you to know that if you and Jeb were ever to, ah, get hooked together—is that how you say it nowadays?—we're cool with it. Jeb's part of the family, yes, but he's not your real brother, and there'd be nothing wrong with it. Not as far as we're concerned."

Dread, cold and heavy, filled her stomach. Were they trying to say they wanted her and Jeb to be together?

"Honey, are you okay?" Gloria's eyes appraised her and Jena swallowed, her throat dry.

"Okay, Mom and Dad, let's get something straight. For the record? I don't need your approval to date anyone. You know me well enough to know I'm going to see whoever I want to, right? As for Jeb—he helped get me out of a tight spot recently, with my Navy job, but it was as a friend. We're not anything more."

Hudson and Gloria exchanged The Look. The one all parents on the planet share. The she-thinks-we-were-never-young look.

"Mom. Please. Stop it."

"Honey, I wasn't born yesterday. You come in here in your little sundress, your hair wet, the dress inside out, a spark in your eyes. You're almost thirty, Jena, and you've done nothing but dedicate your life to service. It's about time you did something for yourself."

"Your mother's right. Don't ever let anyone's opinion, including ours, stop you from your deepest desire." Hudson sounded like a damned preacher.

She looked down at her dress. Sure as shit, it was inside out. Poppy hadn't noticed, or had ignored it. Henry and Sonja had bigger things going on than to notice her dress was on wrong.

"You two have only seen me twice since I got back. My dress is inside out because I was in a hurry to get back down here. It's hot as hell out, and I didn't care about how it looked, frankly. I just had to get dressed. And if there's a spark in my eye, it's because I'm living my dream. I have The Refuge to set up and run. Not everyone wants to hook up and start a family."

Gloria opened her mouth to speak, but Jena's phone pinged. She grabbed it off the table, grateful for any escape from this new, touchy-feely side of her parents. She was happier than anyone that they'd finally dragged themselves into the twenty-first century and the wide, open world of unprejudiced living. But that didn't mean she had to sit here and take romantic advice from them.

"It's from Brandon. The baby's almost here."

Gloria shrieked, and Hudson stood up so fast he knocked his iced tea over.

Jena bit back a smirk, making a mental note to someday thank her niece or nephew for saving her from the Boudreaux inquisition.

"He's beautiful!" Poppy cooed in Jena's ear as she held her newborn nephew. Jena, for her part, couldn't speak past the lump in her throat. Tears of joy trickled down her cheeks as she looked at the sweet little boy.

"He's huge." Sonja spoke up, and Jena exchanged a glance with Henry. It'd been a very long day for Sonja, and it was time for everyone to clear out. Jena was on it.

"I'll see you later, nephew." She kissed William Hudson Boudreaux on his sweet little forehead before she handed him back to Henry. "You two look like you could use some rest. I'll be back whenever you want, otherwise I'll stop over at your place when you give me the all-clear." She kissed Sonja and Henry goodbye and hugged Poppy.

"Thanks for coming in, sis." Henry seemed like he'd get emotional all over again, but the exhaustion was catching up with him.

"Are you kidding? This is what it's all about. Bye!" She turned on her heel and bolted for the door, before the tears of emotions she hadn't begun to untangle ran down her cheeks again.

Gloria, Hudson, and Brandon stood just outside the door. They'd all agreed that they wouldn't have more than two people in there at a time, to keep it manageable for Sonja.

"You headed home?" Brandon looked as slammed by the reality of another Boudreaux generation as she did.

"Yeah. I have to work in six hours." They all laughed, and Hudson shook his head.

"I think I'll stop by The Refuge later tomorrow, if it's okay with you." His eyes, like Gloria's, glowed with a sense of purpose and joy. Clearly, becoming grandparents was easier on the heart than what Jena and Brandon were experiencing.

"You're always welcome, of course, but you don't have to drop in all the time, Dad. Seriously. I know you're taking an interest in my life, and Brandon's and Henry's. That's enough. You've got too long of a drive, anyhow."

"If you're certain—"

"I am." She hugged them all and left, the sense of her heart being left with her nephew so strong she'd have never believed it if she hadn't experienced it.

"Jena, wait up." Brandon's plea stopped her. She turned and faced him. Brandon looked like he'd run a marathon, yet he'd spent most of the night sitting around and waiting with their parents.

"Yes?"

"It's—it's really intense, isn't it? Having little Will come into our lives."

"It is. I don't know what I was thinking, but I had no idea how this would make me feel."

Brandon's eyes filled with compassion. "You deserve to be happy, too, Jena."

Annoyance tugged at her newfound baby bliss. "What is it with you, and Mom and Dad? I know I deserve a good life. Trust me, I have it. I'm working the job I've always wanted, I'm settled here in NOLA for good. Sure, I have to find a more permanent place to live, but I will in time. Even Mom and Dad have finally come around to accepting reality and being better people. And now, there's little Will, like you said. Why does everyone think I'm miserable?"

"You almost died in Paraguay." He lowered his voice so it wouldn't carry. "I don't know what you were specifically doing there, or who you really worked for, but I got enough out of Jeb to know you were in awful shape when he got to you."

"And your point is?" She fought hard to keep her own self-pity and self-recriminations at bay. It'd be easy to give into the martyr narrative and take all the attention she could get from her family. But she didn't need attention—she needed solid bonds, connections.

What she'd thought she'd always have with Jeb. She shoved the rogue thought away, needing time alone.

"All I'm saying is that I do hope you're back home for good, and that you didn't take on Dad's project just to please him, or the family as a whole." Brandon's brow furrowed, and she let out a mental sigh of relief. At least Brandon wasn't chastising her for her non-relationship with Jeb, or trying to get her to make it more, like Hudson and Gloria had.

"Thanks, Brandon. I'm good, really. Yes, I was in a pickle at the end of my Navy time, but that's in the past. I'm over it. And trust me, just like you never wanted to be a lawyer and follow in Dad's footsteps, I never would have taken on The Refuge with your help if it wasn't already my big dream."

"I never thought I'd see the day that you accepted anything from anyone."

"Whoa—it's not a handout, Brandon. You said so yourself. You gave me the start-up funds, but I'm going to have it running on its own. That's what Jeb's doing for us, frankly."

"To be fair, I have to tell you I've asked him to come back to work with me. At Boats by Gus."

"What did he say?"

Brandon shook his head. "I couldn't convince him to. He's determined to move to Atlanta. It's an incredible job offer, and I can't blame him. And underneath it all is the fact that he doesn't think I'll ever completely trust him again."

"Will you? Trust him?"

"With my life. He saved yours."

"Yeah, he did." She savored time with each of her brothers, but not being drawn into more of Jeb's business. Healthy boundaries were a must if she was going to get through two more weeks with Jeb, and then see him leave. "I gotta go. Let me know if you think Sonja or Henry want more help from us sooner."

"Will do." They gave one another a quick hug and Jena headed for home, where she prayed she'd be able to sleep.

And stop thinking about Jeb.

Chapter 10

Monday morning Jeb arrived at The Refuge a full fifteen minutes early to find Jena already at her desk, poring over a stack of grant proposals.

"Good morning." He rapped on the doorframe before stepping into her office. Her face was lined with exhaustion, and the huge steaming mug of coffee on her desk underscored her need for sleep. "You look like you've been here for hours."

"Morning. I've been here for two."

"Congratulations on your nephew."

"Thank you. Brandon told you?" She ran her fingers through her hair, something she did when she was tired or stressed.

He nodded. "Sounds like it was a long day for all of you."

"It was. You never came." She made the statement sound like a question.

"Nah. That was a real family event. I'll meet the little dude soon enough, I'm sure."

"He's a keeper." Soft joy effused her tired features and he took a step closer.

"Wait a minute—is the woman who said she'd never have a baby—who, in fact, detests babies—smitten?"

"Not so fast. Of course I love him, he's my nephew." She stretched her neck and took a sip of her coffee. "We waited forever once I got to the hospital. While we were there, Brandon mentioned that he knew I was a mess when you found me in Asunción. Are you sure you didn't say too much?"

"Certain. Anyone can see the scar on your face, Jena, even with your makeup on. It's definitely faded, but it's still there. I didn't share anything you asked me not to. I've told you that." Exasperation that she didn't fully trust him made him wish he'd skipped coming in to say hello, even if he did have to get the day's list of to-dos. "Do you have anything new to add to my responsibilities this week?"

She gestured to the papers on her desk. "I've started to look at the grant proposals. You've done a hell of a lot of work in such a short time, Jeb. Thank you."

"It's my job."

"How much of the construction work are you still in on?"

"Not a lot—if they need extra hands to paint or someone to sweep up, I'll help. But I'm pretty much on the desk job now." His desk had arrived last week, along with a computer. "I'm happy to paint my office, of course."

"I'd rather you stick to the grants for the short time you're with us, and the budget breakdown. It's worth it if the contractors are on the job an extra day or two to finish the painting. You bring in way more with your financial expertise."

"That's the goal, anyhow." He looked around her office, the fresh paint gleaming as sunlight hit it from the large window that overlooked what used to be a side garden. "We can have some shrubs installed, make your view nicer."

"That's not important to me. I'm just glad to have a window. My Louisiana State job gave me a desk in a shared office with no windows. Very nineteen-seventies."

"I imagine a lot of your work won't be done in here, anyway."

She sighed. "You're correct. Once our clients come in, I'll be working in the meeting rooms and the lounge." Jena spoke about work with an air of detachment, almost distraction. Was she missing her undercover job?

"I can't imagine this kind of work gets your adrenaline pumping. I mean, after your last job."

Laser blue eyes focused on him, trying to look into his soul. "It's not comparable. The satisfaction I get from placing someone with the right agency or job or family—that's what keeps me coming back to social work, what attracted me to it in the first place."

"Sorry. It's none of my business."

"Stop saying things like that. As long as you're working here, The Refuge's business is your business. And when you leave, you and I have our family bond. That doesn't change." Her demeanor reflected nothing less than cool professionalism, but the tone of her voice tore at his conscience. Part of him had thought Jena wanted to keep things like they were back when they'd had their whole lives in front of them. Before she'd taken the clandestine job, before the concept of a sex-only relationship entered their minds. When it'd been just Jeb and Jena, two childhood buddies who trusted one another implicitly.

"Jeb? You're drifting." She turned her attention to her computer monitor.

"Just going over my daily list, is all." *Liar.* He'd never stop wondering if there'd been a point when he could have saved the relationship they'd had, the one they'd only begun to dream about. But it was fruitless—in fact, harmful—to pursue that line of thought. It'd squelch their tentative truce, and for sure destroy any chance at a friendship, no matter how platonic.

"Why don't we meet in the conference room this afternoon? I'll have my dad join us on speakerphone and we'll bring in the new social workers."

"Sounds good." He knew a dismissal when he heard it. He left her office, and it wasn't until he'd finished his third cup of morning coffee that he realized what had bothered him so much about Jena: She'd put on a good show about being a new aunt and all, but she hadn't been able to subdue her basic sadness.

Jena was grieving, but, for the life of him, he had no fucking clue why. Worse, she wasn't going to share any of it with him.

* * * *

Jena covered her face with her hands the minute Jeb was out of her office. That had been so hard, holding back from the one she'd never had to keep anything from.

Of course, if she'd held back that one little line of text after she'd asked him to tell her family her last wishes, they wouldn't be tiptoeing around one another as if they were afraid of setting off a land mine.

She'd barely slept last night, the sounds of the fetal monitor in Sonja's delivery room echoing through her mind, images of little Will sleeping in her arms sending shocks of exultation into her heart.

Starting a family was a very big deal. Until she'd watched her brother help his wife bring life into the world, Jena hadn't given having a family of her own much thought. She thought maybe there was a teeny tiny possibility "someday." Her CIA job had precluded it, as far as she was concerned. And more importantly, she'd never yearned to find the right man. The concept that the right person for her was out there, that fate would bring them together, had always been lost on her.

Then she decided to leave the CIA. She'd known the Paraguay mission was going to be her last. It wasn't the injuries, though they'd been extensive. It wasn't her aging body, either. Still shy of her thirtieth birthday, she knew she had another five, ten years as a full-on case agent if she really wanted it. But the fire in her belly had petered out. At first she'd been lost without it, wondered if she was having some kind of mental breakdown. Ever since the CIA recruiter had convinced her of the impact her duty and service would have on her nation's liberties, she'd been all about her undercover work, but her job as a social worker sustained her need to make a difference between covert operations. It had been the perfect balance for her intellect and athletic abilities.

And then, it hadn't. Maybe she'd seen one too many colleagues suffer at the hands of brutal enemies. Or it could have been watching her superiors call it quits, one by one, as they chose to put family before work.

Jena didn't have anyone but her brothers at that point, since she'd had a strained relationship with her parents for years. Her inability to be at Henry's wedding had hurt, too.

"Good morning, Jena." Her father's beaming face didn't look a bit as tired as she felt.

"Dad! You were taking today off, remember?"

"Turns out becoming a grandfather is energizing. I couldn't sleep, so I thought I'd drive in and spend a half day here."

"And maybe catch another peek at little Will?"

"I don't know. Maybe. To be honest, I don't want to overstep my boundaries." He stepped into her office and motioned at one of the chairs. "May I?"

"Of course." Jena appreciated any distraction from her own thoughts, even if that distraction was her father. She'd been in her own head too much lately, and her head was always a sketchy neighborhood.

He set his coffee on her desk and sat back. "Your mom and I want to be helpful in-laws and involved grandparents, but we don't want to be overbearing. My own parents were rather stifling."

"Grandma and Grandpa?" All Jena remembered about the couple, quite elderly by the time she was born, was that their house always smelled great from Grandma's cookie baking, and the sound of Grandpa's loud, booming laugh.

Hudson chuckled. "Yes, indeed. They were great grandparents to you three, but they put your mother through her paces. My mother was very opinionated, and no woman was going to be good enough for her son. Once she realized your mom wasn't going anywhere, she focused on telling her how to raise you all."

Jena shook her head. "I had no clue. To me, they were loving and sweet, always giving me whatever I wanted." Her grandparents were nothing like the bigots her parents had been.

"As they should have—it's what grandparents do. But the other part isn't desirable, that's for sure." He paused, and she sensed his discomfort.

"Dad, don't worry about it. Your relationship with them is only going to get better with time. Your attitudes were pretty unbearable for a long time. It doesn't heal overnight."

"I appreciate that. And I have to say, it's never fun when your kid takes you to task for your behavior, but I'm grateful for all the times you stood up to me and called me on my bullshit." He shook his head. "I was an ass. For too long."

Jena loved the humble, more open-minded man who sat in front of her. But she couldn't—and wouldn't—defend who he'd been before, the choices he and Gloria made. Hudson had kept his law office in the city, but he didn't do what she and her brothers thought he should—more pro bono work to help the thousands who'd lost everything to the storm.

"We're always learning in life, right, Dad? That's what I'm figuring out, and I'm less than half your age."

"Ouch." He placed his hand over his heart. "I deserved that. What are you learning, besides how to build a safe haven for our community?" She liked that he was taking ownership of NOLA again by using "our."

"I'm learning that work isn't everything." She'd inherited her workaholic tendencies from him.

"You're way ahead of the rest of the crowd then, Jena. What gives me so much joy these days is seeing that despite some of the screwed up values your mother and I could have passed on to you and your brothers, you three didn't take on the bad stuff. You rejected any hint of thinking you were any better than others. Ever since you were a little girl you've never divided people into groups."

"That's a credit to my generation, too, you know." Jena knew her father was right; she'd always known her parents' prejudices were unwarranted and wrong.

"It is, but let me finish. Even though I could have been a better father, you still turned out pretty damned well. I'm proud of you."

She blinked back tears. So many times she'd have paid to have her father speak to her like this, to admit he was wrong. That was what she'd wanted as an adolescent. But now what mattered was that he'd changed and continued to work on himself.

Maybe she could take a page from her father's manual on how to start over.

"Thanks, Dad. I'm happy to see you and Brandon talking again, too."

"Don't think Henry didn't have his issues with me, too. I almost lost him and Sonja. And to think I'd have missed out on that little boy." His eyes misted and she knew he was thinking of little Will.

"You don't have to keep beating yourself up, Dad. What have you always told me? 'It's okay to glance at your past, but don't stare.' You'll be fine, as long as you never forget how awful you were."

Hudson stood and picked up his coffee cup. "That's not bad advice."

"See you later, Dad."

"As long as it's before noon. I want to drive back to Baton Rouge before the traffic hits." He walked out, and it reminded her of *A Christmas Carol*. Her father represented her future. If she insisted on making work her number one priority, and refused to face her own shortcomings, she'd end up with a lot of career success and no family. She didn't want to wait until she was sixty to figure out what mattered in life. Change was inevitable, and at some point the long hours would take their toll, the high from helping people wouldn't hold the same punch.

And unlike her father, who'd been with her mother forever, she'd have no one.

* * * *

Jena could tell Jeb was distracted through the entire meeting. He kept checking his phone—whether for a text or email, she didn't know. She didn't have to. The pain was the same. The realization that no one understood her like he did—and even he didn't know her.

She'd never revealed herself fully to anyone. Intimacy wasn't in her deck of cards. Physical contact of the most intimate kind, sure. Sex for sex's sake? No problem. Having to work side by side with another undercover agent to accomplish a mission? She'd been the first one to raise her hand.

There was no one to blame for Jeb not knowing her better than herself. She'd built and maintained an intricate wall around her.

"I'm not seeing how you think you'll get all of these grants awarded in time to fund the first year of The Refuge, Jena." Brandon frowned as he flipped through the pile of grants and looked at the spreadsheet Jeb had provided. "That's assuming we'll even get them. It's all a gamble."

"It's not a gamble, it's an investment in The Refuge's future." She didn't want to get into it with her brother in front of the growing staff. She, Jeb,

Brandon, two new social worker hires, and a receptionist sat around the conference table that had been delivered just an hour earlier.

"Brandon's correct; the first year or two is going to be hit or miss. But eventually the grants will work out, at least some of them. I expect most of them will come through, but statistically it's best to assume we'll earn maybe fifty percent."

Brandon's brow lowered. "I don't get it." He looked at Jeb, then turned to Jena. "I'm the major donor here. I don't even understand why you're looking for more money. I'm funding it all, aren't I? Or didn't I make it clear enough that I want to?"

Guilt coiled low in Jena's belly. "I know you want to, and that's very generous. But, like I told you in the hospital, if this is really going to work from the ground up, it needs to be fully sustainable. Your donation is crucial to getting the building completed, but it's not enough for The Refuge to keep going on solely the interest." She bit her lip, not wanting to turn this into a family drama, but Brandon had a habit of tunnel vision once he'd made a decision.

"The development of a forward-looking financial plan isn't a luxury or an unnecessary distraction." Jeb commanded the attention of everyone in the room, and Jena saw why he'd been so good at what he did for Boats by Gus—and why The Refuge would never be enough for him. He needed more of a challenge, professionally. The job in Atlanta sounded like it fit the bill, from what Brandon had told her.

"I don't see why it's necessary at all." Brandon was being the stubborn brother she'd arm wrestled with.

"It's necessary because no nonprofit operates well with only one source of income. It's not only bad business, it's an affront to the people we'll be serving at The Refuge." Jeb's quiet authority could smooth the most ruffled feathers. "Besides the grants, there are several different sources of state and local funding. I'm putting those together now."

"We'll go over this again next week. Let's move on." Jena transitioned the meeting to more day-to-day operations, encouraging the newest employees to participate.

When the meeting ended, she left first, unable to remain in the room with Jeb. She didn't trust herself not to ask him why he was checking his phone so much. It could have been his new job. It could have even been a romantic interest. His life wasn't her business anymore. She had to face facts. The day would come soon enough that he'd tell her he was leaving.

What would she do then?

* * * *

Jena stared at her monitor, eyes burning as she studied what had to be the hundredth application for assistance. The Refuge hadn't had its official opening yet, as far as the facility was concerned. But since she'd hired a marketing firm to put the website together and launch it, word got out in NOLA.

Clients ranged from homeless families to alcoholics and drug addicts. There were several requests for help with domestic conflict, and families and couples who needed someone to guide them through conflict resolution about things like home budgets. They also had domestic violence cases, which she was required by law to report to the police.

The initial sense of satisfaction was tempered by the very familiar sense of being overwhelmed.

Which meant it was time for Jena to give it a break until tomorrow. She pushed back from her desk, shoved her feet into her shoes, and stood up. It was a little after eight; Jeb might still have been working in the pantry, but she hadn't heard anything from that side of the building in over an hour. Then again, she'd been engrossed in the requests for aid.

She grabbed her bag and slung it over her shoulder, acknowledging her stomach's grumbles. There was leftover pizza in her fridge, probably too dried out to consider for dinner. Grilled cheese and tomato soup it'd be.

In the corridor, near the front reception area, she heard the click of a door, and she paused. Hadn't she locked up after the contractors left? No, she'd been holed up in her office for the past three hours.

While she didn't miss being a CIA agent, she was grateful for the skills she'd acquired. Setting her bag down, she crept down the hall and waited just out of sight of the high desk. Footsteps, irregular and definitely not Jeb's. Someone had come in off the street.

Before she had a chance to inch closer and get a glimpse of the intruder, a loud thump sounded. Jena ran forward, using moves that assured her safety, but her hackles were no longer on alert. She saw the high-heeled sandals first, the wearer flat on the floor in front of the reception desk. As she peered around the opaque window divider, she discovered an attractive young woman unconscious. She ran to her, kneeled at her side, and felt for a pulse. Very faint, erratic. The woman's purse was beside her, its contents spilled out, including a small plastic packet of white powder and two syringes.

Move.

Jena's training—from basic first aid to advanced trauma aid—kicked in. The woman was coated with sweat and didn't appear to be breathing. Jena shouted on the off chance Jeb was still there. "Is anyone here? Help!" Tilting the woman's head back, she cleared her mouth, then administered several mouth-to-mouth breaths. The woman's lips were still blue, and she tried to breathe but there was only a sick, gurgling noise.

"Jena!" Jeb stood at the woman's feet.

"Call nine-one-one! Probable overdose."

Jena raced to her purse and brought it to the woman's side, dumping the contents. Jeb's voice was background noise as he spoke to the emergency dispatcher.

She quickly gave the woman more emergency breaths, then ripped open a packet of Narcan and prepped it. Placing the nozzle in the woman's nostril, she administered the antidote.

Jena bent to resume rescue breathing, but the woman's eyes popped open and she sucked in a long, full breath.

"What, what, oh, shit..." Her voice, while weak, didn't stop her from letting loose a string of "fucks" and "shits." Jena briefly closed her eyes. *Thank God.*

"You're safe. What's your name?"

"Molly." Her eyes darted around the reception area, never fully meeting Jena's. "Where am I?"

"The Refuge."

Jena placed her hand on the woman's shoulder when she tried to sit up. "Not so fast. You've just survived an overdose."

"Wait—where the fuck did you say I am?" Instinct to fight a perceived threat had her struggling to keep seated.

"Take it easy. You're at The Refuge, a social services center."

Jena looked at Jeb, who stood in place, arms crossed over his chest. His expression was bland but Jena knew the blaze in his eyes. She'd felt the same way the first time she saw a resuscitated heroin OD.

"Oh, shit!" The woman turned her head to the side and vomited. If she hadn't been trained to fight her gag reflex, Jena would have joined her. She rubbed the woman's shoulder, trying to offer calm reassurance. And she was stalling—if the woman knew that an ambulance was en route, she might try to run.

"Here." Jeb handed her a roll of paper towels and a bottle of water. She opened the bottle and helped the woman sip from it, then handed it to her. As she finished cleaning up the vomit, the EMTs arrived through the front door. Two police officers followed.

"I don't need any fucking help!"

"We're here to help you, ma'am." The first EMT smiled and asked Jena what had happened. She explained, and one of the officers nodded. "We know Molly. This is her neighborhood—she lives two blocks over."

"Then I'll leave you all to it."

"We'll need a statement once she's stabilized."

"Of course."

Jena stood back and let the first responders do their jobs. Jeb walked up next to her. "That happen a lot in social work?"

"It didn't used to, but yeah, it's not uncommon. And FYI, I carry Narcan in my purse. Just in case. I'm sure you see the news—we're in the middle of an opioid epidemic."

"This is the first time I've seen it up close and personal." His gaze assessed her. "You didn't bat an eye."

"There isn't time to blink when someone's overdosed. Every second counts. I'm just glad she walked in here and didn't collapse on the street."

"I thought the front door was locked." His frown reflected her thoughts.

"I did, too. I never went out to check it, though. I got so busy in my office." She looked at him. "Why are you here so late again?"

"I was crunching some numbers and planned to do the rest at home. When I got up, I saw that the kitchen needed some sweeping, since the contractors finished installing the cabinetry today."

"That isn't your job anymore—the contractor stuff." They'd gotten laptops for each member of the staff who needed it, and Jeb had plenty to fill his plate as they fought to get the center on solid financial footing.

"It was quick and easy, and gave me a break from the head-pounding tasks."

She wondered if he missed the more physical parts of his work at Boats by Gus, but before she could ask him a police officer approached them.

"Ready for my statement, officer?"

The woman chuckled. "You've done this before."

"Many times." Jena turned to Jeb, but he was gone.

Again.

Chapter 11

"Hey, bro, watch it!"

Jeb ducked in time to narrowly miss being clonked in the head by a falling limb as he and Brandon navigated the bayou in one of the flat-bottom boats their company had manufactured. When they'd had a company.

"Thanks."

"You're distracted this morning." They'd agreed to meet this morning, enjoying time together as they had before what Jeb was beginning to think of as "The Event." When he'd discovered that the woman he'd thought he knew better than anyone in the world was a completely different person entirely.

"I am." No sense fighting it. He was beyond distracted, to the point of obsession.

"Want to talk about it?" Brandon's phrase wasn't new between them. What was new was that Jeb didn't feel worthy of his friend's trust. And yet he'd agreed to join him for something they'd always done: hanging out.

"I wouldn't know where to begin." Especially since Brandon had no clue how close he was to Jena.

"Try me, bro." There it was.

"I have to get past this thing between us first, Brandon."

"You're the only one putting it there." Brandon shut the motor off and handed Jeb an oar. They maneuvered through much more interesting territory the old-fashioned way. Plus, it didn't scare off the critters, which was what had brought them out here as kids.

"Remember that raccoon with the alligator?"

Brandon laughed. "I thought we were going to see that gator swallow him whole."

"Nope—he just caught a ride across the river." Jeb rowed, enjoying the resistance of the current against the oar. "I know I'm the one holding back, Brandon. And to be honest, I don't think I'm ever going to be able to forgive myself for betraying you. I could have at least left you a note."

"And what would I have done? You know me best when it comes to that kind of thing, Jeb. I'm uptight, and when in doubt I'm always the one who'll call for help. I'd have called the police, the FBI, and you'd have never gotten out of the country with the funds."

"You said you didn't care about the money. You'd have wired the money yourself."

Brandon lifted his oar and used it to point. "See that tree? Look up at the branch right over the water."

Jeb's skin crawled at the sight of several water moccasins writhing on the low branch. "We don't want to go over there."

"Let's head out for the middle of the stream." Once they were into a comfortable rhythm, Brandon looked over his shoulder. "You're right—I would have wired the money, but that wouldn't have done jack shit for Jena. They'd have killed her."

Yes, they would have. The sick sense of dread washed over him, his heart pounding against his rib cage. He didn't think he'd ever let go of this—the sheer terror at the thought of losing Jena.

And now he'd been the one to let her go, then send mixed messages by making love to her in the kitchen.

"You aren't disagreeing."

"I can't. You're right."

"What made you go, Jeb? Sure, Jena's been part of your life since you met my family, but what's really going on?"

Jeb stilled. Brandon knew damn well what was between him and Jena—he wouldn't dig into something so personal unless he already knew the answer. Or at least had a good idea of it.

"What are you asking me, Brandon? If Jena and I are more than friends?" He wasn't going to betray Jena, but he wouldn't lie to his lifelong friend, either. A friend he'd already betrayed.

Brandon set his oar down and motioned for Jeb to do the same. He moved to the seat beside Jeb at the stern and fired up the motor. It was relatively quiet for an outboard motor, and that had been a great selling point for their boats. They skimmed along the swampy water, the sun glistening on the brown surface. Several water bugs leaped and flew their way over the bayou, their wings iridescent. He longed to be here with Jena.

And that was the crux of his issues. He always wanted to be with the one woman he'd never have, not in that way. Jena didn't give herself away like that.

"I think we both know the answer to that, Jeb. You don't run to another continent with fifteen million to rescue a friend's sister, unless the friend asks you to. No, my friend, that's what a man in love does."

"That doesn't mean I knew it at the time." He hadn't. He'd simply acted. Like adding up columns, finding a deficit, and knowing it had to be corrected.

"But you're not denying how you feel about her?" Brandon looked at him, his gaze noncommittal. Jeb knew better. Brandon was feeling him out, looking to see if Jeb had thought it all through.

"No." He leaned forward, his arms on his thighs. "It's not what you think, though. I can't have the ending you and Poppy had. Jena and I... We're a lot more complicated."

"How so?"

"Are you kidding me? Should I start with the whole bit about being a part of your family?"

"We all knew there was something there for a long time. You went to prom together in high school, remember? And you're always at odds with one another, at least you have been since college. Henry and I figured something happened between you two there."

"You'd be right." He hung his head. "Fuck."

"It's not a death sentence to care about a woman, Jeb."

"That woman is your sister." It had to carry more weight. She meant a whole hell of a lot to both of them.

"Yeah, but she's her own person, too. And from a brotherly standpoint, I'd much rather see her with the devil I know."

Jeb looked at him, and when he saw the wide grin on Brandon's face, he punched him in the shoulder. Brandon laughed.

"It's never going to be anything more than it was. She and I... We can get along for a while, and it all seems okay on paper, if you will. But we've both kept too much from one another over the years. That's not how it should be with a life partner. I can't be with someone who won't share it all with me."

Brandon nodded. "Yeah, Jena's a tough nut to crack, all right. She's always kept more to herself than either Henry or I. She had the same issues we did with our folks, but instead of throwing it all out there, she quietly planned for college and made a vow to herself she'd leave home for good at eighteen."

"How are you doing with your parents? With your, uh, reconciliation?"

"It's good. I can't pretend the past didn't happen, but it doesn't have to define today. They're doing their best to make up for the lost years, and for how they behaved when Henry announced his engagement to Sonja. Do you know about Henry's ex bothering Sonja after the wedding was called off?"

"A little bit."

"My folks invited Henry's ex to the rehearsal dinner, and the wedding, and didn't tell Henry or Sonja. She was nuts in college, and hasn't gotten any better. It was just a lot of drama for them, on top of Sonja having cold feet *and* finding out she was pregnant."

"Why the hell did they do that?"

"Because they had to make a last-ditch attempt to convince Henry he should marry a white girl."

"Jesus."

"Yeah, Jesus had something to do with them coming around, if you ask me. Only a miracle could have changed my father's ingrained bigotry." Brandon heaved out a sigh, moved the tiller to get around a large patch of cattails. "I'm glad they've both seen the light, but I'm a little bit heartbroken that it didn't happen sooner."

Jeb sat quiet, remembering the many times he'd listened to Brandon vent about his relationship—or lack thereof—with his parents. Brandon cut ties with them when he was in college, furious over how his parents had left NOLA in the aftermath of Katrina.

"Which leads me back to my point, Jeb. I had this conversation with Henry when he was trying to figure out what the hell to do about Sonja and whether to fight it out. You and Jena, you're both very stubborn, and neither of you are the world's most open people."

Jeb didn't argue. He didn't like to talk about his family or the frightening childhood he'd endured at the hands of an alcoholic mother and absentee father. Who would? And Jena didn't talk about anything, beginning with her job with the CIA.

"Trust is central to it all for me, Brandon. I'm not saying Jena's not trustworthy—"

"I get it. You're saying she doesn't trust you, not enough to let you in to her world fully. Take it from me—she doesn't let any of us in. You're the closest ally she's ever had."

It didn't feel like it.

"I don't want to disappoint you, Brandon, but your sister and I, it's not happening."

"All I'm asking is that you think about it. You have something so unique, with having known each other since you were kids. That's rare."

As rare as Jena confiding in him.

"You've known since we were young, huh?" He didn't regret that Brandon and Henry had suspected.

"Hell, yes."

"And you never thought it was icky, or that I'd taken advantage of your family's open arms?"

"Not in the least. You want the whole truth? I saw how Jena idolized you from the moment I brought you home. Until then she'd tagged after me and Henry, but wasn't really a part of our boy stuff. You bridged that gap, taught her to do things like climb trees and roller skate—the things we had no patience for. You two always were a unit, in my eyes."

"But you and I were best buds!"

"We were. And I hope we still are." Brandon pulled out onto the Mississippi from the smaller waterway and headed for his place ten minutes away. He lived in a home he'd built along the river that had its own pier. Boats by Gus had done very well until Jeb made his withdrawal.

"I'm glad you were able to keep your house." He spoke with sincerity.

"Are you kidding me? All you took was the company funds. I had enough put away to make sure I'd be okay if the business ever went under. I would have dug into it, but they're retirement funds. I never would have lost anything, Jeb. And that's what I'm trying to say to you. There's no reason you should lose anything you want to hang on to. It just might take a little extra work."

Was he fucking kidding? Jena wasn't a tricky business proposition, or a column of figures that weren't adding up. She was...

Hell. She was everything to him.

Could he be the one to break through to her, get her to fully open up? Did he even have the courage to do it?

* * * *

Jena dragged home Saturday evening after all day at The Refuge. She wanted to get on top of the paperwork for the grand opening, a week away. She'd arranged catering and ordered a cake from her favorite bakery. It was fun, but also exhausting.

She plopped Chinese takeout containers on her kitchen counter and headed for the bathroom. Within ten minutes she was in her favorite bright green terry cloth robe, had a green mud mask on her face, and was pouring herself a glass of rosé from the box of wine in her fridge, a gift from Robyn's last visit.

Robyn was a huge blessing, a gift for having resigned from undercover work and made the decision to settle down.

Jeb.

She ignored her heart long enough to get settled with her food in front of the television. Tonight was going to be pure escape, and she started to scroll through her binge-watching options.

A knock sounded at her door and she paused, heart racing. The rapping's intrusion through the quiet had startled her, but her fear turned to annoyance as she imagined the landlord outside, asking about some maintenance issue, as she was wont to do, unannounced. Maybe she'd go away if Jena sat quietly enough.

Pound pound pound.

"Holy hell and hairy balls, hang on," she said as she placed her plate and wineglass on the cocktail table. Walking to the door, she told herself to be nice but firm and send her landlord away. Jena needed a quiet night.

She looked through the peephole, a quaint attribute of the carriage house when compared to the super sleek high-tech security system of The Refuge.

Jeb.

Her heart leaped.

Calm down, girl.

"Jena, I know you're there. Please open up."

She moved back from the door, discomfited. Jeb had seen her naked, of course, but never in her shabby shamrock robe. So what? He'd seen her in a towel at Brandon's pool the other day, for God's sake.

She swung open the door. Jeb's brows rose.

"I just got home, and I'm having a quiet night in." Emphasis on "quiet."

"I can see that." He held up a bottle of her favorite sparkling wine and a huge chocolate candy bar. "I come bearing gifts."

"Why?" Sweat began to trickle between her breasts as she stood with the door open, the AC pouring out into the wet blanket that was NOLA in August.

"Can I come in? Your chocolate is going to be fondue in another minute."

"Sure." She turned and left him to follow. "Please lock the door behind you."

"You don't think it's unsafe here, do you?" he asked as he complied, throwing the deadbolt.

She sat on the sofa and motioned for him to take the other end, or the easy chair. "Sit wherever you want."

"Why don't I get us glasses for this? It's chilled." His glance landed on her glass of rosé. "Unless you want to save this?"

"No, no. I can have the boxed wine anytime. Please, help yourself to any Chinese you want, too. The flutes are in the cabinet over the refrigerator."

"I remember." Of course he did. They'd had a particularly wild night of strawberries, champagne, and sex before she'd deployed last year. Correction: before she'd gone on another mission, the one that had proved her last. "This is a very sweet place, Jena, but don't you think it'll get too small for you after a while? Now that you're staying here for longer periods?" The cupboard door opened and closed, the tinkle of flutes and the pop of the champagne cork sprinkled over the rumble of his low voice as he spoke.

"I don't know. And I'm not staying here for 'longer periods.' I'm here permanently." Annoyance scratched at her initial pleasure to see him unexpectedly at her door.

The sofa sagged as he sat on the opposite end and placed her flute in front of her. He hadn't helped himself to any of the food. She popped a shrimp into her mouth and spoke around the food. "Aren't you hungry?"

"I ate. I was with Brandon for a good part of the day, out on the Bayou. We stuffed our faces with crawdads when we got back."

"No one makes those better than he does. Maybe my dad." She was so hungry, she didn't feel bad about eating in front of him. "So what brought you here?" God, she was probably crazy, but she swore she smelled his scent over the steamed shrimp stir-fry. And he looked so, so fresh. His skin was sun-touched without being burnt or leathery, and there were telltale chestnut streaks in his dark hair.

"What always brings me here, Jena. You." His eyes glittered and her insides tightened. She crossed her legs, hoping he hadn't noticed that she was squirming from the instant attraction he always thrummed up between them.

"Cut it, Jeb. We've agreed to a professional relationship. And okay, we're friends from way back. But that doesn't explain why you're here on a Saturday night."

"Can't a friend come over to hang out?" He held up his glass. "To friends."

She warily took her champagne and sipped. An explosion of incredible flavors and delicious aroma filled her mouth. She savored it until she had no choice but to swallow. "This is fantastic, Jeb. What is it?"

"Something I thought you'd enjoy."

"You know me well." She moved to take a second sip.

"Not well enough, Jena. I had no idea you worked for the CIA for the last seven years. None. Nada. Zip. I think good friends should know everything about one another, don't you?"

She froze. "Are you here to berate me? Because if you are, you can take your ass and your chocolate right back where you came from. Leave the bubbly."

He laughed and didn't move from his relaxed position on the couch. "I'm not here for any reason but to talk and spend time with you. I figured you might be alone tonight, and I was, too, so I thought 'why not?' Besides, it'd be foolish to try to 'berate' you when you look like a big green monster." He was clearly holding back laughter, the mirth crinkling the skin at the edges of his eyes. This Jeb she never wanted to lose.

"If you're referring to my robe, I'll have you know it's my old friend." She ran her hand down the nap of the green material.

"Not the robe, Jena, although it's lovely on you. I'm talking about whatever in God's green creation you have plastered on your face."

Oh, shit. She'd forgotten about her pore-eliminating, skin-plumping mask.

Chapter 12

Jeb reached over and put his hand on Jena's forearm, his laughter rumbling between them. "I'm teasing you. Please, don't let me ruin your relaxation. Don't take it off on my account." He was referring to the mask but saw from the way her lips opened, all pink and moist from the champagne, that she'd thought about taking off her robe, too.

His cock swelled but he ignored it—as much as he could ever ignore his arousal around Jena.

She stilled, and warm satisfaction moved through him. He still could ease her anxieties, if only the minor ones. The bigger issue, the reason he was here, was her inability to trust anyone fully. He wanted to prove her wrong—show her that he was one person she could always count on. Not only in the throes of life and death, but in more routine moments like this. Since he'd made the decision to take the Atlanta job, it'd become vitally important to him that Jena remember him that way.

"I can't believe you let me sit here with a green face. Talking, eating, and drinking, without saying a word. You never even smirked!"

"I didn't know I had a smirk."

"Oh, yeah, you are the master of smirks."

"Who knew?" Confident she wouldn't bolt, he broke eye contact and reached for his glass. Champagne wasn't his thing, but he knew she enjoyed it, so he'd asked for the nicest bottle he could afford. He had to admit, it was refreshing on a hot night, even if her air was making it feel like winter. "It's kind of chilly in here. What's your electric bill like?"

She giggled. "I don't usually crank the AC like this, but tonight I needed to relax, take a hot bath, the whole pamper routine, as you can tell." She grinned, wide and clown-like, and the green goop cracked in several places.

But nothing took away from the rich hue of her eyes, the Boudreaux blue that she shared with her brothers and father. A small still voice inside him insisted he was on the way to crazy town, but he forged ahead nonetheless.

He put his glass down and turned to face her fully. "I have an offer for you."

She stiffened, and he swore if she'd had hackles, they'd have been up, pressing through her fluffy green robe. "That sounds like a threat."

"It's not." He fought his doubts. "It occurred to me that you've never met my family. I know yours, inside and out, but you know very little about mine."

"I met them at our high school and college graduations."

"For like five minutes. Tomorrow my grandmother is having one of her big Sunday dinners. She used to do it every weekend, like your mom, but she's getting older and doesn't have the energy as much anymore."

She chewed on her lower lip. "Why now?"

"Why not? We're always going to be connected through your family, Jena. There's no escaping that. I wanted to give you a chance to see where I'm from. It's what friends do." He knew it was a long shot. Growing up, it'd been easy to keep his family in the background as he ran and played with the Boudreauxes. "When we were together in college, neither of us wanted to bring the other home—not until it was more serious. Then we broke up. Our recent time, um, together wasn't something to tell anyone about, either, was it?"

"Exactly. So why now? Why do you all of a sudden want me to meet your family, Jeb? You're leaving for Atlanta in practically days."

"There's finally no pressure. And now that I'm moving away, it's important that the people I've been closest to in NOLA are acquainted. I guess it's like throwing myself a going away party—but in reverse." Jeb couldn't read her expression at first, and fought to fill the void. "This is as friends, as my best friend's sister. Isn't that the best way to meet people, with no expectations?"

She didn't reply right away. Not verbally. But her eyes, the eyes he'd been lost and found in, they measured him. He didn't look away—even though his dick was aching to be inside her and his hands wanted to cup her breasts, her ass.

"I'll go. But you have to promise me one thing, Jeb."

"Name it." Had she really agreed?

"If at any time you start to feel the least little bit unhappy while we're at your grandma's, tell me. We'll go. Whether I've had dessert yet or not." Her mouth loped up in a half smile, her eyes twinkling.

"I've already told you more than I realized, haven't I?"

"Mmm." She sipped her champagne. "It's been a little bit here, a little bit there. Your brothers and sister used to like to show up at your dorm, remember?" Her brow rose and made him laugh.

"It's hard to forget your drunk brother showing up when you're in the middle of romancing your best girl." Mitch had shown up in the middle of a particularly fun Saturday night with Jena. His roommate was away, and they had the whole weekend to be together, alone. Or so they'd thought.

"As I recall, it wasn't that romantic. More like athletic."

He coughed on his drink. "Athletic? Wow. I never thought of our times together as 'athletic.' Boisterous, maybe."

She laughed. "That's the problem with going to college so close to home. My parents and brothers knew it meant death to anyone who showed up at my dorm room unannounced."

"Do you still think we're 'athletic'?" The words rolled off his tongue, which he wanted to use to taste more than champagne. To hell with whatever they'd agreed to. He needed this woman more than any other.

"Olympic-class. Especially those months leading up to my Paraguay assignment. It was like we knew—" She stopped abruptly, and the shadows were back in her eyes, goddamnit. He'd done that, led the conversation here.

"Stop right there, Jena. Give me a minute. I have an idea." He got up and prayed he was doing the right thing.

* * * *

Jena sat on the sofa, feeling stupid. Jeb hadn't come over to seduce her, or to say goodbye, but to ask her to his grandmother's Sunday dinner. She also suspected he was trying to mend fences after their recent rocky road. Fine enough.

A furl of disappointment opened inside her as he spoke, though. Her body was primed for him, always, but she could handle him not coming here for sex, couldn't she? It was deeper than that. A part of her she wasn't too acquainted with wanted Jeb to say he needed her, wanted her to be more than a fuck buddy or platonic friend. The concept of a partner who was the full package was taking hold. Jena had settled for less in her personal life for a long time, if not forever. Certainly since she'd broken up with Jeb senior year.

"Don't move, just lean your head back on the couch." Jeb stood behind her, just out of her line of vision.

"What?"

"Trust me."

"Okay, but if you're going to hit me with a whipped-cream pie or something, I won't go down without a fight. Ohhhh, that is so nice." She sighed softly as he pressed the warm, damp washcloth on her skin, removing the mask. "You don't have to do this, you know," she said.

"Do you want me to stop?"

"Never." It was pure luxury to have Jeb stroking the cloth against her skin, taking off the mask and massaging her at the same time. "You could do this for a living."

"No, thanks. But for you, no problem." As he continued moving his hand over her throat, her awareness skyrocketed from the constant arcing and sparking that always existed between them to an otherworldly need. She grasped his wrists as he ran the cloth up and over her face one last time.

"Jeb." She heard the scratchy edge in her voice, knew he'd interpret it correctly. He slowly pulled his hands from hers, and she closed her eyes. The coolness of the air on her face was her answer. Jeb really did want only a friendship.

Could she do it?

The sofa cushions sank next to her and she opened her eyes in time to see Jeb's face lowered to hers. Happy surprise stoked her desire and she couldn't keep the grin off her face.

"You okay with this? Tonight?" He hovered over her mouth, his breath fanning over her skin, which still tingled from the mask and his ministrations.

"Oh, yes." She turned to face him, reached up, and buried her fingers in his hair, pulling him the rest of the way to make their lips meet.

They'd been together enough to know what turned the other on, to be able to fall into the predictable rhythm that always yielded the most intense, satisfying orgasms. That time in the The Refuge's kitchen had blown all of that away, and now she was no longer totally unself-conscious as she touched him with her fingers, met his tongue with hers. What they shared now was a sense of total awareness of one another and their needs, the realization that what they had together was rare and explosive.

His hands untied her robe and he pushed it off her shoulders, his lips and tongue following, trailing over and up her throat, behind her ear. His tongue swirled into her ear just before he bit on her lobe with the perfect amount of pressure. As he sucked on her ear she couldn't remain seated, and she grabbed the back of the couch as leverage to swing up and straddle him. Her panties were all she had on, her breasts free and full in his face, her sex up against his erection.

"Your jeans are too rough. Let's get them off." She undid his buckle and moved aside long enough for him to remove them, along with his T-shirt. He lay back down on the sofa, fully naked and fully aroused.

Jena moved to take her panties off, and the smoldering heat in his eyes made her pause. She wanted nothing more than to rip them off and plunge onto Jeb's cock, so hard and huge in his want for her. But he'd taught her that patience made the getting all the better.

"Do you want me to take them off, babe?" She gyrated her hips as she straddled over him on her knees, holding a breast in each hand.

"Yeah." The word wasn't more than a grunt, and she knew he was close, so close. Instead of taking off her underwear, she got on all fours and closed her mouth on him, taking his full, hot length to the hilt.

"Jesus, Jena." His hands ran over her head; his fingers tangled in her hair. He gasped and moaned as she sucked, licked, and stroked with the hand that wasn't propping her up.

"Shhh. Enjoy this, Jeb." She continued, using her fingers to gently press just under his scrotum as she sucked on him. His pelvis bucked and he tensed as if his life depended on it, depended on her to get him off. Jena loved how hard he got, how his soft skin moved over the steel length of his erection. He was so, so close. She pressed again in the soft place under his balls, and Jeb's cry split the room an instant before her mouth filled with his salty release. She savored him, didn't stop sucking or licking until he was spent.

"Babe." He tugged her up and pressed her to him, her breasts between them as she lay atop him. His breathing was slow and steady, his eyes closed. Jena rested her head on his shoulder, her fingers playing with the tufts of dark hair that covered his pecs.

"It's your turn to chill, Jeb."

"Just don't put any green goop on my face."

She laughed, and it wasn't just a reaction to his humor—it was the result of the warmth that filled her heart and had to be expressed.

Joy.

* * * *

They lay like that for several minutes.

"You awake?" His voice vibrated through his rib cage, and she loved the feel of it against her ear as much as the way he was running his fingers up and down her spine.

"Yes, but if you keep doing your magic on my back, I'll be asleep."

His fingers stilled. He tapped on her shoulders. "Get up."

"Really?" But she did, sliding up to sit on the edge of the couch, their naked hip bones touching.

Jeb stood in front of her, and even after what she knew had to have been an amazing release, his cock appeared far from replete. When she looked up, his gaze held hers and heat hit her cheeks.

"Caught."

"You like what you see?" Instead of his usual cheeky grin, he smiled, the light in his eyes intent. He reached for her hands and pulled her up next to him. "You." He kissed her deeply. "Are"—another kiss—"amazing." Then he grabbed her buttocks and hauled her against him, and she thought she'd never been more relaxed and full of anticipation in her life.

When he finally lifted his mouth from hers, she reached up and caressed his cheekbones, his jaw. "Jeb, how can you be ready to go again? I know you weren't faking it." They both laughed.

"I can't help myself when I'm around you, Jena. No other woman has ever turned me on like you do." He leaned in to kiss her again and she put her hand on his chest, stopping him.

"That sounds like a lot more than friends with benefits." She damned the tears that blurred his face.

He cupped her face. "We've been more than just friends since that evening at The Refuge, babe."

She nodded. "The kitchen."

He grinned. "That was epic. But tonight will be, too." He took her hand and led her to her bedroom. She'd left the lights on, her messy piles of clothes and rumpled bedclothes in full view.

"Wait, let me straighten this."

"The hell with that." He spun her around so her back was against him, his arm around her waist as he kissed her on the spot between her neck and shoulder that made her knees shake. She gasped, and he didn't relent as he tweaked a nipple while he sucked on her nape. Tight, sensuous desire coiled deep inside, making her pussy throb with need, want. Her nipples pebbled and she arched her back, undulating her hips in reaction. She turned in his arms and pressed herself up against him, bringing his mouth to hers.

The kiss was teasing, playful at first, as they prolonged what she wanted so badly. When he reached between her legs and stroked her wet, swollen flesh, she moaned, needing more. Always more.

"Lie on the bed, babe." She didn't hesitate. The sooner Jeb was inside her, the better. Jena had never professed patience as one of her virtues.

"Hurry, Jeb."

"Scoot up. I need some room."

"Oh, God, you don't have to. We can fuck, please."

"No way. I want it all, Jena." He covered her with his body for a long, lingering kiss before he moved down and placed his mouth on her. Her sighs turned to gasps and she clutched at the sheets beneath her, needing a way to push back against the overwhelming rush of sensation. No one ever made her come to her peak so quickly or so slowly, as Jeb. If he wanted to make her come hard and fast, he knew how to use his tongue and fingers to do it. If he preferred a more leisurely pace, or picked up that she needed to take it slow, he used his mouth to bring her to the edge time and time again.

He looked up at her from between her thighs. "Don't stop, Jeb, please."

"Then stop thinking. Go with it."

His eyes wouldn't let her look away and dismiss him. Her heart soaked up his words, their intent. This was no longer a game between them, a means to an end. She didn't have to analyze his techniques for keeping up a wall.

She lay back and let herself savor every touch of his tongue and fingers, thrilling as everything took on a heightened pleasure. When he circled her clit with his tongue, she felt the pressure rise. She was entirely focused on what his mouth was doing to her sex, how he worked and played her pussy to places she'd only imagined. Time stood still, and all she felt, smelled, and breathed was Jeb. His scent, their scent, as she did as he'd asked and let go.

He shoved one, two fingers into her while he sucked on her clit, and her orgasm exploded from the center out, obliterating logic, catapulting her into pure sensation. Her screams bounced off the carriage house walls, and somewhere in the midst of it she felt him leave her, the coolness of the air moving over her sex-slicked skin. She heard the crinkle of a foil packet as he got a condom, and before she'd completely come down from her climax he was over her, his hands finding hers, moving her arms over her head as he thrust into her without preamble.

"Sweet. So sweet." His words made her pussy clench around him, small waves already building, as if she hadn't just had the orgasm of her life.

"That's it, babe. Don't hold back." She kissed his throat, bit into his shoulder as her nails dug into his back, holding on to him as he rode her. She dug her feet into the bed, moving her pelvis to meet him thrust for thrust, before wrapping her legs around him. They were on a journey and nothing was going to stop them as they came together again and again. Gasps, moans, and grunts were all they exchanged as their bodies moved in unison.

Jena held on as long as she could, waiting for Jeb, but it was impossible to stop the climax that rolled through her. As the cries ripped out of her throat, the primal waves of pleasure gripping her, Jeb shouted her name and collapsed on top of her.

Once their breathing calmed, he slid off and to her side, pulling her up against him in spoon fashion. The thought that they'd never done this, never fallen asleep together afterward, flickered across her mind before she drifted off.

* * * *

Jeb stretched and reached for Jena, but only came up with a handful of rumpled comforter. He opened an eye, remembered where he was, where he wasn't. They'd always gone back to their respective places after they'd had sex. Even after the kitchen they'd gone home solo.

Judging from the angle of the sunlight pushing through the wooden shutters, it was Sunday morning. They'd spent the night together.

Jena.

The woman mystified him. She was all about environmental consciousness except, apparently, when she wanted to take a hot bath. Which he'd never given her the chance to do last night. Hopefully she wasn't upset about it.

The scents of bacon and what he strongly suspected—and hoped— was grits crept into the light blue bedroom. Jeb stood up and stretched, shoved on his boxers and cargo shorts, and walked out into the kitchen. Jena stood at the stove, stirring and singing softly to herself. The fuzzy robe looked sexy on her.

"Do you always cook a full breakfast?"

She looked over her shoulder, her long locks spilling over her back, before she turned to him. "Only on special occasions."

He placed his hands on her shoulders and kissed her. "It smells like heaven in here." And she tasted like it.

She turned her attention back to the stove while he massaged her back. "I hope you like eggs, bacon, and grits."

"It'd be a sin not to, when you're making them for me. God, they smell so good."

"Thanks. I didn't make as much as usual, because you said we'd be eating at your grandma's." She shut off the burners and turned to face him. "Are you still sure you want to take me there?"

"Certain."

"I made coffee—yours is on the table. I don't have a regular coffeepot, so you'll have to settle for a cappuccino."

"Perfect." He walked over to the table and took a sip. "Delicious."

She brought two plates over. "I'm glad you like it." Her smile was genuine, her face devoid of not only makeup, but the usual mask she wore, except on the rarest occasions when she revealed her true self. "What's wrong?"

"I can't believe it's taken this long to find out you don't have a real coffee maker."

She eased herself into one of the chairs and motioned for him to take the other. "We have had a rather different path, that's for sure. I mean, our relationship." She blushed. "Whatever this is between us. And, Jeb—I'm not going to ask you to stay."

He reached over the table and grasped her hand. "Atlanta is not going to change. But we're allowed to end what we have on a more positive note, aren't we? At the end of the day, what we have, what we've always had, is a solid friendship that's lasted years."

She contemplated him, and he wanted to take away the sorrow and doubt he saw in her blue eyes. "That's part of the problem, though, isn't it? We've taken it for granted, not done the work it deserves."

"We're giving it a good start today." He didn't want to tell her what he thought, what he'd begun to hope for. That he'd lied about Atlanta being set in stone. It was too soon, and, based on their history, improbable. "You'll finally meet my family."

Chapter 13

"This is your grandmother's place?" Jena soaked up the bayou beauty that surrounded the small subdivision in the immediate outskirts of NOLA. "I'm surprised it made it through Katrina."

"We were, too. Come on, we never use the front door." He grabbed her hand and took her along a path that ran next to the house, which was stately yet sprawling, the blooming vines and overgrown flowerbeds softening the edges of what otherwise was a very solid structure. It was red brick with freshly painted white trim, and the front door appeared formal and imposing. As the backyard came into view, so did the water.

"Amazing." She stopped in her tracks and breathed in the scent, watched a heron gingerly wade along the grassy bank just beyond a retaining wall. "We're all of what, five feet above the river?"

"That's not the river. It's a tributary, but a big one." He stood beside her, and with the morning sun blistering their backs and the very slight, muggy breeze wafting off the water, Jena felt at one with nature. With Jeb. She looked at his profile, dark against the bright blue sky. He met her gaze and her heart fluttered like the swamp grass, the desire between them a comfortable buzz. A palm-sized dragonfly hovered next to them and Jena laughed.

"What's so funny about a dragonfly?" He held his hand up and the insect zoomed in for a closer inspection before zipping off to skim the water's surface.

"That noise, the low buzz they make? That's how I feel whenever I'm with you." It was the kind of thought she'd usually keep to herself, buried deep. But after last night, acknowledging that Jeb would soon be gone yet still wanted to leave on good terms, she had a sense of freedom. It wasn't just relief that she was free to speak her mind, but more of a letting-go of her former coping mechanism. Around Jeb, she'd always taken the conservative route and kept her emotions to herself, on the back burner of her conscience. But she couldn't do that anymore.

"You mean you think that, like a dragonfly, I'm going to disappear at any moment?" He gave her a puzzled frown, laced with what could only be defined as hurt. She reached up and smoothed the furrow between his brows with her finger.

"Not at all. It's more like an I-want-to-fuck-you-senseless hum."

His concern evaporated when he flashed her a bright smile. "That's a buzz I can handle." He tugged on her hand and she walked with him up to the large screened porch, where they climbed solid wood steps to the door, which he threw open and held for her to precede him.

The porch, true to its southern roots, was a room unto itself. Two large ceiling fans circled, moving the air around enough that she felt she'd stepped into an air-conditioned space. Bright white wicker furniture that matched the house's pristine trim was padded with festive floral print cushions. The chatter of women beyond the second screen door caught her ear.

"Is that your family?"

"Sounds like Grandma and my mother."

Within a couple of heartbeats, she heard footsteps, followed by a loud "Jeb's here, Mother!" A woman of Jena's height stepped through the door, carrying a large tray with a pitcher of iced tea, sugar, lemons, and several tall glasses.

"Mom, let me take that."

"I'm good, just let me set it down." Camellia DeVillier McDaniels bent her knees and slid the cumbersome tray onto a small dining table that was pushed up against one wall of the screened porch. Only then did Jena notice the piles of food on trays and platters of various sizes, including a huge bowl of steamed crawdads. There was enough to feed a ship's crew.

"Come here, son." Camellia opened her arms, stretching her wing-style sleeves open, and enveloped Jeb into a warm hug. She kissed his cheek and Jena bit back a giggle. Jeb had turned into the eldest son of this strong woman in a blink.

"Hey, Mom." He straightened but didn't break eye contact with his mother. "Where is everyone?"

"Ron's in the kitchen with your grandmother, and your brothers are on their way. Your sister is still sleeping—she stayed over with Grandma and helped make all the food last night." Bright eyes moved from Jeb to Jena, and Jena fought to not wiggle her toes like she would have as a child.

She was wearing sandals, and she had a feeling Camellia wouldn't miss the nervous reaction.

"Hi, Jena. Nice to see you again! It's been at least—what, ten years?" Camellia focused her exuberance onto Jena, and stepped forward to give her a hug, too. Her spiky platinum hair and bright gray eyes were in direct contrast to Jeb's dark looks.

"Hi, Mrs. DeVillier. Good to see you again, too." Jena hugged her back, noticing that, while she was on the more slender side, Camellia's muscles and bones were pure steel.

Camellia kept her hands on Jena's shoulders as she looked her over. "It's Camellia, dear. You were a pretty girl when you were younger, but you've really become a knockout." Camellia aimed a glance at Jeb, who looked like he might be holding his breath. Jena smiled reflexively, needing to let him know she was okay with whatever Camellia said. "Don't let this one go."

Jeb's mom dropped her hands and waved to the tea. "Help yourselves."

"Can we do anything?" Jena wasn't ready to plop down on the furniture yet, and caffeine was the last thing she needed as she met Jeb's family.

"No, but if you want to come inside and meet my mother, she's in the kitchen." Camellia looked at Jeb with a raised brow. "You know how she gets before these things."

"I do." Jeb pressed his hand into the small of Jena's back, urging her inside behind his mother. "Grandma Cormier's nerves fire on all pistons when she entertains. It's why my mom doesn't let her do this as often as she used to. She does great through the event, but then later collapses with exhaustion."

"Wow." Jena had to cut her reply short as they entered the old fashioned yet completely modernized kitchen. A tiny woman with white hair like a bristle brush stood at the counter, putting together what looked like tea sandwiches. Jena noted the tuna salad and the egg salad, and how his grandmother was alternating layers between white and rye bread cut into perfect triangles.

"Jeb!" Gertrude "Gertie" Cormier put down her spoon and wiped her hands on a dish towel before she reached her thin, veined hands to his face and kissed him soundly on each cheek. "My boy. Did you bring your friend?" Her eyes, dark brown like Jeb's, alighted on Jena. "There you are!"

"Hi, Mrs. Cormier." Jena bent to get kissed on her cheeks, too, and marveled at the strength still in Gertie's hands. "We met years ago, when Jeb and I graduated high school." Jena wouldn't forget this woman, ever. Clearly the matriarch of the family, and loved by them.

Grandma Cormier grasped her hands tightly, willing Jena to look into her eyes. "You are special."

"Wha—"

"No, no reply is necessary. My grandsons all bring home their girls, my granddaughter brings home her man. But this one here,"—she jerked her head toward Jeb—"he never says anything about his dating life. Never brings home a photograph or tells me that he's met *the one*. Now he's brought you here, and that's all I need to know."

Jena's face grew hot, and she knew that she should be concerned about what Jeb was thinking. Or wasn't thinking—did he want to reassure her that Grandma was reading too much into this one Sunday dinner invite? Instead, she smiled, loving how cherished Grandma Cormier made her feel. With her grandparents all deceased, it was all the more special.

"It's nice to see you again." She had to endure another ten seconds of the old woman's gaze, which normally would have made her uncomfortable. But Gertie and Camellia presented a combined welcome she couldn't ignore.

"What can I do?"

"Stir the grits for me." Gertie didn't have to tell her twice. As she moved the weathered wooden spoon through the creamy, grainy mixture, she listened to the family.

"How's the new job?" Camellia's interest sounded genuine.

"Great. Jena is the director of The Refuge, and my job's to keep the numbers straight."

Jena had to speak up. "Don't let him fool you. He's doing a lot more than crunching numbers. Tell her about the grants you've found." She looked over her shoulder to see him standing in front of his mother with a mixture of pride and his trademark modesty. He cared what his mom thought, which made Jena want to kiss him.

"He's always been a looker, that one. But it's what's in his heart that's special." Grandma Cormier stood next to her, and Jena made a mental note that the octogenarian never missed a thing.

"You'll get no argument from me." Jena tapped the spoon on the side of the large pot and looked at the flame underneath. "These are done. Do you want me to keep them on warm or turn them off?"

"Shut the burner off and move them to that trivet. See it? I need the stovetop for the ham gravy."

Jena's stomach growled. "I love ham gravy and grits."

"There are fresh biscuits, too, if you'd rather." Grandma Cormier got busy making gravy and Jena maneuvered around the small kitchen until she stood next to Jeb.

"This is a beautiful home. I love how it captures its historical roots while having all the modern conveniences."

Camellia's brow rose. "We didn't have a choice. The structure survived Katrina, but we had to gut the inside."

"They were due for a change." Gertie spoke as she mixed hot water into a small jar half-filled with flour. "I would have needed to update everything before I sold it, anyway. That storm did me a favor."

"So you're saying I can sell it now, Mama?"

"Not until I'm long gone. Don't worry, you shouldn't have too much time to wait." Grandma Cormier laughed, and Jena couldn't help but join in.

Camellia shook her head. "Mama'll never sell this place."

"I was born on the dining room table, why should I want to live anywhere else?"

"You complain about cooking and grocery shopping; you could have it all done for you."

"No, thank you."

Jena watched the dialogue as much as she listened to it. Would the day come that she'd be having the same conversation with Gloria? She couldn't imagine it, but she supposed it wasn't too far-fetched, now that her mother had finally let go of her fear-based racist views. If only she'd done it sooner—but then Jena wouldn't have signed on to the CIA. As she stood in the emotionally warm and welcoming ambience of Jeb's family home, she finally got it. She'd become a covert agent because it was a way to strike back at her parents without having to deal with their blowback. Telling them her cover—that she'd joined the Navy—had been a hard enough conversation, albeit satisfying. They'd been aghast that she wanted to leave the life they'd provided. If only they'd known she'd gone farther afield than the high seas.

"Are you regretting your decision yet?" Jeb's low voice vibrated next to her ear, bringing her back. She wanted to lean into it, gain strength from him. But not here—not when she was just getting acquainted with his family.

"Not at all." She turned toward Gertie and Camellia. "Where is everyone else?"

"Clyde, my husband, went out to get a few last-minute items from the Piggly Wiggly."

"The one two blocks away? My family's been shopping there for generations." At least, before they moved to Baton Rouge. But Jena still got her groceries there once a week, and she was pretty sure Brandon still shopped there. Henry and Sonja, she wasn't so sure about.

"Yes, we know. That's the one." Camellia looked up at the sound of a door slamming, followed by heavy footfalls. A tall, silver-haired man around Hudson's age walked into the kitchen. "Speak of my devil."

The attractive man grinned, accentuating his goatee. "You swearing over me again? I found the sugar, lemons, and ice. They were out of straws."

"How can that be?" Camellia unpacked the groceries onto the counter. "Who runs out of straws?"

"It's summertime. Lots of parties and cold drinks. Hey, Jeb."

"Clyde."

The man's twinkling gaze landed on Jena. He stuck out his hand. "Hi, I'm Clyde."

She allowed her hand to be swallowed by his bear paw. She guessed that the man worked with his hands—the calluses and rough patches were like badges. "Jena. Nice to meet you."

"Same." He let go, turned to Camellia, and placed a smacking kiss on her lips before moving behind Grandma Cormier and resting his hands on her shoulders. "How are you doing, Gertrude?"

"I'm good. Get my daughter out of here so I can think, will you?"

Clyde didn't laugh, even though the smile splitting his face indicated he wanted to. "Sure thing."

"Don't waste your breath. I'll take the kids out on the porch. Call me if you need me." Camellia motioned at Jeb and Jena with her hand and Jena stifled a giggle at being called a kid. Jeb nodded for Jena to go ahead of him, which she did, trying to catch more than a glimpse at the heirloom family photos that lined the hallway. So many people, so many years gone by.

On the veranda, Camellia insisted they make up glasses of tea or lemonade and sit on the facing porch swings.

"Woo, it's hot out here." Camellia placed her perspiring glass on her cheek as she closed her eyes. "We'll be inside at the dining table for the main meal."

"Thank you for having me." Jena spoke up, needing to express her gratitude. She'd always been curious about Jeb's family, more so over the past few months—as if she'd been trying to figure him out, once and for all.

Camellia's eyes popped open and she speared Jena with a glance. "You've known Jeb most of his life."

"Since we were both—what, Jeb, eight and ten?"

"Yes." His voice reassured her. She could only see his profile as he sat close to her on the cushioned swing, his leg crossed atop the bottom one that kept the chair still.

"Whatever you've heard about me... I've changed a lot since then." Camellia settled in for what Jena could only think of as a true confession. "I'm not the woman I was when Jeb became friends with Brandon and fell in love with your family."

"Mom." Jeb's tone held warning. Not of violence, but restraint. Jena wished he'd chill. She wanted to know what Camellia had to say. Couldn't wait to know, in fact.

"Go on. Please."

Camellia shrugged. "Nothing to go on about, really. When Jeb came to your family, he needed you. Needed something in his life I wasn't giving him at home." She turned her gaze to Jeb and studied her son before going on. "I'm not sure if you told her everything."

"I told Jena nothing, Mother."

Camellia looked at Jena again, weighing her countenance as if she were sorting gemstones for their worth. "I'm an alcoholic. Been sober for at least ten years now, but it was the hardest on Jeb here. I didn't get sober until he was in college, and my drinking was the hardest on him."

"Mom..."

"Stop it, Jeb, and let your mother speak." When she looked at Jena again, there were tears in Camellia's bright eyes. "My other kids—you'll meet them soon enough—they got the benefits of my sobriety and emotional presence. Jeb had none of that, did you?"

"It doesn't matter now, Mom."

And it didn't. Not to Jena, who'd never seen this side of Jeb's upbringing before.

"It all matters, my dear son." She turned weary eyes on Jena. "As much as I try, forgiving myself for the drinking remains my biggest challenge. Because of the pain it caused Jeb. The other kids got to get the help they needed after growing up in an alcoholic family, but Jeb was in college by then."

"And I turned out okay anyway, didn't I?" Jeb quipped, as if they were discussing the overwhelming chorus of the cicadas, the ebb and flow of the insects' chirping, how they'd been having a particularly tough season.

"You need to know what you're getting, Jena. Jeb has a ton of emotional baggage with our family. You'll be asked to carry it, too, if you stick with him."

"But we're, um, we're not..."

"We're good friends. Period." Jeb reached for her hand and squeezed. While the gesture was always welcome and reassuring from him, she wasn't so keen on the message. She'd thought they were past the pretend-we're not-fucking stage. Or had she misread his signals when he said he wanted her to know his family?

Her heart beat with a familiar thud that matched the chill of dread in her belly. She'd done it again—shoved down feelings related to Jeb. Except this time, she had no other person to place them on.

Before Camellia's emotional intervention on Jeb continued, three men who didn't resemble Jeb in the least came around the porch.

A petite woman holding hands with a very tall, very attractive man followed.

"Jeb! Where the hell have you been?" The first brother didn't waste time yanking Jeb's chain. Jena found she enjoyed watching the interplay. Seeing how Jeb dealt with his family gave her an insight she hadn't had before. Around her family, even though they all thought of Jeb as one of them, he still remained a bit of an outsider. He didn't have the Boudreaux name or earliest history to claim as his.

"Busy at my new job." The seat swung as Jeb stood and greeted the first brother with a hug. "How are you doing, Mitch?"

"Good, good. I'm still in business, if that's what you're asking." A landscaper, Mitch cherished his time outdoors no matter the heat or wet.

"Come over, bro." The second man, a head shorter than both Jeb and Mitch, but much wider with solidly sculpted muscle, greeted Jeb. "When you going to give up that fancy desk job and come work with me? We brought in a record load of shrimp this week."

Jeb laughed. "Not the seagoing type, Fred. You know that. Hey, sis." He leaned down to kiss the raven-haired woman on the cheek, and Jena saw that she had the same high cheekbones as Jeb.

"I second Mitch's question. Where exactly have you been?"

"I swear to God, I've been at work. I already told all of you what happened with my Boats by Gus job."

"Man, that sucked."

"Any chance of a rebuild? Getting your job back?"

"How is Brandon doing?"

"Whoa." Jeb held his hands up. "First, Boats by Gus is over, done. At least for now." He grinned. "Brandon is doing fine. He has a girlfriend, Poppy."

All eyes were back on Jena. Crap. She didn't want to have to explain whatever was between her and Jeb.

"Hi!" She gave a finger wave. "I'm Jena, Brandon's younger sister. I've met most of you, at some point, maybe our high school graduation?"

"Jena, this is Mitch, Fred, Lauren, and Chris."

"Hey. I can't say I remember much of that event, but it's nice to meet you today." Lauren spoke first, a curious smile indicating that she wondered what Jena's presence meant. "This is my boyfriend, Sam."

"Hi, Sam."

The tall man nodded, and Jena wondered if maybe he was overwhelmed by the DeVillier clan, too. Jeb's brothers greeted her before they all were instructed by Jeb's mom to help themselves to the buffet.

Jena piled her plate with biscuits and gravy, grits, ham, and dark cooked greens. At the dining table, resplendent in linen, fine porcelain china and crystal, she found herself seated in between Jeb and his mother.

"I promise I won't interrogate you about your family, or your job, Jena. Here's to new beginnings." Camellia lifted a glass of orange juice and Jena clinked her mimosa glass to it. The rest of the family followed before the hum of conversation again filled the traditional dining room. Camellia used the cover of the other voices to talk quietly to Jena.

"I'm so glad Jeb has you to lean on, Jena. The other kids were still home when I got sober, and I was able to at least educate them about the disease of alcoholism and addiction, so that if they ever need help, they'll get it. Jeb shouldered so much during my drinking years. He's a special person."

"He is." For the rest of the afternoon, Camellia, and then each of his siblings, regaled her with how Jeb had behaved as a child, teen, and young man, and Jena began to see pieces of the Jeb puzzle come together. She had seen one side of him, the more relaxed part, she was certain. He'd been able to just be a kid with her family. But he'd been the acting adult in his house, since the age of ten when his dad left and his mother kept drinking, neglecting his siblings.

She turned to him after they'd cleared their large plates and sat down with dessert. "You've always been the caretaker, haven't you? It's a wonder you didn't become the social worker."

"Don't think I haven't thought that myself. I thought of becoming a counselor, specializing in addiction, too." His answer, low and gravelly, informed her that he hadn't missed an iota of the conversation. He'd been quiet because he was listening, not because he was embarrassed by the impromptu Jeb roast.

She toyed with the tines of the gold fork, his grandmother's finest flatware, pushing her last bite of pecan pie around on her plate. "So why didn't you? Go into more of a service field?"

He bit off a huge chunk of brownie and thoughtfully chewed before he answered. "I'm a numbers guy, was always good at math, especially statistics and probability. Going after a CPA seemed practical and secure. I liked the idea of knowing I'd have a marketable skill after I graduated." She thought back to their college time together. "You got your masters and CPA within—what, a year after we graduated?" She vaguely recalled he'd taken an accelerated program after she'd left for her "Navy" training.

"Yeah. I needed the paycheck to help Mom out until she could get back on her feet. It took two stints in rehab for her sobriety to stick."

As conversations zinged around them, Jena was struck by the unique sense of love and acceptance in the room. She knew Jeb had a larger family than hers, but meeting them put it in perspective. Jeb's family was everything the Boudreauxes weren't—loud, outspoken, at times raw. They didn't brush up the crumbs from shattered bonds and disappointments and hide them away like her family. No, this family put everything out there for everyone to not only see, but inspect, dissect, and scrutinize until there wasn't anything left to mull over.

* * * *

"What's the real deal, brother?" Lauren cornered Jeb in the front sitting room, out of earshot of the kitchen and dining room.

"What do you mean?" Innocence was the best tactic with his younger sister, always. Like a badger, Lauren didn't let go of her prey until she'd shaken every last drop of information from them. But unlike the aggressive animal, her motives were protective. As the only sister in the family, she took over the mothering a little too much for Jeb's liking.

"Knock that shit off with me, Jeb DeVillier. You're speaking to your sister. You've never brought a girl home before. Why now?"

"Why not? And in case you didn't notice, Jena's an adult, as are we." He prayed she'd take the hint to mind her own business.

"I know you grew up with her, practically. You were never home when we were little."

"Not true." She'd obviously forgotten the times he'd tucked her in, signed her homework papers with Camellia's forged signature. All in a day's work for the child of an alcoholic.

She shrugged. "Fine. The rest of us had the next door neighbors to hang out with. You had Brandon, and his sister. I didn't know you and Jena were so close."

"We're friends."

"Do you believe that? Because I'll go along with you if it makes you feel better, Jeb. But friends don't give off the kind of sparkly tension you two do. And friends don't check out one another's asses."

"She did not."

"I'm talking about you." She gave him a sisterly punch to the arm. "Drop the stupid charade. Tell me what's really going on."

He rolled his eyes. "Not everything is so trauma-drama, Lauren. Why don't you tell me how you and Sam are doing?"

She smiled. "We're great. We might be moving in together, I don't know."

"Make sure your credit score's good and locked down."

"Fuck you, Jeb." Her face softened in complete disparity to her words. "I know you mean well, though. He's not like Jim, he's way more responsible."

"Uh-huh." Lauren's string of boyfriends could wrap around the block two times over.

"Now who's playing the parent?"

"I'm not your dad, Lauren."

She frowned. "I don't want you to be. You're great as my big brother. Honest. And I'm not going to ask for money. I mean it. You've always been here for me. But I'm good now." And she was—Lauren was an ER trauma nurse at the local hospital and had recently received a promotion. "It's time for you to take care of yourself, Jeb. I'm only asking about Jena because I think it'd be great for you to find happiness for once. You spent a lot of your life taking care of us."

"You just said I was never there."

"Because you open up more when you get defensive. It's one of your weird superpowers." She grinned and he laughed.

"There's nothing to open up about."

"But if there was? Would you tell me?"

"You'd be the first to know, Lauren."

They talked for a little while longer about work, and Lauren's enthusiasm for his work at The Refuge made the spot under his rib cage warm.

"You know, it makes sense that you like working there. You've always been the family caretaker."

"That's just what I want to hear, after working so hard to not be like that anymore."

"I don't mean in a codependent way. I mean that you have a very caring, compassionate side. Not all guys are in touch with that. The fact that you are, and you have your financial background, makes you a perfect fit to help people with their budgets. And to make sure the social service center gets the funding it needs."

"Thank you." He never sat well with praise, but from Lauren it meant a lot.

She slapped his knee. "Come on, did you see the pile of dishes in the sink? Whoever cleans it up gets first dibs on taking leftovers home."

He stood with her and followed her into the kitchen to help wash dishes. This had always been a comfortable place for him, but with Jena here, it was even more so.

Jena added to everything he did. He poured soap into the dishpan and sighed. Leaving for Atlanta would have been a lot easier before working with her.

Chapter 14

The day passed quickly, with few of the uncomfortable relationship questions she'd expected. Jeb's family was the loving, kind sort that she imagined he'd lacked as a young child.

On the drive home she relaxed into the leather passenger seat of his car, watching the houses blur past the window. "It's nice to not drive. I forget how much I love the colors here."

Jeb stopped at a red light. "But you could get tired of the simple life again, Jena."

She turned to him, met his searching gaze. "I'm where I want to be. If I were to get bored, I'd still stay here, in NOLA. This is home for me. Look at your grandmother—she's lived here her entire life. I want to be her in fifty years."

Jeb shifted the car back into gear and drove. "A nice sentiment, but with the weather changes I don't know how many more storms before Grandma's house is gone. We salvaged her china and heirlooms by moving them upstairs the past several floods. Fortunately, she hasn't had water in the house again like during Katrina. But it's a matter of time, I'm afraid."

"I get worked up when I think about NOLA underwater." She imagined the digitally redrawn city maps that projected into the next century. "The Refuge might have ten or twenty years, tops, if the climate and precipitation predictions hold true."

"We don't have control over that, though, do we? I say keep working at The Refuge, shore up its resources, and if the day comes that you have to move it, you will."

"I suppose you're right." As if caused by their words, big raindrops splattered onto his windshield. He turned a corner where he should have gone straight to drop her at her place.

"Did you miss that turn on purpose?"

"Uh-huh." A small smile came to his full lips. "I have something I want to do with you, but I wasn't counting on the rain."

"Do you have an umbrella in here?" She craned her neck to check out his backseat.

"Yeah, under your seat. We'll be good."

* * * *

Jeb felt the relief of storm clouds clearing when they walked out of Grandma Cormier's place. Not that he'd expected his siblings to be jerks, but he wasn't sure how they'd react to Jena, or how she'd react to them.

His mother couldn't stop espousing AA jargon if she tried. He knew it was a good thing—a very good thing, as it had kept her sober all these years and allowed his youngest siblings to have a decent high school experience. They never had to worry if they brought a friend home that Mom would be splayed out on the stained sofa, passed out in a vodka haze. Or wake up with the sun because of Camellia's Sunday hangover rage, ruining a much-needed rest.

Driving through the older part of New Orleans with Jena, during a pouring rainstorm, was comforting and right.

He parked the car on a street familiar to them both, then reached under her seat to retrieve his umbrella. Her fingers touched his scalp, then his cheek, and when he straightened, he leaned in to give her what she sought, what he ached for—he kissed her.

Jena's lips were the softest thing on Earth, besides the undersides of her breasts. He alternatively licked and kissed her mouth, his tongue darting in and out, playing with hers. When she leaned into him and took over the kiss, her tongue stroking the inside of his cheek, pressing against his tongue with hers, he lost all sense of location. All he wanted was her in his arms. The rain shower turned into a deluge, the sound of the water hitting his car roof drowning out their verbalizations.

He pulled back, his cock throbbing for her, unable to take her the way he needed to in the cramped quarters. "Jena."

"Move your seat all the way back, quick." Her pupils dilated, her breath warm and sexy on his mouth.

He reached down and hit the button to ease the seat as far back as it could go, which wasn't much. "There isn't enough room, not with the steering wheel." *Fuck.* He wanted her so badly.

"Sure there is. Come on over to my side." She'd moved her seat back, too, and turned around and pressed her back against the windshield with her bottom on the dash, leaving a small space for him to maneuver over the center console and slide into her seat.

He groaned as his head hit the sunroof and his knee hit the gearshift.

"There you go." As soon as his ass hit the passenger seat, Jena straddled him, her dress hiked up around her waist. He reached for her thighs and stroked down to her knees.

"Jesus, you're going to kill your knees, Jena."

"Shut up, Jeb." She reached into her purse, behind her on the dash. "Here. Let's get this on, shall we?" She ripped open the foil packet, and his erection strained against his pants.

"Wait." He had to get his pants unzipped. He pulled out his cock, thick and heavy with desire for her, and took the condom from her hands. Close quarters called for desperate measures, and he was desperately on fire for her. The heat of her pussy wafted over his hands as he donned the condom, and he couldn't help but stroke her wetness, plunge his fingers into her.

"Jeb!" She ground out his name as she clenched and unclenched around his fingers, her sex wet and wanting. For him. Her fingers dug into his shoulders and she writhed above him.

"Now, babe." He removed his fingers and immediately thrust up and into her, gripping her hip bones through her skirt and holding on to guide her over his cock as he bucked, entering her to the hilt each time.

Her cries were muffled by the heavy rain, and he felt nothing but her pussy clamping around him, his sex throbbing as he pounded, she pounded, they slammed together in the small space while the world rained down around them.

"Oh. My. God." She cried out his name as her pussy held on to his cock, making him crazy with lust, crazy for her. Within one or two pulses of her sex, he split apart, coming with a thunderous shout, heedless of her eardrums, only feeling his release, his connection to her.

It took them several minutes to come down from the high, from what they'd created together. Still joined, her forehead was on his shoulder and he turned into her nape, breathing in the scent of her hair.

"Jeb." His name, whispered like a prayer, made something in his chest painfully constrict before it released in total relaxation. Total trust.

He stroked her back, kissed the side of her throat as their breath intermingled, the inside of the car a cocoon of intimacy against the storm outside. They could be in the biggest bed in the largest mansion in NOLA and it would still be like this. Jena. Him. Together.

"That was..." She drifted, her nipples still hard and pressed against his chest.

"No words needed, babe." He gently lifted her hips, slid out from her. "I don't know if getting out of this will be as quick as getting into it."

She laughed, low and throaty. The joy of a satisfied woman. It was trivial compared to the depths of his feelings for her, but he enjoyed a burst of pride in knowing he'd made her come, that he'd helped bring her to this satisfied state.

"We're okay. I can get out of the car first, then you come. I mean, get out." Blue eyes on his, full, swollen lips against her flushed face.

"Can you reach the umbrella?"

"Yes." She leaned over him, toward the back of the car, and retrieved the bright green umbrella. Her breasts pressed against his face and he kissed them, sucked a nipple into his mouth through her thin blouse and flimsy bra.

"Jeb, stop." But she didn't move away. Reluctantly, he stopped with the nipple-teasing and eased her back, her spine a C-shape along the windshield.

"You're lovely, Jena." He unlocked the passenger door. "Are you ready?"

She nodded, then flipped the handle and let the door swing wide. Sheets of rain poured down, but the old golf umbrella gave them a bit of respite as they unfolded out of the car.

"You okay with wet feet?" He saw that there was no avoiding the puddles.

"Totally." She smiled, her delight at a walk in the rain shining in her eyes. "I'm so glad you thought of this."

He remained silent as they picked their way across the street and aimed between two larger homes. "This" was the Boudreauxes' old house and property, and he knew she loved it here. The peace in the sheltered garden between the two older houses had been a playtime escape when they were kids, a place to sneak a beer as teens, and then, when they discovered the delights their bodies gave one another, they'd used it as their personal make-out place.

Jeb knew she'd love coming here, but he wasn't so sure how Jena felt about what he wanted to look at together. He wasn't sure if she remembered it, or if the memory was another piece of her former self tossed aside when she decided to take part in the highest levels of secret government operations.

Even if she didn't mind the reminder of their shared history, would she be as thrilled as he was to see it again?

* * * *

The first thing Jena thought of when Jeb pulled in front of her old home was the tree. But he didn't mention it, and their need had outweighed her curiosity. She wanted to ask him, point blank, if they'd come here to see the tree. If yes, why? What was the point of bringing her back here?

Was the tree even still here?

They walked under the arbor, past the benches that had held them at eight and ten years, ten and twelve years, fifteen and seventeen. Past the grove of trees where they'd dared one another to take their tops off the summer she'd turned sixteen. After that, they'd not been able to touch one another without igniting. And they'd kept it from her brothers, from both of their families.

Until today. Now Jeb's family knew that he had her in his life. But what was she to him? He'd called her a good friend, held her hand in front of them. And he'd just made the most incredible love to her.

Love, deeply complicating their sexual chemistry.

"It's way overgrown, isn't it?" His low whisper sent shivers across her damp skin, arousing her as if they hadn't fucked like rabid raccoons in his car only minutes earlier.

"It got this way sometimes, when my parents let it go." Or when the gardeners quit, tired of Hudson and Gloria's patronizing manner. "It's hard to believe they're the same people who lived here, isn't it?"

He stared at her, his expression grave. "They aren't the same. They've really changed, Jena."

"Mmm." She relished the way her hand fit into his, snug and perfectly connected at their palms. No other man had ever made her so happy, given her the sense that she mattered.

"I hope they don't have dogs." He pushed through the small, hinged gate at the end of the arbor and into a garden that sprawled into long stretches of green, the short grass rough underfoot. Puddles of rainwater surrounded them and she gave the ground a closer look.

"I hope the snakes aren't out with this rain."

"Come on." As if he'd scanned the path on the side of the yard, he led her to the red clay garden path that unwound into several hundred yards amongst the brown, dried out shrubs. "I'm counting on the rain to keep anyone from seeing us."

They stayed close to where the trees grew, to the place they'd been told as kids to avoid. *People have gone into those woods and never come out.* Hudson had been clear about why they needed to avoid the very path they walked on now. She laughed. "Remember when my dad put the fear of God into us to stay out of here? It wasn't about snakes or stalkers, was it?" she shouted over the rain.

She felt Jeb's chuckle through her hand, the deluge drowning out the sound of his laughter. "It was more about *my* snake, if you get my drift."

"Do you think he knew what we were doing back then?"

"We were two healthy teens. Your parents have a lot of skeletons in their armoires, but they were never stupid."

They kept walking, drawing closer to where they'd once sworn to be friends forever.

A flutter deep in her heart let her know that what she'd hoped, what she'd been afraid to wish for, was true. Jeb remembered the tree. And that meant he remembered how sacred it had once been to them. As wonderful as the day had been—the last several days, in fact—Jeb was due to leave for Atlanta within a week. She had to look at this as a closure, as a way to let him go—but in truth she had no idea how she ever could.

Another five minutes of walking and they were upon it. The centuries-old oak reached its moss-blanketed arms to the sky, out on either side as a consummate hostess, and down along the ground, offering its oldest, lowest slung branches as steps to reach higher, away from the ground, away from family interference.

He climbed up on the largest bough first, then reached back to help her up. Jena could have easily climbed on her own, but she wanted to feel his touch, the urgency with which he wanted her to see it again. As if no time had passed, as if their lifetimes had passed.

"Here." He stepped to the side, onto a wide, flat limb that easily bore his weight. "I don't know if it's dry enough to sit."

She knelt on the limb she was balanced upon, not an ounce of fear in her at the height of ten or twelve feet. This was her childhood and adolescence, all here in this tree. Her fingers and palm pressed against the mossy upholstery of the branch and she looked up at him. "It's perfectly fine." She eased herself into a crouch before she shimmied onto her bottom and sat against the humongous trunk. Jeb sat across from her, on an equally sturdy branch. Their knees touched; the tree bore their weight as if they were no more than tiny, fragile hummingbirds. Her heart felt as delicate as one, its beats as swift as the bird's wings. Her glance caught on Jeb's gaze, and for a moment or twenty—it didn't matter—they were once again thirteen and Jeb had climbed up here with her to show her what he and his Swiss Army knife had created.

She gasped when she saw it. It was as dominating a feature as when Jeb had first carved it. The heart was at least fourteen inches across—she remembered how he'd pulled out a wooden ruler and demonstrated how it could fit inside the shape. He'd been so exacting about numbers, even back then. The two rounded tops were smoothed with the years, moss covering all but the inside, where the wood had darkened. There, in faint lines made with the sharp point of his pocketknife, were their initials: JDV ∞ JB. Even then, Jeb had been all about the math.

"It's made it through a lot of years and weather, that's for certain." His voice sounded as if he were in a trance, caught in the Spanish moss web of the past. Jena reached out and felt it with her fingertips, letting the smooth edges tell her that through so much, the tree had lived.

"It survived Katrina." A lot of trees had, of course, not just this old oak, but just as many guardians of the bayou had fallen, their stories crushed under the weight of the hurricane.

"And it's still here for us now." Jeb's voice cracked and she shot him a glance. He didn't look like he was crying, but she knew he felt the power of it, too.

The strength of the time that filled the air around them stood still while racing ahead. Forever. This was what forever felt like.

She jerked her hand back from the trunk and wavered on the bough. Jeb grasped her knees with his hands. She looked down and saw the contrast between the strength of his hands and her knees. She covered his hands with hers and raised her face to his.

"Shh." His finger was on her lips, keeping her words inside. Did he think she was going to ruin the moment by saying something he couldn't reciprocate?

"It's the same, hear it?" Jeb's voice reflected awe as he returned his hand to her knee. She'd never felt so safe, so protected. They each sat on their own limb, extensions of this ancient tree that joined at its trunk, making a secure seat big enough for several people. They weren't more than twelve feet off the ground, but it could have been a hundred feet, surrounded by more branches and the hush that only this tree bequeathed on the garden. Then she heard it: the far-spaced but definite creaks as the huge oak swayed infinitesimally in the bayou breeze.

Their lovemaking in the car had been furtive and lust-driven, a quest to reach their climaxes as quickly and forcefully as possible. This was the antidote, in terms of touch and subtlety, and yet Jena felt like Jeb was making love to her all over again.

* * * *

Jena sat and listened to the old tree's groans, which sounded more like clicks and snaps.

"Never was a more perfect tree created." Jeb lifted one hand from her knee to reverently press against the trunk.

"She's seen so much."

"She?" He arched his heavy brow in mock protest.

"I know it's crazy, but I do think of trees as females. Don't ask me why."

"They are nurturing, and they provide shelter, whether out here in the middle of nature's worst events, or after they've been cut down and turned into lumber and then your favorite table."

She ran her fingers over the bark and let a ladybug crawl onto her hand, its bright red a sharp contrast to her pale skin.

"Make a wish." Jeb's prompt spun her mind twenty years back, to long hours spent in this tree, their bare feet dangling just like they were now.

She closed her eyes briefly, feeling secure enough to do it since she had the huge, firm trunk under her palm. When she finished her wish, she opened her eyes and blew on the bug, which flew off in a tiny blur of wings. She met Jeb's gaze.

"I can't tell you, so don't ask."

"Okay. But I can tell you what I would have wished."

"What?" Trembles started in her belly and reverberated to the tips of her toes as she saw every nuance of his expression.

"I'd have wished that we could redo the last two years, before you went to Paraguay." That was not what she'd expected. Sadness and hurt sprang fast, and she blinked rapidly, hoping to stop any tears.

"Oh." So he wished they'd never hooked back up, made their sexy friend agreement. "Well, of course. That makes sense. If we hadn't have gotten together, as friends, you wouldn't have gotten caught up in putting up the ransom." He'd still work for Brandon, and Boats by Gus would be raking in the bucks. And they wouldn't have this awkwardness between them. The need for one another, punctuated by knowing he was going to leave. He'd never indicated anything else.

"Do you really think that's what I meant? Because if you do, you don't know me very well." He leaned forward, his arm against the trunk. His other hand caressed her cheek. "We'd have met at your parents' Christmas party, just like we did. I'd have followed you back to your carriage house, just like I did. We'd make love, and then we'd agree to start a real relationship."

"You mean…dating?"

He chuckled, and the sexy depth of it lit the spot between her legs on fire. "Yeah, for starters. Done it right for once, instead of keeping it quiet. Would you have agreed?"

"Absolutely not." She'd still been focused on her undercover work, had looked at social work as her steady standby. In truth, it had been her dream for all these years—to get out of the secret agent business and throw all of her energy into community service. "I couldn't have, not while I was still active with my former job."

His expression sobered. "I know that. You've never been one for half measures."

"I never meant to hurt you. Back in college, we were young. I didn't know if we were together because we'd wanted it for so long, if it was something for the long haul. When the recruiter spoke to me, she made it sound as if I'd be doing so much for my country. I thought you'd always be here. Immaturity at its finest, right?"

"I know it hurt you when you came home that one summer, from what we all thought was a Navy training exercise."

She tried to summon a smile to show it was okay, but failed. "Yeah, that was rough, when you brought your girlfriend to meet my folks. Whatever happened to her, anyway?"

"We only dated for a few months. She was for show, Jena. I had to prove I had a life that had nothing to do with you."

"It's not like you've been celibate when we haven't been in touch."

"I'm a red-blooded guy. I love women, yes. But none ever knew me like you do."

She nodded. "You know me better than anyone." She was making progress in her friendship with Robyn, and there were a few high school friends who always invited her to girls' nights. She needed to take them up on their offers. But she knew no one else, no matter how much time she ever spent with them, would know her to the depths of her soul. Like Jeb.

"Not well enough."

"We're not back to that, are we? I couldn't have told you about my job if I'd wanted to." A bit of a lie, as there always exceptions—if she'd asked for permission. But that was only ever granted to significant others, and Jeb never had been hers, officially.

"Why didn't you? Want to tell me?"

"I was afraid you'd get sucked into what I did—the emotional ups and downs. I've had more than a few dicey jobs, Jeb. This last one, the ransom demand, that was new. Usually they just threaten my life, no payoff involved."

"What was different this time, that you called me?" Jeb's eyes reflected his need to know, the worry he still must have over the work she'd done and not told him about.

"I've known for a while that it was time to get out of that world. I'd planned for Paraguay to be my last operation, and my required contract time ended last month. Anyhow, when it went south, it had a different feel to it. I wasn't able to compartmentalize my emotions. I was scared." She shook her head, clearing away the dark web of memories. "It's over now. I'm a civilian."

"What is your plan B? Did you have one before you started The Refuge?"

"The Refuge *is* plan B. Or rather, was. It's plan A from here out. I always thought I'd come back here and use my social work degree. Maybe get a doctorate, although that's a long way off." She'd thought of a family, too. But every time she did, all she saw was Jeb. And since he'd always been clear about not wanting more than sex, it was a nonstarter. She wanted to believe that after he left for Atlanta she'd start over, but she couldn't summon any hope.

"What about you, Jeb? What do you want out of life?"

"The bayou's in my blood, and I never had an urge to be anywhere else. I've decided to try something new in Atlanta, which is promising. I always thought I'd travel the world, too. But…" His silence thickened the air between them.

"But what?"

"After seeing what I saw in South America, I'm not in any hurry to get out in the world and travel."

His frankness made her smile despite the gravity of the topic. "You can't judge South America, Paraguay, or even Asunción by what you witnessed. It gets just as ugly here with drug cartels, gangs. Look at The Refuge—we haven't officially opened yet and we've already used Narcan. Bad things happen everywhere."

"The opioid epidemic's not sparing any community." He rubbed his fingers along the trunk's damp bark. "You were brilliant, Jena. Your clarity saved that woman's life."

She brushed aside his compliment. "No, the pharmaceutical genius who came up with an inexpensive antidote to heroin overdoses is brilliant. I did what I'm trained to do. You would have done it if I hadn't been there." She'd provided the training herself to the staff already in place.

Thunder rumbled in the distance, far off, yet close enough that faint vibrations reached them through the tree.

"Time to go." Jeb hauled himself to his feet and she followed, sad that their time in the sacred space had to end. She ran her fingers over the heart, the initials.

"I've missed this so much." She'd missed *them*.

A flash of lightning, followed by a bark of thunder. The storm was moving in.

"Come on, Jena." Just as when they were kids, he took charge of keeping them safe. It was so clear now—Jeb, the caretaker. Classic child of an alcoholic. And now he was an adult. She knew from her work that the effects of his mother's drinking would never leave him, even if Camellia was sober now. He'd spend his life shaking off the disproportionate sense of responsibility toward others, the guilt when he couldn't fix someone else's problems for them.

They made their way down from the tree carefully, having learned decades ago that even though descending seemed easier than climbing, it was more dangerous. A foot could slip on the emerald moss, a T-shirt could catch on a rough patch of bark. Once they were on the wide bough near the ground, Jeb turned, and she ran into him, so focused on following him she didn't have time to stop.

Her breasts flattened against his chest and his hands went to her lower back, steadying her. Without hesitation, his mouth crashed down on hers and she wrapped her hands around his neck, careful not to tug too fiercely, as they'd both end up on the soggy ground, but needing this connection in this place where they'd come together for the very first time.

When he lifted his head, they were both breathless. His eyes glittered with need, and with a question she knew had to be an illusion. Jeb didn't want more, did he? The idea released a different kind of hope, one she'd never dared contemplate.

"Thank you for coming here with me, Jena." He kissed her forehead and stepped off the bough, holding her hand to help her down. A shock of lightning simultaneous with a thunderclap was their only warning before the skies opened again and the winds made the umbrella worthless. They were drenched within seconds.

They ran for the car, across the long lawn and through the garden, across the rain-slicked path and to the curb. Once they were in the car their heat steamed the windows, and Jena turned to Jeb.

"You're welcome, Jeb. Thank *you* for bringing us back here." If only she knew whether he'd meant to bring them back to the emotional place they'd begun their relationship. Free of the complications life had brought their way. When the thought of being anything but together was unfathomable.

Or had he simply wanted a way to keep their friendship intact, mindful that their resurrected sexual connection was about to end?

Chapter 15

"That has to be the most romantic thing I've ever heard." Robyn dipped a huge tortilla chip into bright green guacamole. Mariachi music faded in and out as the accordion player meandered the large restaurant, aglow from hundreds of intricately cut terra-cotta votive candleholders on tables, counters, and windowsills.

"It was more than that." Jena sipped her classic margarita, loving the bite of the lime against the salt. "I think he was trying for it to mean more, but then he didn't say anything to indicate it was anything other than a trip down memory lane. And the fact remains, he's taken a job in Atlanta. It starts week after next." Disappointment flooded her all over again. She hated this part of herself—instead of enjoying the beautiful day she'd had with Jeb and accepting it as it was, she wanted it to mean something new.

"Maybe you're the one who needs to say something." Robyn's eyes sparkled as she cautiously voiced what Jena had been thinking.

"How do you know me this well after such a short time?" She tried to make light of the all-too-accurate observation.

"It doesn't take a lifelong girlfriend to see what we all have in common." Robyn stirred her frozen margarita with her straw.

"Which is?"

"We want it all." Robyn took a big sip through the bright pink straw. "The degrees, the paycheck, the house or condo, the hot guy. Don't get me wrong—we deserve all of the above, and more. But sometimes it's okay to say what we want. Are you afraid that Jeb's going to turn tail and make a run for it if you even hint that you want something more permanent?"

Jena sighed. "We had a semi permanent situation with the sex-only gig. I ruined it when I…" *Shit*. She couldn't tell Robyn about Paraguay, not at all. She started again. "I had a rough time on my last Navy deployment, and I reached out to him in a weak moment."

"Let me guess, you told him you loved him."

"Yes, but—"

"Hold up, girl. There is no 'but' if you said those three words to him." Another chip, another sip. Robyn wiped her mouth with the brightly printed cocktail napkin. "You scared him. But he came back, so it didn't do permanent damage, right?"

Jena looked at Robyn and saw no condemnation, no hint of recrimination. "I suppose not. But it's still temporary."

"We all might be leaving before we want to." Robyn motioned to the windows, where rain poured onto the pavement. "The city can only handle so much of this."

"Yeah." Jena didn't want to talk about global warming, though. Not tonight. She needed to sift through her emotions, something she'd not had to do since she entered agent training. Compartmentalization of any feeling that detracted from the mission was her go-to method. Or rather, it had been. "Too much has passed between me and Jeb. Sometimes it's best to keep a childhood friendship as just that—a friendly bond."

"See this?" Robyn's hand moved as if waving a banner. "It's the bullshit flag."

Jena laughed.

"Here you go, ladies." Their waiter pushed a cart up to their table, a cast-iron fajita pan atop a blue flame. He tossed in the shrimp and assorted veggies with practiced ease and placed the meal in front of Jena, then did the same with Robyn's steak fajita. "Here are your tortillas. Can I get you anything else?"

"No, thanks." She and Robyn both thanked him and dug into their entrées. Jena silently acknowledged that this new Friday night routine with Robyn was a lot more fun than going back to her place to eat takeout or a microwave meal. Definitely better than shoving down a quick meal alone in a tiny hotel room, in a godforsaken place that needed her agent skills.

Anxiety toyed with her newfound bliss. Was it possible to really, truly have it all? A satisfying job and a full, happy life?

For her, the answer was no. Because a full life for Jena had always included Jeb, and he'd made it clear time and again he wasn't in it for the long haul. Plus, looking over their shared history, they always ended up apart. Whether it was her previous occupation or Jeb's mistrust of her or simply life getting in between them, they had never continuously made a go of it.

And the ache in her heart that she'd always been so adept at shoving into the back compartment of her mind wasn't staying put. There was no more locking down her most painful emotions.

Could she live a lifetime with this ache? She'd have to.

* * * *

"It sounds to me like you're getting close to finishing your work at The Refuge, bro." Brandon eyed Jeb as he popped a boiled peanut into his mouth, his posture relaxed as they shared a beer at the old tavern's long, scarred, oak bar. Another Katrina survivor, they'd been coming to this bar since just after college, when their lives and worlds seemed limitless.

When he'd been so busy stoking his resentment against Jena for ditching him and entering the Navy—or so he'd thought—that he'd overlooked a very critical point: She was the only woman for him.

"Jeb?" Brandon nudged him with the bowl of nuts, breaking the exploration of his past.

"Yeah, I heard you. It's complicated. I know it's only been a short time, but I really like what I'm doing for The Refuge. It's making a difference already." But it would never be a full-time position, not for him, even if he weren't moving to Atlanta.

"Problem is that the workload for their grant work and budget doesn't justify more than ten hours a week for me." Especially now that he'd put in the hardest part—laying the groundwork for The Refuge House's cash flow.

"Which means it's a full-time job for a mortal soul." Brandon took a swig of his beer. "Shame you're taking the Atlanta job. Otherwise you could offer to work at The Refuge part time. For example, if you agreed to come back to Boats by Gus full time, you could either work for The Refuge on weekends or donate your time." Brandon was tiptoeing around Jeb's relationship with Jena, not bringing her into the discussion, and he felt a wash of appreciation for his friend. He'd miss Jeb, too.

"Not happening."

"You're worried it'd get sticky if you and Jena don't work out. If you stayed here." Brandon cut to the marrow, one of his talents. A skill that had taken a modest flat-bottom boat production facility to the multimillion-dollar corporation that funded Jena's ransom.

And saved her life.

"There's that." He savored the sip of his Guinness—always a favorite, even in the heat of the summer. "It's just that I enjoy feeling like I'm giving back to something besides the bankroll. I've gone weak, right?"

"No, you've seen what's important. I get it." Brandon didn't push Jeb on working together again. Disappointment flared, and Jeb realized that maybe he'd forgiven himself for pushing the corporation toward bankruptcy. Jena's life on the line had made it a no-other-choice option.

"I don't know if you can get where I'm coming from."

"Jeb, man, why do you think it ended up not being such a big deal for me to take the job I have now? To give up being a boss—being in charge, having a say over every detail—to be another cog in a huge wheel?"

"I thought it was Poppy."

"Hell, yes, it's Poppy, but it's what my feelings for her made me see. I could either focus on the gift right in front of my face, or break down over the loss of my first business."

"Poppy's a catch." For Brandon. The woman was incredibly artistic and always expressing it, whether via the decorating and design she did for Brandon's custom-built yachts, or Brandon's formerly sterile home.

"We're getting married."

"What? Bro, that's fantastic. Congratulations!" He slapped Brandon on his shoulder, all the while surprised at the warmth that spread across his chest. He was truly happy for his friend.

"You think I'm crazy, don't you? It hasn't been that long, if you look at a calendar. But I've been through more with Poppy than anyone else, ever. It was so intense, the highs and lows of how she and I met, got together." By "got together," Jeb knew his friend meant "fell in love."

"When did you know? That she was the one?"

Brandon's mouth hitched up in the grin of a man truly possessed by a woman—in the best way. "Honestly? The minute I set eyes on her, when I pulled up to Henry's pier for his and Sonja's pre-wedding party, for the vows that hadn't happened. She stood out like a...no kidding, like a goddamn poppy flower. You know, the bright red kind they wear on Veterans Day. The ones you donate a buck for."

"Yeah, I know."

"So there she is, like a red flower amongst fucking dandelions. No offense to Henry and Sonja or anyone else. There had to be a couple dozen people at the party, but all I saw was her. At first I thought it was the way she stood—she had this screw-you posture, like she owned the place. But then when I actually met her, saw past the damned sunglasses she was hiding behind, I saw vulnerability. And more than that, because it wasn't pity that drew me to her. The smoking hot chemistry, sure, that's a given. We just connected on a very basic but deep level."

"Jesus, I was only looking for 'when she kissed me' or 'when I found out we like the same music.'"

Brandon jerked his head back, the dreamy look in his eyes cleared, and the man he'd grown up next to cocked a brow at him. "It's not that neat, bro. It's a combination of things, so many events adding layers to the basic attraction. What I'm trying to tell you is that it's not a burning bush kind of thing, at least not for me. It's more subtle, but once I realized that Poppy was the one, it really was like a sledgehammer splitting my skull open."

"Your heart, you mean. It broke your heart." His heart had taken its share of beatings since Paraguay. Since forever, it seemed. Since he'd met Jena, but the last couple of months, for sure.

"No, man, it wasn't degrading in the least. Or sad. Overwhelming? Yeah. But I always *knew*, you know? Once I let my defenses down completely, it was crystal clear that Poppy had always been meant for me, and I knew no one else would ever love her like I do."

"When was that moment?"

"Fuck, bro. It was when it was too late, or close enough." Brandon drank his beer, then set the glass down on the bar. "I never want to have that feeling again. Figuring it out and at the same time believing I'd missed my chance."

Turmoil flipped like a river otter in his gut, and it had nothing to do with his favorite beer or the boiled peanuts that he was absolutely not a fan of. Jeb gripped his glass. He'd waited too long. Jena had laid her cards on the table by agreeing to start up The Refuge with him beside her. She'd continued to see him, to allow their relationship to begin again and go to a place it'd never been before.

The hope of a forever place.

Brandon leaned forward, concern stamped on his face. "You look green around the gills, Jeb."

He swallowed. "I think I've messed it up." He needed to see Jena, now. But she was with Robyn. Part of their new routine was that they left Fridays for their friends, to ensure each of them had more than just each other. It was to avoid what Jena called their previous tendency toward codependency.

"How so?"

"This isn't something I think I need to be talking about with you, because you're her brother, man."

"That's fair." Brandon nodded.

"But if we're speaking in generic terms, women like to know where their guy stands, right?"

"Women do not like to be left hanging, no. No matter what anyone says. Especially an independent, self-sufficient woman like, say, Jena." Brandon winked.

"Right. So why do they say they're cool with a more casual relationship? Or with me leaving?" Hell, he may as well lay all his cards out for Brandon.

"Because they've been hurt. Or they're scared. Or we did something to make them mistrust us."

Fuck. Double—no, triple fuck.

He pulled out a couple of bills and slapped them on the bar. "I gotta go. Leave the change for the tip." He gave Brandon a quick bro hug. "We'll talk next week about working together again, if you're still up for it."

"Wait." Brandon placed his hand on Jeb's shoulder and looked at him. "You mean it?"

"Maybe. Depends. Yes, damn it. Yes."

* * * *

Jena's phone buzzed the minute she dropped it on the kitchen counter after her dinner with Robyn. Hoping it was Jeb, she immediately picked it up, and her heart reacted—but not with joy. It sank to her toes as she stared at the all-too-familiar number.

Her handler. She could ignore it, as she had the last five times he'd called over the past week. Carefully, as if he'd know she was deliberately not answering, she placed the phone facedown on the counter and headed for the bathroom. She'd call him back on Monday. Her margarita buzz deserved a nice long shower and her favorite scented lotion.

Sharp raps on the front door stopped her in the short hallway, her hands on either wall. Jeb. Who else would be here on a Friday night?

She went to the door, allowing the shimmer of sexual anticipation to wrap around her, tighten her nipples, make the heat between her legs throb. The shower could wait, if Jeb was here for a booty call. She really needed to have a heart-to-heart with herself. Jeb was days from leaving for Atlanta, and she still was trying to eke out every last minute of their time together.

She peered through the peephole and recognized the one man she'd thought—she'd hoped—she'd never see again. Grim reality dowsed her desire, and she drew a shaky breath in, then out. She opened the door.

"What the fuck are you doing here, Grant?"

"Answer your fucking phone and I won't have to chase you down to this swampland." The man who'd been her mentor, guide, and sometimes partner pushed past her into the carriage house.

Jena shut the door behind them and followed him to the kitchen, where he took a seat at the small table. "Sit down, Jena."

"Don't mind if I do." She dropped into a chair and offered him a reluctant grin. "You're the worst buzzkill, you know that, right?"

Grant's handsome features revealed no emotion. They rarely did; he was always all business. She had no doubt he was a CIA lifer. Yet he'd never scorned her for leaving. He'd seen plenty of agents come and go. It was a tough business.

"I'm not here to kill anything, Jena. You've got to come with me, though. They need you to go to Asunción and testify against Jardin again. The kingpin this time." "They" meant their supervisors at CIA headquarters in Langley, Virginia. Men and women they never referred to by name, only their code names, which changed with each mission.

"I'm done, Grant. They promised me I didn't have to ever go back, for anything. I gave my statement. It's a closed hearing, right?"

"Yes, but in order to extradite Jardin's head honcho the US has agreed to a live witness. It's part of the process, and it's over our heads, Jena."

"This is the absolute worst time for me to do this, Grant. I'm out. I'm not CIA any longer."

He chuckled, a rare glimpse of his sense of humor—dry, with a twist of dark. "You're memory's not that short, Jena. Your needs versus national security. Let's see…oh, yeah, you lose."

"Fuck going back to Asunción. The Jardin cartel is contained, they've choked all their distribution channels. They don't need me." It was the last thing she'd accomplished before being kidnapped: She'd singlehandedly stopped a shipment of pure cocaine from being smuggled onboard an overnight delivery service headed directly for Miami.

"Resist all you want." He pulled out his phone, tapped on it, and turned the screen for her to read. "You've got a boarding pass to leave in four hours."

Her stomach twisted. She had no choice—and Grant knew it, too. "I'll be there."

"Oh, no, Jena. *We'll* be there. I'll wait out here while you pack. You know the drill." It was to protect her, truthfully, but the standing practice to travel as a team felt more like a measure for a fugitive.

"I'm not going to ignore an official order. I get it, Grant."

"And I get that you want to call your friend Jeb and tell him where you're going, how long you'll be gone. It's best you don't tell anyone about this until your return. For your safety in Asunción. You'll be back in under seventy-two hours."

"I've heard that before. My family will freak out if I vanish." And so would Jeb, wouldn't he? Their relationship had finally shifted into a place she'd only dreamed of. She wasn't willing to risk it all, no matter what Grant said about confidentiality.

"Tell them you're going to Langley, then. For a last checkout procedure. It's no longer classified that you worked for us."

She nodded. "That's fair." It would keep everyone free from worry and safe, away from the knowledge of what she really did and where, and it was best for the safety of everyone working the case, from the State Department to FBI, along with the Paraguayan authorities.

She had no choice but to go. She did have a choice to let Jeb know, though. As soon as they were at the airport, she'd text him and ask him to fill in her family.

* * * *

Jeb pulled up to the curb in front of Jena's carriage house. He had to park farther north on the street than usual because a black sedan was in his usual spot. He paused. Maybe Jena's drinks with Robyn had turned into another girls' night sleepover.

No matter. What he had to tell her was more important, and it wouldn't wait. If Robyn was there, he'd say what he had to say to Jena in private, either in her room our outside on the tiny porch. Then he'd set a time for them to meet tomorrow, at her old house. Because the tree had been such a big part of their growing up, it only seemed fitting that he'd propose to her there. And he had another idea that was slowly taking root, another way to prove to her that he was committed.

He took his time walking up the path, forcing himself to breathe, appreciating every second of this moment. He'd thought that when he found the woman for him, he'd be crazy with lust and the need to have her. Jena incited all that, true, but it was only the tip of what made them a couple. Like a Bayou gum tree, the sexual chemistry they'd shared since adolescence was only the outer branches, sticking above the still water. What bound them together was far more complex, permanent. Their connection was as deep as the roots of the oak tree he'd carved a heart into for her. Their hearts were one. It might not pass any scientific scrutiny, but no one and nothing would convince him of less.

Her lights were on, beacons to him as he crossed the long stretch of garden between the main house and small outbuilding. Her choice of home had never mattered to him before; now he wanted to know if she'd picked the carriage house because of its minimalist function or the history that came with it, tying it to the main house that had stood in New Orleans for three centuries. Did Jena want to own a historical NOLA property? Was The Refuge an example of what she preferred—updating a structure that was so much a part of the city landscape that it would leave a gaping hole once demolished, by man or nature?

There was an unfamiliar flutter in his gut as he approached her door and halted his steps. Holy fuck, were those butterflies in his stomach? He was not the nervous type. After fearing the worst—that Jena was going to die in the deepest recess of Asunción—he'd thought nothing could ever scare him so much.

He was wrong. He stood on her porch, on the verge of calling her out on what she'd offered him, even if it turned out that her "offer"—of staying here forever and leaving her agent career behind—weren't intentional on her part. Because it wasn't a coincidence. Jena wanted permanent roots as much as he did.

Their roots were so intertwined it was impossible to tell where his ended and hers began, which points were twisted or actually one single strand.

Her door yanked open and she stood in the threshold, the yellow bug light casting a fiery glow over her smooth skin. Her eyes widened in recognition, followed by a smile. Her smile died as quickly as it'd flashed, and her perfectly shaped brows drew together.

"Shit."

"That's a fine way to say hello. Look, I'm sorry to come here so late." As he prepared his explanation, he looked into her eyes, let his gaze roam over her face, her delectable lips. "I know you probably have Robyn over, but I'll make this short. I have to talk to you. And then tomorrow, I'll tell you more. Jena, I—" As he looked past her face and saw that she was dressed in the same two-piece athletic suit she'd worn home from Paraguay, he stopped talking. His heart felt like it was going to press out of his rib cage, or stop beating entirely. She wasn't going away again. She couldn't be.

"Jeb, I can't talk right now."

"I know, trust me, it'll only take a minute—"

"Jena, we have to go. Now." A man the same height as Jena stood behind her, his blond hair gleaming, his skin green like a lizard's. Jeb knew it was the bug light—the dude was obviously tan. And incredibly good-looking. This dude knew Jena, and from the looks of it, he knew her well.

"Who the fuck are you?" The words came from a primal place he rarely visited—except when it came to Jena, and life or death.

"Jeb, this is Grant, my, uh..."

"Colleague." The man stepped around Jena, moving her back by placing his hands on her shoulders. He stuck his hand out for Jeb to shake. "Grant."

Jeb ignored the outstretched hand. "Buddy, I don't know who you are, nor do I give a fuck. But if I see you touch Jena like that again, I'm going rip your fucking head off." He glared at the man, this man named Grant, who'd been inside Jena's place with her. His mind told him that what she said was true—this was probably another CIA agent she worked with. He'd met a lot of government authorities when he'd gone to Asunción to deliver the ransom, many of who were simply identified as employees of the US Embassy. He hadn't known yet that she was CIA. Once he did, he was on his way back to the States, after she'd been medically evacuated out of the country.

Grant stepped in front of Jena. His moves were catlike and powerful, hallmarks of an athlete—a trained athlete who might use his skills for other things, like undercover agent work.

Jeb took the man's stare with equanimity.

"It's not nice to talk like that in front of a lady." Grant's growl raised Jeb's hackles.

"I don't take orders from you."

"Oh, for fuck's sake!" Jena shoved herself between them, elbowing Grant in the gut before facing Jeb. "Grant, go to your car. I'll be right out."

Grant backed off, and only then did Jeb see the rolling suitcase that Grant picked up by the handle like a tiny pocketbook. "I've got your bag, Jena."

Jeb couldn't have stopped glowering at the man if he'd wanted to. Once he was out of sight—he didn't assume the man was out of earshot; he knew Jena had the hearing of a bat and assumed it was another part of CIA training—Jeb swallowed his frustration and looked at Jena.

He faced the most frightening part of the evening. She wore her emotionally opaque mask, the one that he'd seen two other times: In college, when she broke it off with him because she had to focus on her career options, and after the last time she came to him, the first time he'd seen her after the return from Paraguay and he'd turned her away. As he looked into her eyes, his heart screamed for her to come back to him.

"Where are you going?" He spoke through gritted teeth.

She shook her head. "Langley." She mumbled the city where CIA headquarters was located and he grasped her chin, made her look at him.

"Bullshit." His sharp reply drew her out of the shell she'd sunk into and tears spilled from her eyes.

"Stop it, Jeb. I can't tell you, okay?" He held her gently; she could have twisted away. He'd never do anything to hurt her. Even if his heart was shattering.

"If you can't tell me, who can you tell?"

She swiped at her tears. "You're making too much of this. It's not a big deal. I've suspected it would come down to this since I got back."

It was like a gunshot hitting his sternum. He dropped his hand and took a step back, fought from sinking to the ground, holding his head.

"You said you wanted to put down roots."

"I did. I am. I mean it."

"But you're taking another mission anyway." Suddenly his motive for speaking to her, reaching out to her tonight, evaporated. He'd imagined her desire to make a life together, with him. She'd been playing, acting as if she'd be able to put her agent life behind her.

"It's not a mission, not really. I can't say a whole lot right now, Jeb. You're going to have to trust me."

"Trust you? Like I did for the last two years while you went off on your 'Navy' stints? Who the fuck do you peg me for, Jena?"

"Jeb. It's late, we had a long week at work. I'll be back by Tuesday, I promise."

"Keep your promises, Jena."

"Everything all right here?" Grant had walked up unnoticed, the bastard.

"Have a nice trip." Jeb spoke to both of them and made his way off the property. The black sedan wasn't Robyn's—it was this guy Grant's. Grant with-no-last-name. If it were another time, and she were another woman, he'd have been certain Grant was her lover. The guy was hot, in that short-dude-in-shape way. But his gut told him that Grant was in the same business Jena had been in. No, goddammit—was still in.

He was done. If Jena could so easily slip out of town, out of his life without telling him, they didn't have the connection he'd thought. It'd been all in his mind. One heart, strong as an oak tree? More like a fucking willow snapped in two by a strategic lightning strike.

He drove off before they did, unable to watch the love of his life reenter her other life. The one without him.

Chapter 16

Jena endured the trip to Paraguay only because she wanted to see the bastards who'd killed so many innocent people behind bars. The days passed in a blur and, true to Grant's word, she was back in NOLA by Tuesday morning. Grant left her in Miami, hopping the next plane to D.C. as she went on to New Orleans.

After a pit stop at the carriage house to shower, she went into The Refuge House. She knew she wouldn't sleep, wouldn't have a minute's rest, until she'd had a chance to talk to Jeb.

He'd gone radio silent the entire time she was gone, refusing to answer her texts. She couldn't blame him, but she had to show him that she was telling the truth, that The Refuge House was her work. That her life was here, with Jeb.

She walked in through the front door, wanting to see the center through a client's eyes. The front of the house was freshly painted and looked like all the other stately homes on the avenue. But the porch had been widened, an accessible ramp installed, and the unobtrusive sign with the "The Refuge House Community Services" painted in script hung on brass chains from hooks screwed into the porch overhang. It was welcoming and professional.

Jena opened the front door to a cacophony of voices of all ages, phones ringing, and the toddler-level television in the play corner blaring a musical cartoon. She looked to the newly hired receptionist, who looked frazzled as she quietly but firmly spoke to a distraught man who held a baby in his arms. It was only eight in the morning—the door had opened minutes ago.

"Hey, Maribel. Can I help?" She stood behind the counter, next to Maribel, and gave the man a smile. The baby was adorable, her bright eyes full of life.

"Welcome back, Jena. This is Mr. Du Bois. He came in on Friday afternoon to find out about educational and counseling services for his five-year-old son, Mickey, who has ADD."

"He's a very smart boy, but I'm not getting anywhere with the school."

"Why don't you come back with me and I'll see what we can do?"

Maribel shot her a relieved look and mouthed "thank you" as Mr. Du Bois bent to pick up a large diaper bag.

"Anything else you need help with today, send it my way." She paused. "Is Jeb in yet?"

Maribel's eyes widened. "Oh, I thought you knew."

Her stomach heaved, and not from jet lag. "Knew what?"

"He resigned, effective Saturday morning. It was the first thing I saw this morning when I came in." She picked up a piece of paper and handed it to her. Jena didn't read it—she didn't need to.

Jeb had finally had enough. He'd left.

"Thanks, Maribel. By the way, I'm going to be out of the office for a few more days, maybe even a week." With Jeb gone, it didn't matter if she stayed here. She could go back to D.C. and get some work done that was waiting for her.

* * * *

The smell of sawdust mixed with welding assaulted Jeb's nostrils, making his eyes smart.

"I've missed this. There's nothing else like it." He spoke to Brandon as they walked through the shipbuilding facility. He'd insisted on showing Jeb what had changed, what they'd been able to salvage when he'd begun bankruptcy proceedings, and what the company would be able to do now that Jeb had brought back five million dollars.

"That's what I was counting on, bro." Brandon stopped at the entrance to the flat-bottom boat production warehouse. His eyes, so much like Jena's, lasered into him. "You're not planning on taking out more money to save Jena anytime soon, are you?"

Hell. He'd neglected to tell her family where she was, as if by doing so it wasn't true and she'd be back. It was Tuesday; she said she'd be back by today.

Not that he'd know. She'd have his resignation, and be either totally pissed at him or relieved to be rid of the constant friction at work. Probably both.

"No, no chance." Dread filled his gut. He should have waited to send the email to the Atlanta firm. He'd done it before he'd gone to Jena's the other night, wanting to be able to tell her that he'd firmly committed to staying in NOLA.

Now he had no choice but to take Brandon's offer, at least for the cash flow—and to do the work he enjoyed most: building boats with his best friend.

"Did you think more about doing volunteer hours for The Refuge?"

"I'd rather work out something here, as a way to give back." He couldn't work around Jena again, ever.

"Keep talking." Brandon's eyes lit up.

"What if we team up with one of the high schools and begin a vocational program here? We'd be able to offer courses in welding and shipbuilding. I'd bet we could add in budgeting or basic finance—I'd teach that part, with an extra aside on embezzling." He waited for Brandon to laugh and was relieved when he did.

"That's all good with me."

"I think I've finally accepted that you're not going to be looking over your shoulder at me."

"No need."

"On that note, I'd like to have another person working the numbers with me. A third party neutral observer, so to speak."

"That's not necessary, Jeb."

"It is. For my peace of mind. I never want you to have to think about what we've been through again."

Brandon quickly checked his phone for texts. They stood in the entrance to the flat-bottomed boat facility, the overhead lights harsh yet comforting. Jeb was back home.

Except a true home for him included Jena.

Not here.

He couldn't think about Jena in front of her brother, no matter how close they were. This cut was too deep. She had ripped the wound back open by reminding him that he hadn't known about her job as an undercover agent. Jena's inability to admit she was still involved with the CIA and unwilling to make a commitment to what he'd thought was their new relationship was a deal breaker.

Jena deserved a man she'd trust with her entire life, the public and undercover. He wasn't that guy.

"Huh. Jena's asking if I've run into you lately." Brandon's puzzlement was fortuitous, enabling Jeb to not reveal his immediate and profound relief. She was back, and safe.

Until the next mission.

"She knows how to reach me."

"Wait a minute—that sounds like you two are Splitsville again. What the hell, Jeb?"

Jeb didn't answer. He couldn't, not without spilling the beans on where Jena had been all weekend. "At any rate, she says she's on her way to D.C. for a few days. Something about wrapping up her Navy commitment."

Son of a bitch. Had she even come back from the weekend trip, then? Another gut punch, but he refused to label it a sucker punch. He wasn't a sucker, unsuspecting of the reality of Jena's career.

So why did it still hurt so damned much?

* * * *

Jena sighed with relief as she boarded her fifth plane in as many days. This trip from NOLA to Dulles, Virginia, was as unexpected as the return visit to Asunción had been, but instead of being told to go, she'd made the choice. She had to go back to Langley and get something for Jeb. Proof that she was truly done with her career as a CIA officer.

A man her height with a slight build bumped her as she placed her carry-on in the overhead bin, and she turned to see him give her a stony glare devoid of emotion, not offering an apology, his expression cold. Immediately her agent senses lit up.

"Excuse me?" She smiled and knew it didn't reach her eyes. She didn't intend it to.

He didn't answer as he continued to stare at her. *What the hell?*

She closed the bin and slid into the middle seat—it was all that was left when she'd bought her ticket for her short-notice trip. The cold seat belt clicked into place and she closed her eyes, forcing herself to calm down. The rude passenger wasn't her problem; if there was an alert on this flight, then a US Marshal was onboard. Not her circus.

Would her instinct to always assume the worst ever go away?

Jeb. He was all the reminder she needed that she was indeed coming back to herself, letting go of her undercover persona.

She was headed back to Langley to sign the last of the paperwork that released her from her tenure with the CIA. She could have had it express mailed to her, but she wanted the documents in hand. In eight hours she'd be free, one hundred percent civilian, The Refuge House her only employer.

With a jolt she realized what she had to do. She needed to make a grand gesture. Grander than the paperwork she would hold in her hand, saying her CIA employment was final. A grand gesture like Jeb had made, taking her to their tree after introducing her to his family.

She pulled out her phone and texted him.

Meet me at my place tomorrow night, eight o'clock.

Normally she slept on flights, but on this one rest eluded her. Her life since she'd graduated college had revolved around being able to handle any situation thrown at her, from basic agent training, to advanced training, to taking down enemies with her bare hands. But for the life of her she couldn't figure out how to reach Jeb, to prove to him that she was ready to let go of her past fear of commitment and trust someone with the rest of her life.

Jeb.

She ate the sack lunch she'd purchased in the NOLA airport, the hard-boiled egg not sitting well with her stomach. Something was bothering her; what was it? Aside from the overwhelming sense of grief that she'd lost Jeb forever.

Pay attention.

Her intuition alerted her, making her sit up and surreptitiously look around the cabin. She stood up and stepped over the sleeping man in the aisle seat, heading for the restroom at the front of the plane even though the rear bathroom was closer. Jena silently counted the passengers as she moved forward, noting that the flight was almost full. The bulkhead row had two empty seats, and she stopped in her tracks at the sight of the man who'd bumped her earlier. He leaned forward in his seat, making a slice across his throat with his finger before he pointed at her.

What. The. Fuck.

"Excuse me, do I know you?" She'd give him one last chance to come clean before she used her phone midair to contact Grant to raise the signal and have him detained upon landing. The chances of him being related to the Jardin cartel were slim, but she had just testified against them, ensuring the kingpin would spend the remainder of his life behind bars.

Cool mental clarity flowed over her, putting her into the headspace she needed to face a potential enemy. Jena wasn't a stranger to having her life threatened—it was part and parcel of working for her soon-to-be former employer. Back when she'd foolishly thought she had nothing to lose, being followed by a creep like this dude wouldn't have fazed her.

Now she stood to lose her last thread of hope for a life she'd never dared imagine. A life with Jeb.

The man stood up and gave the cabin a quick perusal with his unfeeling eyes. In a blink he was in her face, not touching her, but definitely crossing all her personal boundaries.

"You're dead, bitch. This is from Jardin." He flicked out a blade at least three inches long and jabbed at her midsection. Jena acted on instinct, lurching her core backward while forcing her arms between his, breaking his momentum. The knife flew from his grasp and a female passenger screamed. The sound of running footsteps rose above the roar of the jet engines, but to her it was all white noise. She grabbed the bastard's head and knocked it with her forehead. His groan wasn't satisfying—she never enjoyed hurting anyone. But it told her she'd hit her mark. Shoving her knee into his groin gave her the necessary result, as he bent in two and crumpled to the cabin floor. The passengers roared and clapped. Jena had never had such a large audience while taking out an attacker.

A tall brunette woman in jeans and a blazer stood at the front of the cabin, speaking to the flight attendants. She took the microphone.

"Ladies and gentlemen, please remain seated while the authorities handle this situation. I'm US Marshal Williams. There is nothing to be concerned about. This man is a suspected felon who will be taken into custody upon landing."

Jena never took her attention away from the man she'd leveled. He lay in the fetal position, his face contracted in extreme pain, but she was prepared if he attempted any further action against her or another passenger.

"This almost hit me." A passenger held the criminal's pocketknife in her palm, her hand held out for Jena to take it.

"That's mine, I believe." Marshal Williams reached over with an evidence bag to take possession of the knife. She smiled at Jena. "US Marshal Serenity Williams." Marshal Williams opened her blazer wide enough for Jena to see her holstered weapon. "I witnessed the entire event, Ms. Boudreaux. I've got this." The suspect was still conscious, so Serenity read him his rights and cuffed him. She addressed the flight attendants who hovered over the scene. "We'll keep him here until we land. If he's up to it, I'll buckle him into his seat for landing."

Jena shook her head. "Why the hell didn't you sit up here? There were two empty seats next to him."

"Sorry about that. But to see you take him out—that's a paying ticket."

"I'll have to give a statement to TSA upon landing."

"We'll make it brief, I promise." The respect in Marshal Williams's eyes caught Jena off guard. Of course the marshal had the flight manifest, and since Jena was a possible target of the Paraguayan cartel, it raised the risk against this particular flight. The marshal would have been thoroughly apprised of the situation.

"Good." Jena looked at Jardin's henchman one last time. "Don't give him any special treatment. His colleagues have caused enough devastation to last ten lifetimes."

"Agreed."

* * * *

The next night, Jeb waited on Jena's porch for two hours past the meeting time she gave him. His initial elation that Jena had told him the truth—her truth—quickly turned to despair. She'd said in her text that she had to leave this one last time.

He'd been a fool.

He looked at the trees around her carriage house as he turned to walk back to his car. The Spanish moss hung limply, as if the trees were weeping along with his heart. Something more important had kept her in D.C., or she'd arrived back home only to realize she didn't want to be with him after all.

Whatever the reason, it led to the same result:

They were through.

* * * *

By the time Jena got to CIA headquarters for her final discharge ceremony and paperwork, three different videos had made it onto social media. It didn't matter that Marshal Williams had instructed the passengers to turn over any cell phones they'd recorded with and warned that if anyone publicly shared images they were subject to prosecution. The sight of a female taking out a man with a knife was too juicy to ignore.

"Good thing you've resigned. Your cover is totally blown." Grant's voice was level in the cubicle next to hers, where they'd shared their workload for the better part of the last decade.

"No one knows I'm CIA—was CIA." Only a few more minutes and she'd be walking out the door, away from her life in undercover service of the United States of America and toward her life with Jeb.

"The social media posts got picked up by the Associated Press. They connected the suspect you took out with the Jardin cartel, which led them to the trial."

"You're kidding me. This is your last little way to jerk my chain, right? Please tell me that's what it is, Grant."

"Afraid not. But hey, they don't have your name, and you're returning to a quiet life in NOLA. Your fame will die a quick death—as long as no one recognizes your face on that grainy video."

"Right." Her heart began to pound. "But my friends and family might recognize me." She had to call Jeb.

"Let them know you're okay, that they shouldn't confirm it's you with anyone." Grant's mouth was its usual straight line, but the skin around his eyes fanned and his eyes twinkled.

"I'm glad you think this is funny."

"Aw, come here. I'm going to miss you." He opened his arms and she regarded him warily.

"You've never hugged me before." He hadn't—through all their missions, all the life-threatening and heart-stopping work they'd accomplished together, not one iota of affection had passed between them. They were partners, trained agents.

"We weren't about to become friends before."

She awkwardly stepped forward, accepting his brief, tight, bear hug, during which Grant whispered in her ear, "Go and get your man, Jena. You've earned every drop of happiness you can get."

Chapter 17

"Jena!" Jena's mother's cry signaled she'd finally come back to NOLA for good. She'd walked out of the arrival gate and into the welcome arms of her family. Her mother's voice had reached her over the others', Gloria's mascara running on cue. Her parents had texted continually while she was gone, asking when she'd return—another sign of their desire to turn over a new leaf.

The news about her midair takedown had only added to their angst to have her back home.

"Mom." She hugged her mother, allowed the familiar grasp of her arms to sooth her, before she pulled back and took in everyone else: Hudson, Henry, and Sonja, with baby Will, Brandon, and Poppy.

No Jeb. Disappoint sucker punched her gut, solid and low.

Don't go there.

She'd find him, wherever he was. And do her best to convince him what she knew. They belonged together no matter what.

"Honey, don't you worry about anything. You're home safe now." Hudson hugged her, kissed her on her cheek before he gave her shoulders a tiny shake. "I can't believe we fell for your Navy bit!"

"Dad." This wasn't the place to have that discussion.

"Hey, sis." Henry stepped forward, planting a kiss on her cheek, followed by Sonja, who handed her Will.

"We were so worried when we saw the video on the news," Sonja gushed. "And to see you do those moves…."

"Way to go, Jena." Brandon hugged her, followed by Poppy.

"How did you all know it was me?"

"Your profile. Poppy is a social media expert—she was able to compare it with the photo I have of all of us, from last year before you were deployed."

"I knew it was you because I'm your mother, honey." Gloria squeezed her arm.

"We'll talk about it another time. Just let it drop for now, okay? I mean it." She didn't need the press trying to get an interview about the scary Jardin cartel or her part in bringing them down.

Jena looked around the airport, and continued to do so as they all began to walk toward the parking lot.

"He's not here." Brandon spoke quietly next to her.

She jerked her head and stared at him.

"Who?"

"Cut it, sis. Jeb. He said to tell you that you'll know where to find him."

Jena gulped. She knew Jeb had gotten her text from the flight—before she'd been detained for three additional days of testimony with TSA in Washington, D.C.—because he'd replied with an "ok." But he'd ignored her follow-up texts and her calls over the last few days. She wondered if he'd even listened to her voicemails, which were increasingly desperate since she hadn't heard back from him.

Where to meet him, though?

* * * *

Jeb waited on the lowest limb of the old, familiar oak. The tree was part of a wooded lot that backed up to a public park, a no-man's-land between two long-standing homes with lots of acreage. What he'd taken for granted as a great place to play was a rare find. He was lucky to have grown up in the same neighborhood as the Boudreauxes, even if his mother's house was basically a shack three blocks away.

He felt her close before he saw her slim figure appear through the overgrown trellis a couple hundred yards away. It'd always been this way. His heartbeat sped up, his stomach tingled with anticipation. And his dick—it did a hell of a lot more than tingle when he was near her.

She wore a long, gauzy skirt, and he grinned. She'd have to hike it up to climb, but it would prove most convenient for what he planned, what he hoped, would be the evening's activity after they had "the talk."

He figured there were three kinds of talks in life. The informative, revelatory kind, like when you told your kids exactly how they'd been created. Or when your mother told you she'd knock you upside your head if she ever had a hint that you drove drunk. The second kind of talk was never good; it involved a firing, or losing a job, something you'd worked your ass off for. The third kind of talk was far riskier, as murky as the bayou after a heavy rain, when the sediment had been stirred up and you had no warning before an alligator slid its nostrils above the surface. Talk number three could be a clarification before talk number two. It could be a clearing of the air, like after a loved one finally got sober and wanted to make amends, make sure they were accountable for all the harm they'd inflicted. He'd had that with his mother, after she got out of rehab.

Talk three could also be a precursor to some of the most pivotal moments in life. Whether to end a relationship gone stale or start it anew. Deciding if you were really on the right career path or maybe needed to quit, go back to school and start again.

Or. Jena closed in on the tree, and as their eyes met in the early evening light the same shock of connection hit him, warming his chest and wasting no time reaching his cock. It'd been like this since they were ten years old. Not the cock part—though that had come along as they'd matured and trusted one another with their first kiss, and, years later, their first time making love. He used to tell himself it was sex, but that lie's power died the moment he read her text from Paraguay.

The sun cast a golden aura around her and he saw that her sleeveless top was as flimsy as her skirt, but instead of bleached white it was a soft rose, a shade lighter than her most intimate parts—parts he hoped to reacquaint himself with soon. But as with all talk number threes, there were no guarantees.

"Hi." Jena's voice, all silk and wonder, wrapped around him and he briefly considered chucking the talk and hauling her to him, kissing her, having her straddle him right here. They could work things out afterward.

"Hey, Jena." No, he had to talk to her first. He checked her out, head to toe, relieved to not discover any new bruises or scars. "I see you're no worse for wear."

"'Wear' is an understatement, right?" She kicked off her sandals and stepped up onto the thick bough. Her toes were painted pale pink, like her top, and he knew all he had to do was reach under her skirt to the apex of her legs to feel what he so very much missed.

He shifted on the bough, his erection too much of a distraction.

"Is it going to be a problem, all the media exposure? For your cover?"

She didn't answer right away, but settled in next to him on the bough, not touching, but close enough that he felt her body's heat and the constant sexual need between them. The bough was almost two feet wide, and their feet swung not more than six inches off the ground. The magic of the oak was that it gave the ambience of being high in the tree canopy without the inherent risk.

"I want to talk to you about that."

"No. I get to talk first." He leaned over slightly so that she'd look at him. Once he had those beautiful blue eyes on him, he spoke. "I've had a lot of time to think over the past week. First, I'm sorry I resigned the way I did. It was an asshole move, and you didn't deserve to find out with a letter. I owed it to you to tell you in person."

"Thank you." She opened her mouth to say more, but he held up a finger, halting her.

"Second, unless I'm even more of an obtuse jerk than I think I am, you have demonstrated beyond measure that you're committed to us." He saw her eyes get watery, but he kept going. He had to, before he took her in his arms and kissed her until she begged him for more. "We didn't talk about it, but the very fact that you took on your father's project, came with me to meet my family, and still wanted to be with me—it's more than I could have ever hoped for. And I want to give you the trust you've given me, Jena. I don't care if you want to stay with the CIA for another year or thirty years. It's who you are, and no matter how much I think it'll kill me with worry, I can't take that from you."

The tears trickled down her cheeks, and from the way the sun hit them they looked like perfectly round, iridescent pearls. Her eyes became a brighter blue, and he reached over and allowed himself to touch her enough to wipe the tears away. "Don't cry, babe."

She sniffled. "I'll do whatever I need to." She nuzzled her cheek into his palm and closed her eyes. The weight of her head in his palm couldn't have been more tender. After a second or two, her eyes popped open and she fixed him with her trademark stare. "Is there anything else you want to say right now?"

He shook his head. "Nothing that can't wait. Your turn."

"Why didn't you answer any of my texts or pick up your damned phone all week?"

"Pride. Heartbreak. Wanting to make this moment all the more special by waiting."

Jena's mouth dropped open, her expression slack. "Well, that's anticlimactic." She looked out past the tree and into the woods beyond. Her profile was the perfect intersection of femininity and fierce female passion.

"I'm so glad that you accept my life as an agent, because it means you accept all of me. No one's ever done that before." She kicked her feet, swinging them as she'd done thousands of times with him. "But it's not necessary. I meant it when I told you I was done with that part of my life. I had to go back for out-processing this time, to pick up my official discharge papers. It was only supposed to be for a day. I had no idea I'd been targeted by Jardin's thugs."

"What about for the future? Are you worried they'll come for you here?" Because he sure as hell was. "I know I told you I'm a born and bred Louisianan and never want to leave, but I'll make a new life with you wherever we have to go."

"You will?" She started to cry again, and she swiped at her tears. "We don't have to. That guy on the plane was the last in a long line of that cartel's henchmen. Most were killed during the shootout that happened after you rescued me, or locked up. While it was a horrible, lethal group of thugs, that cartel wasn't as far-reaching as it liked to think it was."

"I still think going away for a while would be a good idea. Does the CIA offer you some kind of temporary witness protection?"

She shook her head. "Trust me, Jeb. I'm safe from the cartel. They're a done deal. And…" Her hand disappeared into the folds of her skirt, into a pocket he hadn't noticed. "Here." She pulled her hand out, holding a slim, black wallet. "Take it. It's yours now."

He took the soft leather and opened it, seeing her agency identification on the left side and a blank right side. "I don't get it. Where's your badge?"

"I never carried a badge while working as a case officer. The one I was issued stayed in my desk most of the time. But that's the spot for it, and it's not there because I had to turn it in as part of my out-processing. I'm officially done. No more security clearances, no more 'Navy' deployments." She made air quotes when she said "Navy."

The air left his lungs, and he fought against an explosion of joy in his chest. "You can't do this because of me, Jena. I want you to be who you are, do what you want to do with your life. The thing is, I was never really upset that you were with any kind of law enforcement. It's the fact that you didn't tell me that stung. I had to get over myself."

"I couldn't tell you, not unless we became—our relationship was more permanent. And when we agreed to be friends with benefits, I thought that was it, that you weren't in the market for a girlfriend, much less a spouse."

"Spouse?" He kept his expression straight. His restraint was paid off by her blush.

"I'd only be authorized to tell a life partner or husband about what my job was. And even then, details are never up for discussion." She turned to him and grasped his hands. "I don't think I ever made it clear enough that what I did, texting you when I realized I was in a life-threatening situation, was highly abnormal. I only did it as a last resort."

"Is that what made you quit? Or did it get you fired?"

"Both. I knew the minute I picked up my phone to tell you I loved you, to ask you to tell the same to my parents, that it was a career-ender. I wouldn't have done it, either, if I didn't think it would save our other team members from the cartel without repercussions. I didn't plan on you convincing me to tell you where I was. Or to show up with fifteen million dollars ready to go."

"I know."

"You know what?"

"I know you believed you were about to die. You're the most loyal person I know. You wouldn't have ever risked a mission to reach out. You're a national hero."

She shook her head, as he knew she would. "It was my job. I'm only glad it all worked out—my teammates made it. And we put the bad guys away, always a plus."

"You're going to miss it, Jena."

"No, that's just it, Jeb. I don't, I won't. All I've been focused on these past weeks is having my final debrief and saying farewell to my CIA career. It's a younger person's job."

He laughed. "You're twenty-nine."

"Thirty next month, and you'll be thirty-two. Yeah, we're still young enough for a good life ahead of us, but it's hard staying in that kind of shape. Mentally more than physically, to be honest." She motioned at the identification wallet. "That's all that's left of my CIA life. It's not classified that I worked for them, by the way. But some of my missions are."

He fingered the laminated card, looking at her photograph. "You look so serious."

"It was a serious vocation. It's over. I don't want to discuss it anymore, Jeb. And believe it or not, that's not why I wanted you to come to my place when I sent that text."

He was ready to listen to her, he'd said all he had to say. Except one thing.

"Before you go on, Jena, I have to tell you one more thing."

* * * *

The light in Jeb's rich brown eyes had nothing to do with the sun's slanting rays as twilight drew close. Her center coiled into tight anticipation, and she couldn't focus on one single emotion as joy mixed with hope and wrapped into the one constant that had always been there with Jeb.

Love.

"Don't." She placed her fingers on his lips, their soft, firm texture in deep contrast with his scratchy stubble. Desire swirled, made her stomach dip and her pussy wet. It had only ever been Jeb. "Not yet."

His lips curved in a smile before he grabbed her hand and gave her a sweet kiss on her fingertips, his eyes never leaving hers.

She swallowed, aware of a heightened urgency to everything they shared while the soft blanket of impending nightfall wrapped around them, reassuring as only routine can be. Jena wanted it all with Jeb. The exciting, the daily, the routine.

"My plan was that I'd cook you the best meal I know how." She fingered the white cotton of her skirt, the only way to keep her hands off him. "And no, before you ask, it wouldn't be takeout, or even catered. I'd make you meatloaf, rice, crawfish."

"That sounds delicious."

"I know you like a wide variety of choices on the table. I've been watching you, Jeb DeVillier, from the day you ran into that backyard over there and rocked my world. You never turned down one of my mother's buffets. Your favorite, real favorite, is fried chicken and cheese grits, but you like to eat healthy so you don't do fried very often. Then I was going to pour you a nice cold beer, because I know you buy champagne and fancy wine for me but you don't really care for it. You enjoy trying new beers at Abita's but you're happiest with a good lager. You're a dog man, but you'd probably put up with a cat or two. And you never, ever hurt an animal on purpose. You don't even like to fish, and while you do like crawdads, you don't want to be the one to steam them."

He'd gone still, and she knew she had his full attention. "You're a stickler for tradition, but you're a modern dude—you'd never tell me what to do with my life, my career choices." Damn it, her eyes were burning again. To hell with it—it's why she'd put on waterproof mascara and eyeliner. She let the tears fall, felt them drop off her jawline, and kept talking.

"While I appreciate that you had no problem if I wanted to stay with the agency, you didn't have to." She cupped his face. "Because I already knew it, babe. I feel you here." She moved his hands to her heart, pressed them into her breast. "Feel that? It's for you. My life, my heart, my love. It's for you, Jeb."

She watched him and waited for his response. It was okay with her if he wanted to stare at her, blink back a tear or two of his own. This was their time, and she'd waited her entire life to be here with him in this moment.

"You already told me that. I was the fool who didn't accept it."

"You were angry after Paraguay."

"I was a jerk after Paraguay."

Their laughter intermingled until, inevitably, Jeb stood and took her hand, pulled her up and to him.

In the quiet of the bayou setting sun, their hands touched as they smiled at one another like two fawning kids.

"I feel like we're starting all over, but we have so much we've learned together." Her voice caught with the depth of her emotion—her love for Jeb.

"We are starting over—in the best way."

"You can finish what you wanted to say earlier." She looked up at him. "But I want to say it first."

"I love you, Jena."

"I love you, Jeb."

Their shared laughter at their familiar synchronicity cut off as their lips met. Jena wanted to pour everything she was feeling into this kiss. As Jeb's tongue stroked deep inside her mouth, she knew he did, too. Desire rose swiftly between them, and her knees shook.

He let go of her hands and reached around her waist, pulled her up against him. She gasped as he bent his knees, making sure she felt the length of his arousal.

"Jena, I want to do this properly, in a bed, but it's been too long." She got it, got him. Days apart felt like years for them.

"We have our whole lives to be proper." She pushed at his shoulders, forcing him to back up to the wide trunk of their tree, where they'd first climbed its strong limbs as kids, kissed, and lost their virginity. Today it offered them the same shelter from prying eyes, and nightfall provided the rest.

He kissed her until her head spun, then lifted her leg by leg until her limbs were wrapped around him. With her arms around his neck and legs around his waist, he turned and gently rested her up against the tree.

Jena's need made her wild with lust, with love for this man. Her man. Her Jeb.

"Now, Jeb. Fuck me now. Please." She licked, nipped his earlobe, trailed her tongue down his throat in the way she knew made him hard.

He braced himself with one hand on the trunk and reached between them, shoved her skirt up and aside, found the center of her spread legs. "Holy fuck, Jena, no panties?"

Her laughter vibrated in her throat and her toes curled as his fingers took advantage of her bare pussy. When he shoved his fingers inside her, found her walls slick with her need. He moved them until she cried out, begging for release. His thumb gently teased her clit and she wriggled against his hand, seeking relief from the deep ache of her need for him.

"Jeb," she panted. "Please."

"Enjoy it, babe." He kept her right at the apex of need and release, his fingers doing things she swore he'd never done before, taking her to a new level of arousal.

"Please," she sobbed, clutching his shoulders, unable to do anything but allow him to hold her. If she reached for him, she'd fall, and the magic he was doing to her pussy would stop.

His lips hovered over hers. "For you, babe." His mouth crushed hers as his thumb pressed on her clit, no longer teasing in its caress. The rush of her climax blindsided her, her keening howl swallowed by Jeb's passionate kiss. Before she came down from it he donned a condom he'd drawn from his pocket and entered her in one strong thrust, the angle of their joining allowing him sink to the hilt, his skin hitting and grinding against her clit. His gasps filled the air as he moved again and again, taking her to the place where there was nothing but Jeb and their joined bodies.

"Jena." He ground out her name the moment before he thrust one last time, grunting his release in the night air.

They clung together for several minutes, forehead against forehead, still joined, Jeb's hands cupping her ass, her back resting against the solid trunk.

"I love you, Jena." He kissed her deeply before helping her unwrap her legs, her feet hitting the dew-chilled ground.

"I love you, too." Her skirt fell around her and he leaned in to kiss her again, his scent filling her.

"There's another thing I want to show you." He zipped up his pants and reached for her hand. "I hadn't planned for it to be this dark."

Curious, she slipped into her sandals and allowed him to lead the way as they left the tree and wound through the garden. Once back on the street, they walked to the front of the large house that had been so much a part of her life until her parents had sold it right after Katrina.

Jeb stopped, looking at the house, not seeing what Jena did.

"Jeb, did you know this house is for sale?" A large for-sale sign on the front lawn she'd known like the back of her hand made her inexplicably sad. "It'll be the second family to own it, since Dad and Mom sold it." It made her sad, her family home traded like any other commodity.

"Huh." Jeb stood still, as if on the verge of a cliff.

"What?" He looked nervous, quite a feat after the bayou-pounding sex they'd just had—no, after how they'd made love beneath the stars, she corrected herself.

"What's going on, Jeb?"

He pulled a small object from his pocket, but it wasn't another condom packet. He pressed it into her hand and got to one knee.

"It's not a ring, not yet, because I want you to pick out your own ring. It's a key, but not just the key to my heart—you've had that since we met, and it's yours forever. We started a lifelong friendship in this house, Jena, on this property. I want to start a new life together here, to let our kids enjoy the love and NOLA for as long as the hurricanes let us."

"Jeb." She choked out his name, unable to verbalize the tsunami of love washing over her from all sides.

"Will you marry me, Jena Boudreaux?"

"Yes, yes, yes. I will marry you, and be with you the rest of our lives, Jeb." She tugged him up, opened her palm to reveal the house key he'd placed there.

"It's really, really the key to this house?"

He grinned. "It is. Look here." He drew her around the metal sign, and she saw the freshly placed SOLD sign plastered diagonally across it.

"Jeb." She reached up and kissed him. "I can't believe this."

"So you're not thinking it's over-the-top, too many childhood memories? Because you had some awful times with your folks here, too, once you were a teen and realized how backward their bigotry was."

She shook her head. "That's what makes this the perfect engagement ring, Jeb." She dangled the key in front of him. "It's a chance to make new memories, to raise a family open to whatever the world has to offer."

He kissed her, holding her tight. When he lifted his head, he grinned. "I was hoping you'd see it that way. Are you ready to be carried over the threshold?"

"Only by you."

Chapter 18

Three months later

"You're beautiful, dear." Gloria Boudreaux sniffed back tears as she adjusted Jena's wispy white veil, careful to untangle the delicate lace from any seed pearl beads on her bodice.

"Thank you, Mom." Jena couldn't wait until the day was over and she was in Jeb's arms again. She lived for their nights together in the rambling old house, half of which was currently under renovation.

"I'm glad you went with the bluer white." Robyn squeezed her hand affectionately and Jena savored the burst of love.

"I'm glad you agreed to be my maid of honor."

Robyn smiled, and Jena knew she had a lifelong friend in the woman whose skills had rebuilt The Refuge House.

"You look stunning." Sonja walked up to them, her mother next to her, an older version of Sonja's regal beauty. Sonja's dress was a pale ivory, the perfect shade to highlight her deep brown skin. She'd forgone a veil for a fresh flower headpiece made of baby's breath. A freshwater pearl necklace finished her look.

"As do you. Did Henry give you the pearls?"

Sonja's hand reached for the necklace, her smile full of joy. "He did. And the earrings are from Will." They laughed, as Will wasn't even crawling yet.

"My nephew has great taste." Jena looked across the room to the vanity, where Poppy was putting the finishing touches on her makeup. "Poppy, are you doing okay?"

"Yeah, hurry up already," Sonja chastised her best friend. "We have to be downstairs in five minutes."

"You look fine, honey." Poppy's mother had flown in from New York, and while clearly overwhelmed by the triple wedding, had been a trooper through all the pre-wedding festivities.

"I'm ready." Poppy finished with a flourish and turned to face them all. "And guess what?"

Sonja held up her hand. "Do. Not. Say. It."

"What?" Jena looked from Sonja to Poppy and back again.

Sonja never took her eyes off Poppy. "She looks like she's ready to tell us some very special news, and I'm sure it can wait until after the wedding. Don't do what I did, Poppy."

Poppy smiled, shaking her head. "I've already told Brandon. Unlike you, I don't believe in keeping my husband-to-be out of the loop."

"Told Brandon what?" Jena had no clue.

Poppy walked up to Jena, her pale pink gown a perfect foil to her flushed skin. "You're going to be an auntie again!"

Jena squealed and began to jump up and down before Gloria interrupted with a faux stern look. "Honey, settle down. We'll celebrate after the vows."

Jena eyed her mother. "You already knew?"

Gloria's eyes misted, and her lips wobbled. "Yes. Hudson and I are so blessed."

"We all are." Jena looked around the room. Sonja and Poppy had each asked their sister to stand up for them. Robyn and Gloria stood on either side of Jena. "I think it's time."

* * * *

Jeb stood next to Henry and Brandon under the new trellis he'd constructed in front of the tree. The minister stood behind them, waiting for the three brides to come out of the house. Jeb could wait forever if he had to. He had Jena at the end of it.

Jeb's back and shoulders ached from the last few weeks. He and Jena had singlehandedly cleared out the back of the property, doing their best to return the garden to its original splendor. It would take years to make it into the beautiful spot Jena envisioned, but it was good enough for today.

Their wedding.

Once she'd agreed to marry him, they quickly devised plans to make it official in this house. They moved into the empty place immediately, renting it from the previous owners and closing on it the day before yesterday. The event that kicked everything into supersonic high gear was when, at their impromptu housewarming and engagement announcement, Jena's siblings had voiced a desire to get all the Boudreauxes married at once. Together. A triple wedding. Since it was now December, they wanted it done before the crush of the holidays. So he and Jena had agreed, and now he waited for his love to join him under their tree, to make it all official.

It had been a whirlwind, and they'd barely had time to be together, except at night when they collapsed into bed. Between The Refuge, cleaning up the house, and readying the garden, it was a wonder they were still standing.

He credited that to the healing powers of lovemaking. Despite their exhaustion from working long days, and then nights at home on the house, they'd continued the celebration they'd begun that night against the tree three months ago.

"Who do you think will come out first?" Brandon's voice cracked, a sure sign of his nerves.

"Sonja. I'm the oldest." Henry's certainty made Jeb laugh.

"It's not primogeniture, brother." Brandon wasn't going to let his older brother get away with anything.

"It'll be Jena. It's our house." Jeb shot them both a glance and offered his widest grin.

"Piss off." Henry's rejection was given with a smile.

"You're about to become an official Boudreaux, unofficially, so it's our house again, too." Brandon patted him on the shoulder.

"I appreciate your generosity with the family name, boys, but your sister is about to become a Boudreaux DeVillier. It has a nice sound to it, doesn't it?"

Both Boudreaux men groaned, yet within a heartbeat they were all laughing.

The sound of the screen door creaking open caught Jeb's attention first. Crap, he'd forgotten to lubricate the hinges. His focus had been on the front porch and walkway, leading to the garden.

But it wasn't the brides that came out. The mothers of the brides, along with their witnesses, came forward and walked down the paved path to the trellis, taking their seats as planned. There were too many brides and grooms to have the entire wedding party standing during the vows.

"Where are the brides?" Henry sounded concerned. He would—he'd been jilted not six months earlier. But since Sonja and he had made up, and now had little Will, Jeb wasn't worried. Sonja was a shoe-in to show up.

As was Jena. He began to sweat, and not from the early evening New Orleans heat. His mind fired salvoes of memories he wished would remain buried forever, including Jena leaving for "deployment."

"They'll be here." His voice sounded a little too high-pitched.

"Poppy is no doubt keeping them in line." Brandon's voice was steady, but he rocked back and forth on his feet, his polished shoes belying his anxiety. "She's all about being prompt."

The agreed-upon processional music sounded over the wireless speakers, which Jeb was quietly proud he'd thought of. Now all he gave a damn about was Jena, here, next to him, sealing the deal that began over two decades ago. Immediately he saw her as she was at eight, running across this same lawn, to the huge tree behind them, providing protection from the harsh sun even still. He quickly looked over his shoulder, and the sight of the gnarly old tree in all its humongous majesty stilled him, grounded him. The heart was visible through wisps of Spanish moss, as though the tree winked at him.

This was home, where he and Jena belonged.

He turned back around at the same time the guests collectively gasped. All three brides walked out from the front of the house, around the corner, arms linked in a single line of beauty.

The only one Jeb saw was Jena. She was in between her two soon-to-be sisters-in-law, and her eyes met his with complete assurance and the one thing he'd been blind to for too long:

Love.

The music swelled, the brides grew closer, but all Jeb knew or cared about was that Jena walked toward him without hesitation, with no sign of the nerves he'd had. This was a woman who knew what she wanted, and she wanted him.

Jena reached where her father stood, and Hudson lifted her veil, kissed her on the cheek, and handed her over to Jeb. A traditional gesture for a very untraditional road taken.

Jeb took Jena's hand and kissed her on the cheek—to hell with waiting until after the vows.

"I've been waiting for this my entire life," he whispered in Jena's ear. "You're beautiful."

"I'm yours, Jeb DeVillier. Always have been."

They turned to face the minister and the oak tree's branches swayed in the light breeze, blessing their union.

Love the Bayou Bachelors?

Read the whole series
FULLY DRESSED
BARE DEVOTION
BAYOU VOWS

Available now
Wherever ebooks are sold
From
Geri Krotow
And
Lyrical Caress

Meet the Author

Geri Krotow is the award winning author of more than thirteen contemporary and romantic suspense novels (with a couple of WWII subplots thrown in!). While still unpublished Geri received the Daphne du Maurier Award for Romantic Suspense in Category Romance Fiction. Her 2007 Harlequin Everlasting debut A Rendezvous to Remember earned several awards, including the Yellow Rose of Texas Award for Excellence.

Prior to writing, Geri served for nine years as a Naval Intelligence Officer. Geri served as the Aviation/Anti Submarine Warfare Intelligence officer for a P 3C squadron during which time she deployed to South America, Europe, and Greenland. She was the first female Intel officer on the East Coast to earn Naval Aviation Observer Wings. Geri also did a tour in the war on drugs, working with several different government and law enforcement agencies. Geri is grateful to be settled in south central Pennsylvania with her husband.

Fully Dressed

**There's nowhere hotter than the South, especially with three men who
know how to make the good times roll. But one of the Bayou Bachelors
is about to meet his match...**

New York City stylist Poppy Kaminsky knows that image is everything,
which is why she's so devastated when hers is trashed on social media—
after a very public meltdown over her cheating fiancé. Her best friend's
New Orleans society wedding gives her the chance hide out and lick
her wounds . . .

Brandon Boudreaux is in no mood to party. His multi-million dollar
sailboat business is in danger of sinking thanks to his partner's sudden
disappearance—with the company's funds. And when he rolls up to his
estranged brother's pre-wedding bash in an airboat, a cold-as-ice friend
of the bride looks at him like he's so much swamp trash.

The last person Poppy should get involved with is the bad boy of the
Boudreaux family. But they have more in common than she could ever
imagine—and the steamy, sultry New Orleans nights are about to show
her how fun letting loose can be . . .

Bare Devotion

Sweet and sultry, hot and wild...that's desire, Louisiana-style. And there's no one better to explore it with than one of the Bayou Bachelors...

Returning to her flooded New Orleans home to face Henry Boudreaux, the man she jilted at the altar, is the hardest thing attorney Sonja Bosco has ever done—even before she discovers she's pregnant. Sonja backed out of the marriage for Henry's sake. He wants to be part of his father's law firm, and his parents will never approve of an interracial marriage. Better to bruise his heart than ruin his life.

Henry can't forgive Sonja, and doubts that he can trust her again. But learning that they're going to be parents means there's no avoiding each other. Springtime on the bayou is already steamy enough...now they're living in the same small space while their damaged house is repaired. And with each passing day they're getting a little more honest. A lot more real. And realizing that nothing—not even New Orleans at Mardi Gras—glows brighter than the desire they're trying to deny . . .

Printed in the United States
by Baker & Taylor Publisher Services